She wanted him to kiss her.

Kiss her thoroughly.

Kiss her until her blood heated to an impossible pitch.

Tess's heart thundered in her chest, and her knees felt weak. Her desire was so strong, she was sure David could sense it. The very air seemed to throb with her need.

He reached out, and for one impossibly long moment, Tess thought he was actually going to fulfill her wish. But his fingers just brushed her cheek, and he said gently, "It's cold. You'd better go inside."

After he left, Tess wondered if the bargain she'd struck would have far too high a price tag.

She had once thought not being married to the man you loved would be the most devastating thing that could happen to a woman. Now she wondered if that was true.

Perhaps being married to the man you loved when he didn't love you was even worse.

Dear Reader,

This March brings you a very special event—the publication of *Convincing Alex*, by Nora Roberts. This extraspecial SILHOUETTE SPECIAL EDITION title is the fourth tale in Nora's bestselling THOSE WILD UKRAINIANS series, and features Alex Stanislaski—definitely the sexiest detective in New York! Don't miss this wonderful story—it's destined to become a classic!

The March selection of our THAT SPECIAL WOMAN! promotion is *One Last Fling!* by Elizabeth August. This warm, wonderful tale is sure to win hearts! Our THAT SPECIAL WOMAN! series is a celebration of our heroines—and the wonderful men that they fall in love with.

This month also brings you stories from more of your favorite authors—Emilie Richards, Diana Whitney and Trisha Alexander—as well as a super debut book in the Special Edition lineup by Kate Freiman. A wonderful March will be had by all!

I hope that you enjoy this book and all of the stories to come.

Sincerely,

Tara Gavin
Senior Editor

Please address questions and book requests to:
Reader Service
U.S.: P.O. Box 1325, Buffalo, NY 14269
Canadian: P.O. Box 1050, Niagara Falls, Ont. L2E 7G7

TRISHA ALEXANDER

SAY YOU LOVE ME

Silhouette®

SPECIAL EDITION®

Published by Silhouette Books
America's Publisher of Contemporary Romance

This book is dedicated to all the wonderful females in our family: Wanda, Kim, Shelley, René, Gerri, Margie, Norma, Susan, Bev, Kay, Theresa, Lisa, Brigitte, Ingrid, Elizabeth, Allison, Shari, Gail, Erin, Beth, Dawn, Kelly, Chris, Kaylee, Jackie, Alex, Brittany, Lindsay, Ashlyn and Kara; and one very special male!—my new grandson, Ryan Alexander Kay.

 SILHOUETTE BOOKS

ISBN 0-373-09875-8

SAY YOU LOVE ME

Books by Trisha Alexander

Silhouette Special Edition

TRISHA ALEXANDER

has had a lifelong love affair with books and always wanted to be a writer. She also loves cats, movies, the ocean, music, Broadway shows, cooking, traveling, being with her family and friends, Cajun food, *Calvin and Hobbes* and getting mail. Trisha and her husband have three grown children and two grandchildren and live in Houston, Texas. Trisha loves to hear from readers. You can write to her at P.O. Box 441603, Houston, TX 77244-1603.

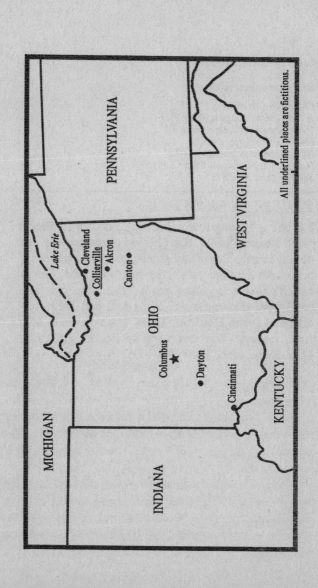

MICHIGAN

INDIANA

Lake Erie

Cleveland
Collierville
Akron
Canton

OHIO

Columbus ★
Dayton
Cincinnati

PENNSYLVANIA

WEST VIRGINIA

KENTUCKY

All underlined places are fictitious.

Prologue

Collierville, Ohio
Early January

"Tragedy struck a Collierville family today," intoned the 11:00 p.m. newscaster in an appropriately solemn voice.

Tess Collier stiffened. Her hand—the one scratching the neck of her cat Budge—stilled as she stared at the screen. Collierville was a small town. Everyone knew everyone else.

The newscaster continued. "About three o'clock this afternoon, a truck driver, while trying to pass another vehicle on Interstate 90, lost control of his eighteen-wheeler and sideswiped a car. The car was pushed into the guardrail, and one of its passengers was killed. The

dead woman has been identified as thirty-seven-year-old
Leah Bannister.''

Tess clapped her hand over her mouth. *Leah Bannister!*

''Two other occupants of the car were injured in the
accident, and have been life-flighted to Collierville
Memorial Hospital. The injured are David Bannister,
the dead woman's husband, an employee of Medlock
Chemical Company, and Francesca Bannister, his seven-
year-old daughter. The extent of their injuries is not
known at this time.

''Officials at the scene said the heavy snowfall and
blizzardlike conditions were contributing factors to the
accident. Cleveland-area motorists have been under a
weather advisory since early this morning.

''The death of Mrs. Bannister is the second traffic fa-
tality so far this year....'' The newscaster's voice faded
as Tess absorbed the impact of his announcement.

Leah Bannister. Dead.

And Francesca and David...injured.

''Oh, dear God...'' Tess said, the words half prayer,
half plea. Her heart contracted painfully in her chest,
and she bit her bottom lip to still its sudden quivering.
Francesca Bannister had been her piano student for a
little over a year, and in that time Tess had grown to love
the child. Tess had also come to feel as if David Bannister was her friend, and even though she and Leah Bannister were never more than casual acquaintances, Tess
had admired the other woman. Admired and envied her.

The Bannisters.

Her family. The family she'd secretly fantasized
about. The perfect family, as she'd always thought of
them.

The television droned on in the background as Tess stared unseeingly at the flickering images. Her mind grappled to assimilate what she'd just heard. Leah. Bright and shining Leah. The most alive person Tess had ever met, was dead.

Tess vividly remembered the first time she'd met Leah Bannister. It was right after the school year had started the September before last, and Leah had called Tess to inquire about piano lessons for her daughter.

"You come highly recommended, Miss Collier," she'd said in a low, throaty voice. *A sexy voice,* Tess had thought. Idly, she'd wondered what the woman looked like. Three days later her curiosity had been satisfied when Leah brought her daughter Francesca—who had just turned six—for her first piano lesson.

Tess saw at a glance that Leah Bannister was everything she herself was not. Tall and lush, with high, full breasts shown to advantage in her bright red dress, Leah had short, swingy, black curly hair and intense dark eyes. Everything about the woman was vibrant and colorful and radiated energy.

She placed a slim, tanned hand with long painted nails on her little daughter's shoulder. "I'm Leah Bannister," she said. Her full red lips parted in a poised, assured smile, exposing perfect, large white teeth.

There was nothing indistinct or dull about her, thought Tess. She'd probably never experienced a self-doubt in her entire life. *Not like me.*

Leah's dark eyes appraised Tess quickly. Tess could see her assessing the inexpensive, cotton, shirtwaist dress and plain patent-leather pumps. Her gaze lingered for a moment on the strand of real pearls that had belonged to Tess's great-aunt Millicent, then moved to Tess's straight, brown, waist-length hair that she wore in an old-fashioned braided coronet, and finally rested on her nondescript gray eyes.

Tess felt like a sparrow in the presence of a cardinal. She wondered how anyone gained that kind of self-assurance and air of authority. She wished, for probably the thousandth time, she had even a small measure of it herself. And it wasn't as if Leah Bannister was so much older than she was, because Tess guessed they were close to the same age—mid-thirties. But age was the only similarity between them. In all the important ways, it was painfully obvious to Tess they were worlds apart.

After taking Tess's measure, Leah introduced Francesca, and Francesca, with a gravity and poise well beyond her six years, held out her small hand and said, "Hello, Miss Collier."

Tess smothered a smile and shook the proffered hand. She was immediately smitten by the little girl who had inherited her mother's creamy complexion and dark hair. There, however, the physical resemblance ended. Francesca's eyes were a lustrous green dusted with gold, and her smile was touchingly sweet and shy.

Tess's heart immediately went out to her, for Tess understood what it was to be shy and how especially difficult a move to a new town must be.

Within weeks, Francesca became Tess's favorite pupil.

Tess didn't meet David Bannister until Francesca's first piano recital in April. Francesca performed beautifully, playing one of Mozart's early minuets without making a single mistake. Feeling like a mother bird who has just sent her fledgling out of the nest, Tess looked on proudly.

Afterward, Francesca, green eyes glowing with pride, led her father forward. "This is my dad," she said.

"I'm David Bannister," he said. "It's really a pleasure to meet you." He smiled warmly. "Francesca talks about you all the time."

Something in Tess's chest tightened under his friendly green gaze. *Francesca's eyes,* was her first thought. *And her wonderful smile,* was her second.

That was the beginning of Tess's love affair with the Bannister family. And ever since, she'd been fascinated by them and garnered every tidbit of information she could. Like how the former Leah Parrish, a gifted and brilliant fashion designer, had met the equally brilliant and gifted David Bannister, a research chemist. Like how they'd moved to Collierville only weeks before Francesca became Tess's pupil in September. Like how, a few months after the move, Leah resumed work for her New York design firm and how she often made trips back to the city.

Some of Tess's information was gleaned through the small-town grapevine, but most came directly from David Bannister, because once Leah began to travel, he was the one who brought Francesca to her lessons. He fell into the habit of staying and watching his daughter play, and afterward, because Francesca was the last student of the day, he would linger.

He and Tess would talk, sometimes for as long as thirty minutes or an hour, while Francesca played with Tess's cat. Several times, confessing that Leah was out of town, he and Francesca had stayed to share the evening meal. He'd laughingly called his weekly commitment to Francesca "a good excuse to play hooky from work." Tess knew he really loved his job and that he normally put in long hours. She also knew—with a secret thrill—that he enjoyed his growing friendship with her.

She treasured her growing friendship with David, and she stored her nuggets of knowledge about him and his family the same way a squirrel stored his cache of food against the lean winter months. Each time she was around any of the Bannisters, she pretended she belonged to their magical circle and basked in their golden aura. All three of them were so beautiful, so interesting, and so exciting—each in a different way.

In Tess's mind, the Bannisters were never lonely and bored the way she was. They never had self-doubts or were unhappy. Even Francesca's shyness didn't disguise her innate intelligence, and Tess knew that by the time the child grew to adulthood, she would be a wonderful woman.

Yes, fortune had smiled on the Bannisters.

Nothing in their world could ever go wrong.

But now, something *had* gone wrong. Terribly wrong. One horrible accident, and the perfect world of the Bannisters had been destroyed.

Beautiful Leah was gone. The blazing comet would shine no more. Tess closed her eyes. Poor Francesca. Poor baby. She had adored her mother.

And David.

Tess could only imagine how he must feel. The pain. The heart-wrenching grief. The desolation and loneliness.

Slow tears slipped down her cheeks.

What would happen to David and Francesca now?

Chapter One

Tess pushed open the heavy glass door of the Collierville Public Library and emerged into the sweltering afternoon heat. It always surprised visitors to this part of the country, but northern Ohio could be just as hot in the summer as states much farther south, and today was a perfect example.

She wished she'd driven to town, but it had seemed so lazy to drive when she only lived four blocks from Main Street. But now, feeling the blaze of the sun on her shoulders, she regretted that decision.

Her sandals slapping softly against the pavement, Tess started down the steps to the sidewalk and thought how nice it would be to get home. She intended to pour herself a tall glass of iced tea and lay in her hammock under the shade of the big elm tree for the rest of the afternoon. She was grateful that her only piano students today had been this morning. Maybe, if she was lucky, Hazel would have baked some fresh sugar cookies while she'd been downtown.

She smiled, thinking of Hazel Wancheck, who was her housekeeper and had been her great-aunt Millicent's closest friend until Millicent's death eight years earlier. Tess's mind thus occupied, she was only vaguely aware of the man who had just exited the City Building next door to the library.

"Tess?"

Tess looked up, and for one stunned moment forgot to breathe. "D-David," she said, shock causing her voice to wobble. "You're back home! I had no idea! W-when did you—?"

"Francesca and I got back yesterday."

She stared at him, incapable of saying anything sensible. One thought hammered at her: David Bannister was home. He was standing there, on Main Street, in the flesh. "I . . . I'm so glad to see you," she finally said.

He smiled—a poignant smile that tore at her heart. "I'm glad to see you, too," he said softly.

They stood there awkwardly for a few seconds, then Tess finally got her emotions under some semblance of control and said, "How's Francesca?"

He shrugged, a bleak look clouding his eyes. "Not good." His gaze met hers. "Physically she's fine. Emotionally she's not."

"Oh, David, I'm so sorry."

He nodded, then looked away, his jaw set in grim lines.

Tess swallowed against the painful lump in her throat. He looked so unhappy. She wished they weren't in public. She wished they had the kind of friendship where she could put her arms around him. Make the pain go away. She wished she could say something, anything, that wouldn't sound inadequate or stupid. She'd never felt so impotent.

He looked up, studying her face for a long moment. "Listen, Tess . . . I . . . I'm not very good company these days, but, well, I could really use an understanding ear. Could we go to Dalrymple's and have a cola or something?" He grimaced. "You're probably busy. . . ."

Tess tried to smile but she was too close to tears to be very successful. "I'm never too busy to talk to a friend."

She still couldn't believe he was home. For the past seven months not a day had gone by that she hadn't thought about him and Francesca and wondered if they were all right. Wondered if she would ever see them again.

Tess forgot the heat. She forgot how much she'd been looking forward to getting home. She forgot everything but the man walking beside her. Covertly, she studied him as they walked the short block and a half to Dalrymple's, an old-fashioned ice-cream parlor that also sold the best cheeseburgers in Collierville.

He looked older, she decided, noticing the strands of silver threading his almost-black hair—a silver that hadn't been there seven months ago. His nose, always a little too large for his face, looked more pronounced and deep grooves were etched into his forehead. He was thinner, too, which made him look even taller than his. six feet.

But despite these changes, he still looked wonderful to her. Tess had always thought of David as the ideal man. Perfect husband, perfect father, and—she had imagined—perfect lover. David was handsome, successful and intelligent, but he also possessed qualities that Tess valued even more: kindness, understanding and compassion. She saw all those things in his eyes, in the way he had always treated his wife and his daughter, in the way he had always treated *her,* an insignificant little piano teacher who had never commanded much attention from anyone.

Five minutes later, settled across from each other in a booth overlooking Main Street, Tess knew the months since Leah's death had not been easy ones for him. It must have been earth-shattering to lose Leah—the kind of woman no man would ever be able to forget.

After Leah's funeral, David had closed up their home and taken Francesca with him to Switzerland, where he had an assignment—an assignment that was already in the works when Leah died. When David had called Tess to explain he wouldn't be bringing Francesca back for piano lessons, they'd talked for a while, and he'd confided the information that he'd agonized over whether to go or not but had decided that maybe the change would be good for both him and Francesca. Tess had wished him luck, and they'd said goodbye.

Tess had missed them. She'd missed them terribly. She hadn't realized how much she'd always looked forward to Francesca's weekly lesson until the child no longer came. She also hadn't realized how much she'd looked forward to her conversations with David. Or to seeing them in church. Or to hearing about them around town. The Bannister family's sudden absence left a gap in her life. A gap that sometimes reminded her of a sore tooth—always there, throbbing in the background, impossible to ignore.

Now the remaining Bannisters were back. Father and daughter. David and Francesca. The knowledge played in Tess's mind like the words to a familiar song that refuse to go away.

And David Bannister was sitting across the booth from her. Looking at her with his beautiful green eyes. Making her feel special again.

"Are you back to stay, David?" Tess asked softly. She took a sip of her cherry-flavored cola, determined to ignore the hollow shifting in her stomach. Determined to pretend that David Bannister's sudden reappearance in her life was not that important. That he was a casual friend and nothing more. That she did not, absolutely did not, have a silly, schoolgirl crush on him.

He nodded. "Yes. The Swiss assignment is over, and it's time to get my life on track again. To try to, at least."

"Has it . . . has it been very hard on you . . . and Francesca?" *Stupid, stupid question. Of course, it's been hard. His wife died—his beautiful, brilliant, beloved wife died, for heaven's sake! What's wrong with you?*

He shrugged. "Yes, it's been hard. Especially hard for Francesca. She . . ." He hesitated, his gaze meeting hers. "Ever since the accident, Francesca won't talk to anyone."

"She won't talk to anyone! Oh, David! Why? I thought her injuries weren't serious!"

Another shrug. "Her physical injuries *weren't* serious. The doctors think it's shock. Shock and denial." He laughed without humor. "But they really don't know. They're just guessing because they think they have to give me some kind of answer for her behavior." He rotated his glass in his hands. "Francesca hasn't stopped communicating entirely. She says things like 'yes' and 'no,' and 'I guess,' but not much more."

"Even with you?"

"Especially with me." His face twisted. "She blames me."

Sympathy tore through Tess. She swallowed hard. More than anything in the world she wanted to comfort him, to reach across the table and place her hand over his. She clasped her hands tightly together in her lap to prevent herself from doing just that. "Oh, David," she said again, not knowing anything else to say.

"Why shouldn't she blame me?" he said bitterly, the bleakness back in his eyes. "I knew better than to be out in that weather. I shouldn't have allowed—"

"The accident wasn't your fault. *You* weren't driving that truck!"

His gaze locked with hers. "It doesn't matter whether I was driving the truck or not. Leah's dead. And Francesca ..." His jaw clenched. "Nothing really matters to me right now except my daughter. Unfortunately, she *does* blame me, and I have to try to do something about it. I thought maybe getting her away for a while... I even tried therapy. While we were in Switzerland I took her to a psychologist who worked with her for six months. But nothing's helped." He turned and gazed out the window. "I'm hoping that coming home will be good for her." Slowly, his gaze met Tess's again. "God knows, I've run out of other ideas."

Tess's heart ached for him. It was bad enough that he'd lost Leah. Now he'd lost part of his beautiful daughter, too. "If there's anything I can do..."

"Well, you know, there is. As a matter of fact, it was funny that I should run into you today, because I had intended to call you this afternoon, anyway. I was going to ask if you'd be willing to take Francesca back as a piano student."

"Of course! Why *wouldn't* I be willing?"

Sadness flickered in his eyes. "Because I must warn you, Tess. It's not easy to be around Francesca. She can really depress you."

"That doesn't matter. Nothing matters but helping her, although I don't know how much help I'll be."

"I have a feeling you'll be good for her. She's always liked you a lot. She talked about you all the time."

"She *did?*"

He smiled, and this time the smile carried a trace of the old David—a gentle warmth that enveloped Tess. "I've told you this before. She used to repeat things you'd said as if they were gospel." His smile expanded. "Sometimes Leah would get irritated by Francesca's obvious hero worship. I think she was a bit jealous."

A curious elation coursed through Tess at the thought that there was anything about her that Leah Bannister might have envied.

"Dr. Rickstein—that's the Swiss psychologist who's been treating Francesca—said I had to find someone she'd talk to. I immediately thought of you and how, from the very first, Francesca seemed so drawn to you."

"I don't know what to say. I—I'm flattered." More, she was touched. And a little scared. His trust in her suddenly seemed a great responsibility, and she didn't want to let him down. She smiled gently. "I've missed her, you know. It'll be wonderful to see her again."

For the first time that day, David's eyes glowed with some of their past brilliance. "I'm really grateful. I've about run out of options."

"Is there anything special I'll have to do?" Tess frowned. "It's not as if I have any training or anything. I mean, I don't want to do or say anything that would make things worse."

"Don't worry," he said. "I know you're not a therapist or counselor. Francesca just needs a friend."

Tess nodded. "I can be that, David." *I think you need a friend, too.*

He smiled again. "Thank you, Tess. I can't tell you how much I appreciate this."

Tess's heart beat faster under David's approving gaze. "You don't have to thank me," she said softly. "I love Francesca. I want to help her."

They agreed that David would bring Francesca to Tess's house on Wednesday at four-thirty. Then Tess stood. "I'd better be going. If I don't get home soon, Hazel might send out the cavalry."

He stood, too, fishing some money out of his pocket and laying it on the Formica tabletop. They walked out together. Tess squinted against the bright sunlight.

"So Hazel's still working for you?"

"Yes, she is. Actually, she lives with me now."

"Oh, really? As a boarder?"

"No, not exactly. It got to be a little too much for her, keeping her house and mine, too, plus I think she was a bit lonely." *Like me.* "Anyway, I'm not sure whose idea it was—hers or mine—but earlier this year she decided to sell her house and come and live with me." Tess smiled. "It's worked out great. She still looks after me, and I can keep an eye on her, too." She looked up, meeting his interested gaze. "She's seventy-five, you know."

"She *is*? I never would've guessed it." Suddenly he grinned. "Does she still have that salty old tongue?"

Tess laughed. "Oh, yes. Believe me, I bear the brunt of it all the time. She'll probably be ornery and cussing out the doctors on her deathbed." Then her smile faded. "I hate to think of Hazel dying. She's been an institution in the house since I was a child. She's still pretty spry, but I can see subtle signs of aging. She's a little slower than she used to be."

"She's lucky, having you." He frowned. "Which reminds me. I'm looking for a housekeeper. Do you know anyone?"

"Isn't Jane Cooney coming back?" Jane had worked for the Bannisters before Leah's death.

"She's got another job. I couldn't very well expect her to sit around until I came home again."

Tess nodded. "I'll ask around."

"If you hear of anyone, would you call me? Right now Tammy Littlefield is going to stay with Francesca when I go back to work, but Tammy'll start school in a couple of weeks, so I've got to find someone else."

By now they had reached the parking slot in front of the City Building where he'd left his car, and he turned to her. "Can I give you a ride home?" he asked.

"Thanks, David, but it's only a couple of blocks. I'll walk." Tess knew she needed some time alone before she had to face Hazel, who was nothing if not curious. Her emotions were still too chaotic over the surprise of seeing David again.

"Well, okay, I guess we'll see you Wednesday afternoon." Taking her hand in his, he clasped it warmly. "You've made me feel a lot better, you know. It's good to be back home."

David felt as if a great weight had been lifted from his shoulders as he drove home. He couldn't believe his luck in running into Tess Collier today. He'd gone down to the City Building to pay his utility deposit, and as he'd exited through the revolving door, he'd been thinking about Tess and how he needed to call her.

And then he saw her.

She looked exactly the way he remembered her, as fresh and clean as a balmy spring breeze in her bright yellow sundress. For a moment, he'd just looked at her. Her shining hair was braided and twined around the top of her head in an old-fashioned style that he'd always liked. Everything about her was simple yet attractive, from her lightly tanned skin to her shapely bare legs to her unmade-up face. And when he spoke to her, her soft gray eyes lit up, and David knew a moment of quiet pleasure.

Running into Tess today was a sign, he decided. A sign that his feeling she might be the one person who could get through to Francesca was right.

He'd meant it when he'd told Tess that Francesca had been drawn to her from the beginning. And it was obvious to David that Tess had felt the same way. He'd noticed the connection between them immediately, had even once mentioned his feeling about them to Leah.

He grimaced, remembering. Leah hadn't liked his observation. Her dark eyes had glittered in annoyance. "Oh, that's ridiculous," she'd said. "That mousy piano teacher? She has *nothing* in common with Francesca!"

But it hadn't been ridiculous. He knew it, and he knew Leah had known it. She just hadn't wanted to admit it.

It was funny about Tess.

Leah could say she was mousy and plain. And it was true that Tess wasn't the kind of woman to dazzle a man with her beauty or charm or wit. She didn't wear the latest fashions or tell the latest jokes.

Yet she had an inner glow. Francesca had responded to it immediately. *Hell, admit it. You responded to it, too.* Yes, that was true, David thought. He *had* responded to it. In fact, he had come to look forward to his weekly visits with Tess Collier. They'd been a tranquil interlude in an otherwise tumultuous life.

He had missed those visits after he and Francesca went to Switzerland. He'd never realized just how hard it was to find a person you could talk to—really talk to. Tess had always been easy to talk to because she was such a good listener. Because she always seemed to understand, not only what he said, but what he felt. He had found himself telling her things he'd never told anyone else.

No wonder Francesca had responded to Tess.

Now all David could do was pray that she would respond to Tess again.

Chapter Two

All afternoon Wednesday, Tess watched the clock. She taught the students who paraded in and out, part of her mind functioning the same way it always did. The other part of her mind fastened on the knowledge that in just two hours, one hour, half an hour, David would arrive with Francesca.

Finally, when Tess's stomach had settled into a permanent case of butterflies, the grandfather clock in the foyer chimed four-fifteen, and she knew it wouldn't be long.

She had purposely scheduled Francesca's lesson in a slot where there would be no one preceding her and no one following her, so that if Tess wanted to take extra time with the child, she could.

And there was another reason, wasn't there? You were also thinking that David could stay and talk after the lesson, just like he used to... weren't you? Come on, admit it.

Yes, she thought as the minutes crept toward four-thirty, that thought *had* crossed her mind. Tess stood in the front parlor and gazed out the open bay window. Sounds floated through the screen—familiar summer sounds that Tess had heard all of her life. The soft drone of a bumblebee as it worked the hollyhocks rimming the front porch. The rattle of little Jason Mahoney's wagon as he pulled it along the uneven front sidewalk. The pure note of a robin as it flitted through the leafy branches of the maple trees lining the long street. The wail of a baby from a neighboring yard.

And then—causing her heart to skip—the sound of a car coming slowly up the street.

David. David and Francesca.

As the familiar black BMW nosed into view, she put her right hand against her chest, willing her heart to stop its mad flutter. When the BMW stopped in front of her house, she forced herself to breathe deeply. She knew it was ridiculous to be so nervous and excited, but she couldn't seem to help herself.

David was counting on her. She didn't want to let him down. This is what she told herself, yet Tess knew her emotions were much more complex than just apprehension over whether or not she'd be able to help Francesca.

Despite her agitation, the deep breathing helped and gradually her heart slowed. Calmer now, she smoothed down the skirt of her blue cotton dress, then walked into the foyer and stood just inside the screened front door.

The door on the driver's side of the BMW opened. David, dressed in gray cotton casual pants and a white knit shirt, his dark hair shining in the dappled sunlight, emerged and walked around to open the passenger door. Tess watched as he reached for Francesca's hand; saw how the child seemed to hold herself back, even as she allowed him to help her out of the car.

Eyes downcast, Francesca walked beside David. She, too, looked different. It hurt Tess to see how much thinner Francesca was, how bony her shoulders and knees looked in her short-sleeved pink T-shirt and matching pink shorts. Even though Tess knew the child had grown, she seemed so fragile and vulnerable as she approached the house.

Tess opened the screen door when the two of them started to climb the four shallow steps leading to the front porch. "Hello, Francesca," she said, stepping outside. Francesca, eyes haunted and sad, looked up.

For a long moment, no one moved. Then Tess, fighting against tears, opened her arms, and Francesca, after a brief hesitation, walked slowly forward and allowed Tess to hug her.

Tess could feel the child trembling, and she smoothed her hand over her silky dark curls, murmuring, "It's okay, honey. It's okay." Swallowing hard, her eyes met David's over the top of Francesca's head.

What Tess saw caused her heart to contort with a painful wrench. His green eyes were filled with despair, and she knew it must be even more terrible for David to witness his daughter's obvious misery than it was for Tess.

Tess took Francesca's hand and they walked inside the house together, David following.

Tess led Francesca into the front parlor. Tess usually taught her students on the spinet piano in the library. Tess herself always played the beautiful old Steinway grand piano that had been in her family for generations, but she only allowed her students to play it when they were readying themselves for a recital or some other public performance.

However, Francesca was different. This situation was different, and Tess had already decided she would teach Francesca on the Steinway. She wondered now if Francesca would say anything about the change of instruments. So far the child hadn't uttered a word.

"I thought we'd have our lessons here," Tess said, but Francesca still said nothing.

That look of profound sorrow in Francesca's eyes wasn't going to be easy to endure. Yet instinctively, Tess knew the worst thing she could do was treat Francesca with pity. Pity was the last thing the child needed. She needed understanding and, as David had said, she needed a friend. A nonthreatening friend. Tess groped for something to say, something to alleviate the awkwardness and tension permeating the room.

At that moment, Tess's cat, Budge, walked into the room, his bushy yellow tail an exclamation point behind him. He sidled up to Francesca, said "Meow," in his superior I'm-here-at-last-you-lucky-person voice, and Francesca finally reacted with some semblance of her former self. With a happy cry, she let go of Tess's hand, sank to her knees and embraced Budge, who in typical Budge fashion, endured her petting for as long as he could stand it, then twisted out of her grasp. With an arrogant swagger, he padded over to the bay window, leaped up onto the window seat, and sank down in a pool of sunlight, where he immediately began to bathe himself.

"I think Budge missed you," Tess said. "He doesn't show himself to everyone, you know."

She was rewarded with the barest of smiles. Then Francesca slid onto the piano bench, and Tess's gaze met David's. She could see the indecision in his eyes. She wondered if he planned to stay. *Don't stay,* she tried to communicate with her eyes. *It'll be better if we're alone.*

"I have a couple of errands to run," he finally said. "I'll be back at five."

Tess nodded. She smiled reassuringly. Some of the worry left his eyes. She wished she could say the things she was thinking. Instead she gave him a wave, then turned back to the waiting child.

"Well," she said brightly, sitting next to Francesca on the bench. "Where shall we start?"

Francesca shrugged.

"Have you done any practicing at all since you stopped your lessons?"

Francesca shook her head, and now her eyes had taken on a hesitant look, as if she were afraid of what Tess's reaction to this disclosure would be.

Tess smiled. She put her hand over Francesca's. "That's okay, honey. Don't worry about it. Why don't we start with the scales? Let's see how you do with those."

For the next ten minutes Francesca played scales. At first her playing was stiff, and she made a lot of mistakes. But gradually her fingers limbered up and her natural talent and affinity for the piano resurfaced. Soon her scales were light and almost error free.

"That's wonderful," Tess said, smiling again.

Francesca smiled back. The smile wasn't even a glimmer of her old joyous one, but still, it was a start, and Tess felt the first real stirring of hope.

"How about playing some simple pieces?" she suggested.

Francesca nodded.

Together they went through the book Francesca had been working in when her lessons had been discontinued. Francesca pointed to the pieces she wanted to try. She started with Beethoven's "Für Elise." For the remainder of the lesson, she attempted to play several other pieces she had formerly mastered. She stumbled several times in each, but Tess felt encouraged by how little she'd lost over the past seven months.

"Well," Tess said as the grandfather clock chimed the hour, "you've done beautifully for your first time back. Do you still have a copy of this book at home?" It was a book of classic pieces arranged in a simple style, with the difficulty of the melody divided between the two hands.

Francesca nodded.

"How about practicing each of the songs you played today? Then next week, if you want to, we can start on something new." Tess racked her brain. Then, suddenly remembering, she grinned. "Maybe even the 'Spinning Song.' Would you like that?"

Francesca looked up, and Tess was gratified to see that there was a spark of enthusiasm in her eyes. She smiled shyly and whispered, "Yes," so low Tess almost didn't hear it. Before Tess had time to react to Francesca's first verbal communication, she heard David's footsteps coming up the front walk. Obviously, so did Francesca, for the happy light in her eyes vanished.

David was right, Tess thought. Francesca must blame him. Otherwise, why would she act this way at the reappearance of her father? Why would she act as if she didn't want to see him? Tess wished she had time to try to talk to Francesca about her feelings, but David had already tapped on the screen door.

"Come in," Tess called, watching Francesca's face. The child sat stiffly beside her on the bench as David walked into the parlor. She didn't meet his gaze.

He smiled—first at Tess and then at Francesca—as he advanced into the room. "How did the lesson go?"

Tess hesitated a second, looking at Francesca, wondering if she might answer. But she didn't, so Tess said, "It went just fine. Francesca hasn't forgotten what she learned."

Francesca bowed her head.

"That's good." There was a warm light in David's eyes as his gaze met Tess's again. Tess wondered what it would be like to always bask in the warmth of David's gaze. "Thanks," he mouthed silently.

Tess smiled her acknowledgment.

"Francesca," David said, "why don't you go on out and swing on the porch swing while I talk to Miss Collier for a minute?"

Silently, Francesca stood. Tess said, "Now, don't forget to practice this week."

Avoiding her father's eyes, Francesca walked over to the bay window where she leaned over and hugged Budge. Still not looking at either David or Tess, she then turned and walked out of the room.

A couple of seconds later, Tess heard the creak and whine of the porch swing as it moved on its rusty hinges.

David sighed and shook his head, then ran his right hand through his hair. "What do you think?" he said in a low voice, his forehead furrowed with worry.

Tess motioned with her hand, and he followed her into the foyer and down the hall so they'd be out of earshot of Francesca. "I don't know for sure," Tess said slowly. "It's easy to see she's a very troubled child. But I don't know...always bearing in mind I'm no expert...she doesn't seem *hopeless,* David. There were flashes of the old Francesca today. I'm hopeful." She wanted to tell him that she agreed with his assessment of Francesca's mental state. That she thought he was right in feeling Francesca felt antagonism toward him. But no useful purpose would be served. Not now, anyway.

"I hope you're right," he said wearily. "I wish she'd talk to me. I know she blames me for Leah's death." He shrugged. "Can't blame her, can you?"

"Oh, David... don't be so hard on yourself."

He grimaced. "You don't understand."

"I think I do."

"Look, my feelings don't matter at all." He looked in the direction of the porch, where the faint creak of the swing could still be heard. "Well, at least she seemed happy to see you. That's a start, anyway." He reached into his pocket and extracted a checkbook. He opened it and ripped out the top check. "Here," he said, handing it to her. "This is for the first month's lessons."

Tess accepted the check, folded it and put it into her skirt pocket, then she walked outside with David. When Francesca saw them, she stopped the swing.

David smiled at her, but she didn't smile back.

"Did you find a housekeeper yet?" Tess asked, remaining on the porch as first Francesca, then David, walked down the steps.

David turned, looking up to face her. Francesca kept on going. "I'm interviewing two women tomorrow. As a matter of fact, I was going to ask you if you knew either one of them."

"Who are they?"

"Janet Witherspoon and Peggy Kaminski."

"I know both of them. Janet goes to our church, and Peggy's one of the singers in the Collierville choral group. They're both very reliable, I would think." Tess hesitated, wondering if she should say more. Privately she thought Peggy Kaminski was the best choice of the two, but David hadn't asked.

"What?" he said, obviously realizing she wanted to add something.

"Well . . . even though Janet's a nice woman, I think Francesca would be better off with Peggy. Peggy's got a more cheerful personality. She's more upbeat, and I think Francesca needs someone positive right now."

He nodded. "Thanks, Tess. I appreciate all your help. We'll see you again next Wednesday."

Tess stood on the porch and watched as he got into the BMW. He started the ignition, then tooted the horn as he pulled away from the curb. Francesca stared out the passenger side window as the car moved off down the street. Tess smiled and waved, and after a moment, Francesca waved back. She didn't smile.

Tess knew the picture of Francesca's sad little face would haunt her the entire week.

David glanced at Francesca often as they drove the fifteen minutes or so it took to reach their home at the outskirts of Collierville. If only she'd talk to him. Hell, if she'd even *look* at him!

She did neither. She kept her face resolutely turned away from him while she stared out her window. She didn't look in his direction even once.

Tess had said Francesca needed someone upbeat right now. That was certainly true. David needed someone upbeat, too. For too many months he and Francesca had lived in a silent, gloomy world. A world where Francesca thought her thoughts and David thought his thoughts. A world where she blamed him and he blamed himself. A world without laughter or joy or hope.

David knew he couldn't stand much more of this. Something had to give. He had tried everything, and so far, nothing had worked.

Tess was his last hope.

When they reached the house—a large, stone, split-level set against the backdrop of a densely wooded area—Francesca bounded out of the car the moment David pulled it to a stop inside the double garage. He sighed as she disappeared into the house before he'd even opened his door.

He got out, closed the garage door, then slowly entered the house. He didn't even have to look. He knew exactly where Francesca would be. Heart heavy, he walked through the large combination kitchen and family room with its gleaming copper pots and the very latest in kitchen gadgets, and into the hallway. Bypassing both his study and the formal dining room, he entered the L-shaped living room with its enormous plate-glass window that covered most of two walls and overlooked the street on one side and the woods on the other.

He clenched his teeth.

Just as he'd known she would be, Francesca stood in front of the fireplace, her gaze turned up to study the big family portrait hanging over the mantel.

David grimaced as he, too, looked at the portrait. There they were, the three of them. The perfect family. David, dressed in a dark suit, stood behind an ornate carved chair that reminded him of a throne. His hand rested on the top. Seated on the chair was Leah—a smiling Leah in a vivid red dress. Francesca, leaning against her mother's knee, was outfitted in dark green velvet trimmed with lace.

The portrait had been Leah's idea, taken only a month before she'd died. Its very size had seemed pretentious to him, not to mention the lie it perpetrated. They were not the perfect family. Once David had thought they could be, but that delusion had been long gone when the portrait was taken. Yet Leah had been adamant in her desire to have the picture taken and to display it prominently afterward.

"It doesn't matter that *we* know our marriage wasn't exactly made in heaven," she'd said. "In this world, appearances are everything."

David, as he'd been doing more and more often, had found it easier to accede to her wishes than to provoke another argument. That last year they'd argued much too often. He'd known it wasn't good for Francesca to hear them, but Leah had had no qualms over airing any of their disagreements in front of their daughter. In fact, she'd seemed to relish his discomfort and disapproval when she did. He'd known Leah well enough to know that she'd enjoyed provoking him. That she hadn't cared how much turmoil she'd caused her daughter as long as she'd remained in control. He'd also known the time would come when he would have to make a stand. Yet he'd continued to delay, because he'd known that the moment their marriage fell apart for good, Leah would have taken Francesca back to New York.

So now the portrait mocked him. He wanted nothing more than to remove it—bury it somewhere where he'd never have to set eyes on it again. And he would have taken it down, except for Francesca. He couldn't do anything more to upset her, and if she derived comfort from the portrait, it was the least he could do to allow her that solace.

But he hated the portrait, and he always would. It was a constant reminder to him that he had failed. As a husband.

And now as a father.

Tess grinned as she navigated her way through the maze of children's toys littering Summer McKee's front walk. An abandoned roller skate, an upended wagon, and a forlorn-looking doll lay scattered like forgotten pieces to a jigsaw puzzle.

Summer was Tess's best friend. Had been her best friend since both were toddlers living next door to each other. Summer was the exact opposite of Tess, and Tess had always wondered why the lively blonde with the effervescent personality had singled out quiet, shy Tess Collier to be her friend.

Sometimes Tess thought Summer liked having her around because of the contrast between the two of them. But those thoughts came during Tess's gloomier moments. Most of the time she realized Summer genuinely loved her, that Tess brought some balance into Summer's hectic life.

From inside the house came the sounds of children's voices raised in laughter. Yes, definitely hectic. And noisy. But whose life wouldn't be hectic and noisy with four children under the age of twelve? And usually, in addition to her own four, Summer had at least two or three of the neighbors' children around, too.

Just then there was a loud crashing noise from the direction of the kitchen, followed by an exasperated, "Lisa! Didn't I tell you not to try to carry all of those at once?"

Tess rang Summer's front doorbell.

"Will one of you kids see who's at the door?" Summer's voice shouted over the din.

A few seconds later, Lisa—Summer's six-year-old—unlatched the screened door. "Hi, Aunt Tess," she chirped, blue eyes shining. "Mommy's in the kitchen." Lisa was Tess's godchild, although all of Summer's children called her Aunt Tess.

After exchanging a hug, Tess followed the youngster back into the large kitchen. Summer and her husband Mitchell had built this modern two-story home three years ago after their twin boys were born and the family had outgrown their first house. Today, the smell of spaghetti sauce floated in the air.

"Tess!" Summer said, turning from the sink. She grinned. "Gee, I didn't know you were coming over."

Even though Summer was flushed from the heat, surrounded by kids—Tess's quick count showed there were five children around the big table—and elbow-deep in soapsuds, she looked beautiful. Her blond hair was secured by a rubber band and tied up in a ponytail, and she wore no makeup. She was dressed in tight-fitting cut-offs and a red and white striped T-shirt. Still, her tanned skin, large blue eyes and sparkling smile were all she needed. Summer was a natural beauty—her name a reflection of her golden good looks and optimistic disposition.

"Hi," Tess said. "I didn't know I was coming over, either. I was on my way to the supermarket and decided to stop in." She looked around. "It's not the best time, is it?"

Summer wiped her hands on a dish towel and walked over to Tess, hugging her. "It's always a good time to visit with you." She clapped her hands. "Okay, kids. Outside."

"Aw, Mom," said Lucas, her eight-year-old. "We were just startin' the game."

"Play it outside on the picnic table," Summer said firmly. "I'll bring you a pitcher of grape juice."

"But we wanna talk to Aunt Tess," Lisa argued, pouting.

"You can talk to Aunt Tess later."

"We don't wanna play outside," Lucas said. "It's hot outside!" His freckled face settled into mutinous lines.

"It's hot inside, too."

"But Mom-mm..."

"Don't *Mom-mm* me. School starts in nine more days," Summer said, "and you'll be inside all day long then. This is your last chance to play outdoors. Now no more arguing. Git!"

Finally, after a few more grumbles and dragging of feet, the kitchen was cleared out.

Tess smothered a smile.

"Thank God," Summer said, shaking her head. "Sit down. Do you want a glass of lemonade?"

"That sounds great. Where are Scotty and Sandy?" she asked, referring to Summer's three-year-old twins.

"Mitch's mother took them for the day."

"And instead of enjoying the respite, you've got three of someone else's kids here."

"Well, Lisa and Lucas would never entertain themselves!"

A few minutes later, glasses of cold lemonade in front of them, they began to talk of other things. Then Summer said, "Guess what? I've applied for a part-time job with Schwab Travel Agency. You know Nettie Schwab, don't you?"

"Yeah. But how are you gonna work? Who's going to watch the twins?" Tess asked.

"I'll put them in Mother's Day Out three times a week."

"But wouldn't all the money you make go for day-care expenses?"

"Making money isn't the point," Summer explained patiently. "Getting out of the house and relating to someone other than a child is what it's all about."

"But you love your children!"

"What does love have to do with it?" Summer countered. "Of course, I love them, but that doesn't mean I want to spend every waking moment with them."

Tess sipped at her lemonade and didn't answer. She didn't trust herself to answer. She didn't want Summer, or anyone, feeling sorry for her. So she didn't say what was in her heart. She didn't say, *You don't have any idea how lucky you are. I'd give my soul to have a child of my own, and I'd gladly spend every moment with that child.* Instead she pushed her thoughts aside and asked, "What will you be doing there?"

"Learning the reservation system. Helping people plan trips. It's straight commission, but I'd get great training. Doesn't that sound like fun?" Summer's blue eyes lit up with eagerness. "I can hardly wait for school to start. Nettie said I could begin then."

Tess nodded slowly. Actually, the job *did* sound like fun. A whole lot more fun than teaching piano. Still, she wondered why Summer felt the need for this job.

"You don't look convinced," Summer said.

"It's just that...oh, I don't know...I've always thought you had everything. I've always envied you your busy life with Mitch and the kids, and now...well, now you're saying you need something else, too."

"But, Tess, I complain all the time about how I hate being stuck in the house."

Tess shrugged. "I know, but I thought you were just, you know, letting off steam. I didn't think you really *meant* it."

"Heck, yes, I meant it." Summer leaned forward, her expression earnest. "I know my attitude must strike you as selfish," she said slowly. She hesitated, her blue eyes clouding imperceptibly. "But things are not always what they seem. Sure, I love Mitch and the kids, but I need a life of my own. Something apart from them. Something I can feel is all mine."

Tess struggled to set aside her own yearning for a child so that she could understand Summer's feelings.

"Actually," Summer continued, "I've always envied you a little bit."

"Me!"

"Yes, you. You're strong and self-sufficient. You're independent. You have a career. You don't have a lot of responsibilities." Summer grimaced. "Sometimes I imagine what it would be like to be in a quiet house. No one else around. Just me and a book or a bubble bath." She sighed. "Dream on, Summer."

Tess's mind was stuck on one word. "Strong? I've never thought of myself as strong." She laughed a bit self-consciously. "I've always thought of myself as a wimp."

Summer stared at her. "A wimp! Tess! Didn't you drop out of college so that you could stay home and take care of your great-aunt? Didn't you, all by yourself, not only nurse her back to some semblance of health but build a career, as well? Didn't you, after your aunt died, manage to not only support yourself but hang on to that house?"

"I did what I had to do."

"That's my point. You were strong enough to do what needed to be done."

"Well, I'd hardly call what I do a career," Tess said. "Besides, you have the most important career in the world. You're a mother. You're creating a home for your family."

"Oh, I know, I know. That's not what I mean. I wouldn't trade my family for anything. But what's wrong with wanting it all? My kids aren't going to be little forever. And once they're grown, then what? Am I supposed to sit around twiddling my thumbs? Going to garden club meetings and playing bridge? No, no. That's not for me."

I don't want it all. I just want what you have.

"Well, that's enough about me," Summer said. "Tell me what's going on in your life."

Tess hesitated. She fiddled with the skirt of her mint green sundress. Then she lifted her eyes and said, "I've got a new student."

"Oh? Who?" There was genuine interest in Summer's voice.

"Francesca Bannister."

Summer's eyes widened and her mouth opened. "Francesca Bannister! You mean, David Bannister is back in Collierville?"

Tess nodded.

"I hadn't heard. When did he get back?"

"A week or so ago, I think."

"Have you seen him?"

"Yes. I ran into him downtown last week. And he brought Francesca for her lesson on Wednesday."

"How are they doing?"

Tess shrugged. "As well as can be expected, I guess. Francesca is having some serious emotional problems, and David's worried about her."

Summer's expressive face contorted with pity. "Poor little thing. What kind of problems?"

So Tess explained about Francesca's self-imposed silence. How David thought Francesca blamed him for her mother's death and that's why she wouldn't speak. "Anyway," Tess finished, "he thinks maybe I can help her."

"If anyone can help her, you can," Summer said loyally. "You're wonderful with the kids."

Tess sighed. "I hope I can. I'm sure going to try."

"Why don't you bring her over here some weekend?" Summer suggested.

Tess nodded. "That's a good idea. I'll mention it to David and see what he thinks."

"You've always liked Francesca a lot, haven't you?"

"Yes. She's pretty special."

Summer smiled. "David Bannister's pretty special, too."

"He's a very nice man."

"He's more than nice. He's a hunk." Summer eyed her thoughtfully. "Don't you think so?"

Tess froze. Was Summer implying something with her remark? Did she suspect Tess was interested in David? Had Tess somehow given away her feelings? Carefully, Tess studied Summer's face, and relief gradually washed over her. There was no innuendo in Summer's gaze, no hint of suspicion. Her remark had been an innocent one. Simply an observation of fact. And Summer was right. David *was* special. After all, Tess certainly thought so, and she was sure every other female under the age of ninety who had ever met David would think so, too.

Summer grinned. "Gee, now I'm really looking forward to church tomorrow. Do you think they'll be there?"

"I don't know. I guess so." Tess hoped so.

"Won't it be fun to see the women buzzing around him?" Summer's grin expanded. "I'll bet Pamela Gates is even now rubbing her hands in glee!"

Tess knew how she was supposed to respond, but it was hard. Pamela Gates was aggressively husband-hunting, and Tess could just imagine how she would try to latch onto David. Eligible bachelors were few and far between in Collierville. And handsome, successful, eligible bachelors were even more scarce.

"So tell me what he looked like. How he acted. What he said," Summer said enthusiastically.

"He's sadder, older and quieter."

"But still handsome, I'll bet."

"Yes, still handsome."

A speculative gleam appeared in Summer's eyes. "You know, Tess, David Bannister would be perfect for *you.*"

"Me!" Tess could feel her face getting red. She shook her head. "Oh, no. Not me."

"Why not?"

"He'd never be interested in me. I'm too...too boring."

"Honestly, Tess! Quit that! Quit thinking of yourself in such disparaging terms. You're not boring at all."

"That's not what Howard Simmons said."

"Oh, Howard Simmons!" Summer said. "I never realized he was such a jerk. He just wanted someone to gush all over him and tell him how wonderful he was, and when you didn't, he said you were boring. Don't pay any attention to him."

Howard Simmons worked with Summer's husband, and Mitch had invited him and Tess to a barbecue earlier in the year. Summer confessed later that Mitch had thought he was doing them both a good turn. But the evening had been a disaster.

"Oh, I haven't let Howard's remark bother me, not really," Tess said.

"Yeah, sure. Then why did you bring up his name?"

Tess shrugged. It hadn't taken Howard Simmons's opinion to plant the idea in her mind. After all, she *was* boring. What nineties man wanted to be around a woman who taught piano lessons to children all day long? Who wasn't sexy or exciting or stimulating to be with? Who didn't have a talent for snappy repartee?

"Seriously, I think you should make an effort to befriend David Bannister," Summer said. "Believe me, he's not going to last long on the marriage market."

"I want to be David's friend, but I couldn't...I couldn't go after him...." Even the thought of pursuing David made Tess flinch.

"Well, mark my words. Once the unmarried women in town find out he's back, they'll all be after him. He'll be invited to dinner parties and cocktail parties and birthday parties. You name it, they'll ask him. They won't be the least bit shy about showing him they're interested in him."

Tess bit her bottom lip.

"Think about it, Tess. If you want him, you've got to show him you do. Now is not the time to hang back and wait for something to happen. You've got to make it happen!"

Chapter Three

You've got to make it happen.

Tess thought about Summer's advice throughout the rest of that day and evening. Summer made it all sound so simple. So easy.

Make it happen.

As if, just because Tess might entertain secret thoughts of David, she could, by the sheer force of her desire, make him notice her as someone other than a friend to his daughter. Make him aware of her as a woman. A desirable woman.

Oh, sure, Tess thought. Fat chance. David had never once—not while Leah was alive and not after her death—given Tess the idea that he was attracted to her. Tess might not have much experience with men, but she'd had enough to know the subtle signs of interest. She'd received her share of looks over the years—from married as well as unmarried men.

No, David had never indicated his awareness.

Or his interest.

And now Summer had hinted that Tess might provoke it. That she had the power to shape events to her liking. The trouble was, for people like Summer, who were full of self-confidence, making the things happen that they wanted to happen *was* easy.

For people like Tess, who were full of self-doubts, nothing was ever easy. Summer could never understand, because everything she'd ever wanted she'd gotten. Mitch was a perfect example.

Summer had met Mitch when both were in college. As she'd later told Tess, she'd taken one look, told herself Mitch was the man she'd been waiting for all of her life, and that had been that. Six months later they were engaged, and two years later they were married.

Tess, in contrast, had also met the man she'd thought was her destiny while she, too, had been in college. They began to date in the spring of her sophomore year. But when her great-aunt Millicent fell ill during Tess's junior year, and Tess had had to drop out of school to care for her, Glenn hadn't been willing to wait around. When four months went by and Tess was still at home caring for her great-aunt, he came to Collierville to see her.

Tess would never forget that day. It had been a blustery, frigid February afternoon, and the wind off Lake Erie was cold enough to freeze even the hardiest plants.

There was a big fire going in the fireplace in the parlor, and after greeting Glenn—a greeting that included several satisfying kisses—Tess led him into the parlor. She was thrilled that he'd made the four-hour trip to see her. Her body tingled from his caresses, and her heart was full of hope and happiness.

"So when are you coming back?" he asked without preamble. He held his hands out toward the fireplace and grinned down at her with the offhand charm that had captivated her from the very first.

Some of Tess's happiness faded as she remembered how sick Aunt Millicent was. How guarded Dr. Torok was when he'd talked to Tess about her aunt's prognosis. "Oh, Glenn, I wish I knew. Things don't look good right now."

He frowned. "What does that mean?"

"I . . . well . . . I just can't be sure. Her doctor doesn't think Aunt Millicent will be able to live on her own, even if she *does* get better. And if she doesn't . . . well . . ." Tess blinked back the tears that threatened as she thought of her aunt lying so frail and sick upstairs in her bed. "Th-they don't know how long she'll last. They said things could go on like this for years."

"For years!"

Tess nodded miserably. She'd been just as shocked by the possibility when she'd first been told. Not because of what it meant to her, but because she hated the idea of her aunt suffering for so long.

"Does that mean you intend to stay here until your aunt either gets well or . . . dies?" he asked bluntly.

For the first time since his arrival, a chill crept down Tess's spine. But when she spoke, her voice was calm. "Well, yes. Surely you wouldn't expect me to do anything else?"

A frown marred his handsome face. "Tess, be reasonable. You can't stay here for years. What about *your* life? What about me?"

"I can't just abandon my aunt. I'm all she has."

"I'm not saying you should abandon her. But you could put her in a nursing home. Or you could hire a nurse to come here and stay. You don't have to take care of her yourself."

"Maybe not. But I also can't do what you're suggesting, either. I told you how Aunt Millicent took me in when my parents didn't want me! I explained how good she's been to me. I can't just palm her off on some stranger. Besides, I don't want to do that—"

"Look, babe," he said, putting his hands on her shoulders. "I know you're grateful to your aunt. And I admire you for it. But that doesn't mean you have to devote the rest of your life to her, does it? She wouldn't expect that."

Tess stared at him. Why was it she'd never noticed how cold his blue eyes could look? "I couldn't live with myself if I abandoned her." She told herself he didn't mean to sound so unsympathetic. He just didn't fully understand. His own parents were young and healthy. He couldn't imagine facing the kind of situation Tess was facing.

"Where does that leave us?"

Tess's chest felt tight as she touched his arm. "Glenn, please, please understand. I have to do this. I owe her."

He shrugged off her hand. "Okay, fine. Stay here if you have to. You've made your choice. But don't expect me to be waiting around forever." He reached for his jacket, then bent, dropping a quick kiss on her nose. "So, hey, babe, no hard feelings. Maybe I'll see you around sometime."

Many weeks later, Tess realized how much she'd always hated being called "babe."

As Tess dressed for church the morning after her visit to Summer's house, she once more thought about her friend's advice. She knew Summer was right about one thing: David Bannister would not remain a bachelor for long.

Tess walked over to the cheval glass mirror in her bedroom. She studied herself dispassionately. She was thirty-five years old—almost thirty-six—but she knew she looked younger. She'd inherited her mother's beautiful skin and her father's wide-eyed look of innocence.

She figured her youthful look was a point in her favor. Most men David's age seemed to like younger women.

Her gaze traveled downward from her face to her body. She was thin, too thin, she thought—only weighing one hundred and fifteen pounds on her five feet five inch frame. She knew that *wasn't* a point in her favor. In her mind's eye she could see Leah Bannister, with her sexy, lush figure—her high, full breasts and her rounded hips. No, Tess's thinness wouldn't win any points with David. She was certain of that.

She wasn't sure about her hair. Her hair was unusual, she knew. Not the color. The color was just an ordinary light brown. What was different about her hair was its length and weight. She'd been letting her hair grow since she was fifteen years old. It now hung to below her hips and was so long she could sit on it. It was very thick and very straight. Today, like everyday, she had brushed it until it gleamed, then braided it and twisted it into a coronet around her head. But even though Tess liked her hair, it was nothing like Leah Bannister's hair, which had been chin-length and curly and as black as midnight.

The rest of Tess was just plain ordinary, she thought. Gray eyes, which were large but not spectacular. Straight nose. Ordinary mouth—not thin, not full, just ordinary.

Tess looked at her hands. Her fingers were long and supple and perfectly shaped. She was secretly vain about their appearance, indulging herself with an occasional professional manicure. But what man cared about long fingers?

Don't forget your legs.

Tess stared at her legs. Summer and others—including Glenn—had told her she had pretty legs. Like her fingers, they were long and shapely, but as far as Tess was concerned, they weren't much of an asset. She wasn't the type to wear miniskirts or shorts, so what good did they do her?

She sighed again, smoothing down the skirt of her peach silk shirtwaist dress. Not much to work with. Certainly nothing to compare to Leah Bannister's sultry good looks and vivid personality.

So no matter what Summer had advised, Tess knew she wouldn't make any overt moves in David's direction. Just the thought of how she'd feel if David rejected her caused her to flush with embarrassment. Or worse, what if he felt *sorry* for her? No, she couldn't risk it. At least now she had David's friendship and his company. And that was infinitely better than nothing.

When David, holding a reluctant Francesca's hand, walked into the sun-filled church, the first person he saw was Tess. She was seated at the pipe organ in the chancel to the left of the pulpit, and she was playing "When Morning Gilds the Skies."

Nodding to familiar faces along the way, he led Francesca to an empty pew about two-thirds of the way down. Once they were seated, he looked around. Several people smiled and nodded, and he smiled and nodded back. A good-looking blonde dressed in a pale blue suit waved at him, giving him a beaming smile.

David smiled back, but inwardly he was wondering who the devil the woman was. He knew her face, but he couldn't remember her name. Her brilliant blue gaze still rested on him, and he shifted uncomfortably. There was something almost predatory in the way she was looking at him. He turned, still trying to pry her name from his subconscious, and his own gaze once more settled on Tess. She had just finished the hymn and was turning the pages of her three-ring binder. She glanced up, and their gazes met. She smiled shyly, and the uncomfortable feeling the blonde had caused slipped away.

David returned Tess's smile, thinking how restful she was. She had that rare ability to soothe and calm just by her presence in a room. It had been the first thing about her he'd ever noticed. At this very moment he could feel the hard knot in his stomach dissolving under her serene gaze.

She looked very nice today, he thought, in her peach dress. Sunlight pooled around her, burnishing her with soft, golden light. As he watched, she began to play again, this time "The Church's One Foundation." Pleasure warmed him as he watched her graceful hands move over the keys of the organ. David hummed along under his breath. He'd always liked this hymn. It reminded him of his boyhood, when, on Sunday mornings he had sat between his mother and his father and, instead of paying attention to the service, had daydreamed about what he would do for the rest of the day.

He smiled as he remembered those wonderful, carefree days of childhood. He had always felt so secure in the love of his parents. They had clearly adored him and told him many times how surprised and thrilled they were by his birth nearly twenty years into their marriage. He was still thinking about his parents when he glanced down at Francesca.

Immediately, David's feeling of well-being disappeared. His daughter sat stiffly upright, her face turned straight ahead. Her rigid profile told him, without words, that her childhood was not carefree and wonderful. Her childhood had been filled with unhappiness and stress—first by the arguments that had escalated into an ongoing battle between him and Leah—and then by the abrupt and traumatic loss of her mother.

A loss that could be laid directly at David's door.

Because, no matter what Tess, in her kindness, or anyone else, in their compassion, had said, David knew that he and he alone was responsible for Leah's death.

And Francesca knew it, too.

When the service was over, Tess gathered up her music. She quickly changed from her flat ballet slippers to her pumps, then slowly joined the membership exiting the church. Her eyes searched the throng as they shuffled through the narthex. Almost everyone stopped to exchange pleasantries with the Reverend Humble, who stood in the open doorway.

Tess wished they'd all hurry. She was impatient to get outside, but her way was blocked. She stood on tiptoe and looked for David. At first she didn't see him, and she was afraid he was already gone.

Then his dark head bobbed into view as the crowd shifted, creating an opening. Her breath caught, and her heart gave a quick skip as her gaze rested on his handsome profile. He was smiling, talking to someone. He looked wonderful today in his dark blue suit paired with a striped shirt and burgundy tie.

Unlike a lot of women who seemed drawn to muscular types who displayed a lot of skin, Tess had always thought there was something wonderfully appealing about a man in a well-cut suit. Today, when she'd first seen David walking up the aisle with Francesca, a rush of emotion had caused her hands to tremble and she'd almost misplayed a note. She had hurriedly looked down at her music, telling herself to settle down.

Later, after he and Francesca—who looked adorable in a red and white checked pinafore—were seated, Tess had covertly watched as people nodded and smiled at him. She felt a thrill of pride as she realized David was well-liked, that people were glad to see him back. Tess knew she had no reason to feel proprietary toward David, but she couldn't help it. Then Pamela Gates, looking polished and beautiful in a blue suit, waved and made a big show of smiling at him, and Tess had a violent urge to slap her. Shocked at the intensity of her feelings, Tess had looked away.

She wondered where Pamela Gates was now. She was probably lying in wait for David. Ready to pounce the moment he walked outside. Tess couldn't help grinning at the picture she'd created in her mind, even as her stomach clenched at the thought of all the women who were sure to want David.

Well, there's not a thing you can do about it, so paste a smile on your face and act normal.

By the time Tess reached the spot where Reverend Humble stood, she had gotten her emotions under control again. She murmured her greetings, then turned to exit the church. As she did, someone slipped a hand around her waist.

"You look nice today," Summer's voice said in her ear.

Tess grinned. "Thanks. Where were you? I didn't see you in church."

"We were sitting in the back."

Summer looked beautiful, as always, Tess thought as they walked outside into the heat of the morning. She was wearing a short, black and white striped linen dress with a big white collar. Her hair was held back from her face by a black headband, and on her ears were clipped huge black and white earrings in the shape of stars.

For the millionth time, Tess wished she had some of Summer's breezy style. *I always look like a school teacher,* she thought glumly, looking down at the sedate length of her own simple dress. Their choice of earrings alone pointed out the marked contrast between them. Looking at Summer's jaunty stars, Tess touched the small pearls in her own ears.

They started down the steps. "Where're Mitch and the kids?" Tess asked.

Summer looked around. "I don't know. Somewhere. Scotty needed to go to the bathroom, so Mitch took him and Sandy off in that direction. And the other two dashed outside earlier."

Tess nodded. Just then she saw David again, and her heart fluttered. He stood off to one side of the wide front walk, still holding Francesca's hand. Francesca didn't look at him. She didn't look at anyone. She stared down at her white patent-leather shoes as if she were a prisoner being punished. Tess's heart immediately went out to her. The child looked so forlorn.

Forgetting all about Summer, forgetting about everything except Francesca and David, Tess started in their direction. At that precise moment, Pamela Gates rushed toward David from the opposite direction.

"David Bannister!" she exclaimed. "It's wonderful to see you back again!" She planted herself firmly in front of him, partially blocking Tess's view. Tess stopped, and Summer bumped into her.

"Sorry," Summer muttered. "What's wrong?"

Tess wet her lips. She inclined her head toward David and Pamela. "I was going to go over and talk to David, but I think I'll wait until Pamela Gates is gone."

"Why?" Summer nudged Tess in the small of the back. "Get over there. Don't let Pamela stop you." Tess shook her head, but Summer continued to push her in David's direction. "I'm going to go find Mitch and the kids. You go talk to David. I mean it, Tess."

By now David had noticed her approach, and Tess had no choice but to keep going.

"Hi, Tess," David said with a smile. "Francesca, look, it's Miss Collier."

Tess smiled back. "Good morning, David. Pamela." She looked down. "Hello, Francesca."

Pamela Gates turned, an annoyed look sliding across her face. "Oh," she said. "Hello, Tess." There was no welcoming warmth in her voice. Obviously Pamela Gates was not pleased by Tess's appearance.

Francesca immediately let go of David's hand and moved to Tess's side. Her warm little hand slid into Tess's, and Tess smiled down at her. "That's a pretty dress," she said.

Francesca smiled shyly, and her hand tightened. "Thank you," she said, her voice barely above a whisper.

"I enjoyed your music today," David said, his green eyes sparkling in the morning sunlight.

"Did you?" Tess started to say something else, but Pamela Gates interrupted her.

"As I was saying, David, I'm having a few people for dinner on Friday night, and I'd like you to come."

Tess looked down at Francesca and tried to act as if she wasn't the least bit interested in David's reply. *Say no,* she willed him. *Say no.*

"I appreciate the invitation," he said, "but I'm afraid I'll have to pass."

Yippee!

"Oh, David!" Pamela protested. "Please come. I was counting on you."

He shook his head. "I'm sorry, Pamela. I can't."

"But why not? Have you got other plans?"

In a perverse way, Tess admired Pamela's dogged persistence.

"No, it's not that." David glanced at Francesca. He lowered his voice. "Right now, I don't like to leave Francesca—"

"Oh, bring Francesca, too!" Pamela gushed. "I understand completely, *believe* me. After all, I have children myself." She gave him a we-parents-understand-each-other conspiratorial look that effectively excluded Tess. "Of course, you don't want to leave Francesca by herself."

"It's really nice of you," David hedged. "Could I take a raincheck?"

No, don't take a raincheck!

Coyly, Pamela wagged her finger at David. "I don't intend to take no for an answer, David."

David laughed. "You never give up, do you? Okay, you've talked me into it."

"Good!" Pamela said. "Come at seven. Do you remember where I live?" When David indicated that he didn't, she gave him directions, then said, "Well, I'd better get going. I'm having lunch with some friends, and if I don't hurry, I'll be late." Her gaze slid to Tess. Her eyes sparkled with triumph as she said, "Goodbye, Tess." She patted Francesca's head, then turned back to David. "See you Friday, David."

As she walked away, Tess decided she could cheerfully strangle Pamela.

David, still chuckling softly, turned to Tess again, saying, "As I was trying to say before Pamela steamrollered me into accepting her invitation, hearing you play this morning reminded me of Sunday mornings when I was a kid. The music was always the highlight of the service for me."

Tess smiled with pleasure, even though she wished he'd stood his ground with Pamela. He was much too nice for someone like Pamela. "Thanks. I'm glad you enjoyed it." Then, because she couldn't think of anything else to say, she asked, "Have you found a housekeeper yet?"

"I took your advice and hired Peggy Kaminski."

"Oh, I'm so glad! Peggy's awfully nice. You'll like her."

Just then Ange and Margaret Bell, longtime members of the church, walked up to talk to David, and Tess thought this was a good time for her to leave. She knelt down to Francesca's level and said, "I'll see you on Wednesday, Francesca. Don't forget to practice."

"I won't," the little girl whispered.

Tess grinned, glancing up to see if David had heard, but he and Ange Bell were shaking hands and greeting one another, so she was pretty sure he hadn't. She squeezed Francesca's hand in farewell, then stood and walked away.

She wondered if David noticed that she was gone.

* * *

Francesca's second lesson turned out to be an almost exact duplication of her first. She only spoke a couple of words, but she seemed very happy to see Tess, and she played well.

"You've been practicing. It shows," Tess said.

Francesca smiled in response. As the lesson progressed, her initial stiffness disappeared, and she relaxed. And as Tess had promised, she worked with Francesca on Ellmenreich's "Spinning Song." Tess could see that the child completely forgot about herself as she worked to master the fingering and notes.

Resuming her piano lessons was exactly what Francesca had needed, Tess thought, and would have been a good idea even if she hadn't felt close to Tess. Because now she had something different to think about. An interest that had nothing to do with her mother or her father.

But when David arrived to pick Francesca up, she immediately crawled back into her unresponsive shell.

"What do you think?" he asked after the lesson was over and Francesca had walked outside.

"We're making progress," Tess said. "I don't know if you noticed, but she talked to me on Sunday."

"Yes, I did notice. And that reminds me, why did you leave so abruptly? I was going to invite you to lunch with me and Francesca, but all of a sudden, you just disappeared."

Tess's heart jumped. Lunch! He'd been going to invite her to lunch! And she'd left before he could. "You . . . you were busy. I figured you'd be tied up talking to your friends for a while." *Don't get all excited. Lunch with him and his daughter is not a date.*

His expression was one of genuine bewilderment. "But they're your friends, too."

"I know them, yes, but we don't move in the same circles." She had no intention of explaining to David that she'd felt like a fifth wheel. That even though she was well acquainted with people like the Bells, she didn't consider them real friends. "Has Peggy Kaminski started working for you yet?" she asked, to change the subject.

"Yes, she started Monday." Some of the perpetual worry lines around his eyes eased. "I think she's going to work out well."

"I'm glad."

He looked down at her, his green eyes glittering in the afternoon light. "I have you to thank."

"Me? What did I do?"

"You steered me in the right direction. I have to admit, left to my own devices, I'd've probably hired the other woman." He smiled. "Thanks."

Tess felt absurdly pleased by his compliment. "Does Francesca like her?"

He shrugged. "She seems to. But who knows about Francesca these days? You're the only one she communicates with." Sadness had crept into his voice again.

Tess laid her hand on his arm, an instinctive gesture of comfort. "David, be patient. You said yourself that it hasn't been very long since...Leah died. And you've only been back home for a couple of weeks. I think, given some time, Francesca will come around."

"Do you?" Hope lit his eyes again and he gave her a warm look.

Tess dropped her hand. It was dangerous to her well-being to get too close to David Bannister. She already knew she cared for him far more than it was sensible to care. She'd be foolish to allow herself to fall in love with him. Because she knew this friendship between them would never flower into anything more. Once Francesca was back to normal and David's grief had had time to heal, he would find someone with whom to share his life.

And that someone would not be Tess.

Chapter Four

David tapped his pen against his desk blotter and stared unseeingly at the report his assistant had placed on his desk earlier that morning.

He was having a hard time concentrating today. He kept thinking about Francesca. It was late October now, and he and Francesca had been back in Collierville for nearly ten weeks. She had been taking piano lessons with Tess for nine of those weeks, but the improvement David had hoped for hadn't happened.

Oh, there were some changes in her behavior. But the changes didn't last. He frowned as he mulled the problem. The trouble was, Francesca seemed much better right after her Wednesday piano lesson, but then, a day or so later, she reverted right back to her brooding silence.

Both Peggy Kaminski, his housekeeper, and Miss Wilson, Francesca's second-grade teacher, had remarked on this phenomenon. "She seems much more responsive on Thursdays and Fridays, much brighter and happier," Miss Wilson had said at his last parent-teacher conference. "Then by Monday, it's like a wall has gone back up, and she's on the other side of it."

David swiveled his chair around and stared out the big window comprising the south wall of his office. The maple trees outside were shedding their fall finery, and the grounds were covered with a carpet of gold and scarlet leaves. After an interlude of Indian summer, the weather had turned cooler earlier in the week, and this morning there was a definite frosty chill in the air.

His thoughts continued to dwell on Francesca. He wondered what he could do to maintain the positive progress she showed when she was around Tess. He hated seeing the child she had become. Since Leah's death, Francesca had gone from a bright, happy, active child to a troubled, lonely, quiet little girl who tore at his heart.

Another thing that concerned him was Francesca's continuing obsession with that family portrait. Every day, every blasted day, the first thing she did when she entered the house was head for the living room and the portrait.

David had to grit his teeth to keep from saying anything. He wondered if he was doing the right thing. Maybe he should just remove the damn thing—tell his daughter that it was time to put it away. Maybe if the constant reminder of her mother wasn't in such prominent view in their home, Francesca would be able to move on. But the one time he'd suggested taking the portrait down, Francesca had begun to cry, and he simply hadn't had the heart to carry through.

David sighed heavily. He knew he had to do something more than he *was* doing. The question was, what? Once more, his thoughts drifted to Tess, the only person who seemed able to put a smile on his daughter's face.

If only Tess could be with Francesca more often than once or twice a week, perhaps then Francesca would begin to put the past behind her and forget. Above all, David wanted Francesca to be happy, and if being with Tess made her happy, then that's what he needed to accomplish. Only Tess couldn't be with Francesca all the time.

Or could she?

David twirled his pen in his hands. Would Tess consider giving up her students to become a full-time companion to Francesca?

No, of course, she wouldn't. And he couldn't ask her to, either. After all, the day would come when Francesca no longer needed Tess, and what then? He could hardly expect Tess to give up her life simply because it would suit his purposes.

He continued to stare out the window and think about his dilemma. Problems were David's forte. As a scientist, he spent his days solving problems. Experimenting. Trying this and trying that until he found a solution. Surely he could find a solution now, when the stakes were so high.

What if Tess came to live with him and Francesca, and continued to teach?

As quickly as that idea had formed, David dismissed it. Tess had a home. She couldn't just leave it.

Besides that, Tess was a Collier. She had a certain position to uphold in Collierville. During one of their conversations, she had told him her family's history and how it was sometimes a burden to be a Collier. The town was named for her great-great-grandfather, Thaddeus Finley Collier. "Colliers live in a goldfish bowl," she'd said. "Everything I do is watched. Watched and judged."

Yes, there was a standard of behavior expected of Tess, and living in the home of a man unrelated to her was not part of that standard. No matter what the reason.

So that idea was definitely out.

He had been so sure coming back to Collierville would do the trick. That here Francesca would get better. That she just needed familiar surroundings and familiar faces. Now he wasn't so sure. Maybe they would both have been better off back east, where Leah's parents and sister lived. But he hadn't wanted to leave Medlock Chemical. He really liked his job, and he knew he had a promising future with the company.

Still...what was more important? His job? Or his daughter?

For the rest of the day, as David worked, he tried to decide what would be best. If he could only think of a way to bring Francesca and Tess together without causing gossip, harming Tess's reputation, or interfering with her career.

Surely there was a solution to his problem. Maybe if he applied the same analytical thinking he used with a complex scientific problem, he would find it.

Tess carried her bowl of buttered popcorn into the downstairs study. There was no television set in the parlor, so she normally spent her Saturday nights curled up on the chintz sofa in the study—a book on her lap and the remote control within reach. On cold winter nights,

Budge was likely to crawl up next to her and park his hefty body against her hip.

Hazel rarely joined her, because most nights she retired to her upstairs bedroom about eight o'clock. She had a small television set up there, and she would watch it until she fell asleep.

Tess sighed. How many Saturday nights had she spent in just this way, her only companion a cat? She wasn't sure she wanted to know. Worse—how many more would she endure in her lifetime?

Perversely, almost as if she wanted to torment herself, Tess's mind began to calculate. Fifty-two Saturday nights in a year. She was almost thirty-six years old, healthy and strong. Collier women were long-lived, so her reasonable life expectation could take her to eighty or more. Forty-four years times fifty-two....

Oh, stop that! Quit feeling sorry for yourself. Think of everything you have to be thankful for.

She was young, healthy and strong.

I won't be young forever.

She had a career. And even though it didn't pay much money, she wasn't starving.

Teaching other people's children. Wouldn't you rather have your own child? This was a thought Tess rarely allowed herself. To think about a child of her own caused an impossible yearning. An ache that refused to go away. Tess had often wondered why a family of her own seemed so important to her. There were many women who seemed perfectly happy on their own, but no matter how many friends she had or how busy her life was, Tess had never felt as if it was complete.

She wanted a husband. She wanted children. She wanted to belong to a family. She wanted that picture-perfect life that Summer had. That Leah Bannister had had.

Stop that! Stop wishing for what you don't have and keep remembering what you do have.

She had a home. A beautiful, old Victorian home filled with antiques. Okay, so the house was beginning to need a lot of repairs—repairs she couldn't afford—but she'd figure something out. She had to. The house was a landmark in Collierville. It had been in her family for generations. Her great-aunt had left it to her because she knew Tess was the only one who would understand the historical significance of the house.

So what? You can't snuggle up to a house. A house won't be a companion when you're old.

She had Hazel, and she had friends. She even had parents.

Uh-huh. Parents who dumped you on your great-aunt when you were a baby and really don't seem to care whether you're alive or dead. Face it, your parents have always preferred performing their music all over the world to the company of their only child. Neither of them has ever even said they love you!

Forcing herself to ignore that relentless inner voice, Tess reminded herself that Summer actually seemed to envy her. Tess really *was* independent and self-sufficient. She also had no real responsibilities, other than figuring out how to keep the family homestead from falling down around her head.

That was a lot. More than many women had. So why did she feel so discontented? Why did she want more? Especially lately?

Oh, you know why. Because David came back. Because his reappearance in your life has brought it home—loud and clear—just exactly what you're missing.

Yes, Tess thought sadly. That was indeed the reason she was so acutely aware of how lonely and barren her life really was.

She closed her eyes. The truth settled into her chest like a dull ache. She was more than halfway in love with David Bannister. She wondered what David was doing right now. She wondered if he, too, was spending Saturday night alone. He never talked about his social life. Tess had no idea if he was being invited out, or if he was accepting the invitations. She really didn't want to know. It would be torture to imagine him going out every weekend. She remembered how tormented she'd felt back in September when she knew he was at Pamela Gates's home.

Thinking of that episode, Tess grinned. She had, oh, so casually, said to David the following Wednesday, "So did you have a good time at Pamela's on Friday?"

He'd smiled sheepishly. "I didn't go."

"You didn't go!" Tess had wanted to cheer but contented herself with a curious smile. "Why not?"

"Francesca didn't seem to be feeling well," he'd answered.

But Tess knew that just because he had ended up not going out that night didn't mean he hadn't gone out dozens of times since.

And there's not a darned thing you can do about it.

She knew that was true. No matter how much she might wish she could step into the shoes Leah had vacated.

Because she wasn't Leah.

And she never would be.

* * *

Monday afternoon Tess was in the middle of a difficult lesson with her most fractious student—Teddy Farrell—when Hazel called her to the phone.

"David Bannister's on the phone," Hazel said, opening the door to the study. "Do you want to talk to him, or should I take a message?"

Tess jumped up. "Oh, I'll talk to him."

Hazel gave her a knowing look. "I thought so."

Tess flushed. Honestly, she must be so transparent. Even Hazel had noticed that David was special in her life. Then she frowned. David never telephoned. What could he want? Had something happened with Francesca?

"Uh, Hazel," she said, eyeing Teddy, "would you mind keeping Teddy company while I take this call?" She knew Hazel would understand that what she really meant was that Hazel was to watch him like a hawk. Left to his own devices, there was no telling what mischief Teddy might get into. "Teddy, you practice your scales while I'm gone."

Hazel nodded grimly and marched into the room. "Now, young man, let me see what you can do."

Tess hurried to the kitchen phone. "Hello?" She could hear Teddy's uneven scales in the background.

"Tess? This is David."

"Yes, hi, David. Is something wrong?"

"No, of course not. What made you think something was wrong?"

"I...I don't know."

"Well, nothing's wrong. The reason I'm calling is Francesca is flying up to New York on Friday. Leah's parents are celebrating their fortieth wedding anniversary Saturday, and they wanted Francesca to be there for the party.''

"Oh, how nice. Is Francesca happy to be going?"

"It's hard to tell. You know how she is with me, but she didn't refuse to go. Anyway, I wondered if you'd like to have dinner with me Saturday night. I thought we could go to the Lodge."

Tess's heart shot up into her throat. At first she wasn't sure she'd heard him right. "D-dinner?"

"Yes. I've been giving Francesca's situation a lot of thought lately, and I'd hoped we could discuss her progress and see if we can come up with some kind of plan that might speed things up a bit."

"Oh, of course. I—I'd love to go to dinner with you."

"Good. We'll decide on a time when I bring Francesca for her lesson on Wednesday. Okay?"

"Yes, fine."

Tess's hand trembled when she hung up the phone. She told herself not to be ridiculous. This wasn't a real date. David had simply asked her out because he wanted to discuss his daughter. Nothing more.

But knowing she would spend Saturday night with David, having the evening to look forward to—she couldn't help but be excited. In fact, Tess wasn't sure how she would manage to get through the week.

On Thursday night Tess went to the weekly practice of the Collierville choral group. She sang contralto and had been a member of the group for five years. Shortly after she'd joined, their accompanist had left, and they'd asked Tess to take the woman's place, but Tess had declined. She played the piano or the organ all the time. Playing for them would have been too much like work. But singing with them was pure fun. Normally, she thoroughly enjoyed the weekly practice and the get-together afterward at a local pizza parlor.

But on Thursday night, after the women had ordered their pizza and drinks, the conversation at the table turned to David.

"Boy, that David Bannister sure is a sexy-looking guy, isn't he?" said Heather Baird. She lifted her straw from her glass of soda and sipped at it noisily.

All the women agreed.

"Well, you can quit drooling, Heather," Marsha Guinness said. "Number one, you're too young for him. Number two, you're married."

"Maybe married, but not blind," Heather retorted, tossing her red hair back.

Then Joanne Flack said, "I hear he's finally started dating."

Tess's heart stopped.

"Oh?" said Heather. "Who's the lucky woman? Pamela Gates?"

Joanne laughed. "I'm sure she *wants* to be, but I don't think it's Pamela. I heard he was dating someone he works with out at Medlock."

Tess looked down at her drink. *Dating someone he works with... Dating someone he works with...* The words pounded at her.

"Do you know who it is, Tess?"

Tess looked up. The question had come from Sue Dawson, the head librarian at the Collierville library, and one of Tess's closer friends in the group. "No, I don't have any idea," she said, hoping her voice didn't betray her unhappiness.

"How would Tess know?" Joanne asked.

Sue explained that Tess taught David's daughter, and that she and David were friends.

"Oh, *really?*" Joanne said, her brown eyes alive with curiosity. "Lucky you!" She leaned across the table. "So give us the scoop!"

"I don't know any more than you guys know," Tess said. She prayed someone would change the subject.

Thankfully, Sue did, and David was forgotten. The conversation turned to the dresses they would wear for the upcoming annual Christmas performance. They'd finally settled on floor-length, red and green plaid taffeta skirts, white cotton blouses with ruffled necklines, and dark green velvet cummerbunds.

But Tess couldn't enjoy the talk or the food. The evening had been ruined for her. As had much of her pleasure over the coming dinner with David. Because now she knew for a certainty that she had been absolutely right when she'd told herself not to get excited about it.

Saturday dawned clear and cold, with the first hint of winter in the air. Most of the leaves had fallen from the trees, and squirrels raced around foraging for food to store for the long months ahead. Deer hunting season would start soon, and already the hunters in Collierville were gearing up for their favorite sport. Thanksgiving was less than four weeks away, and pumpkins, apple cider and sweet corn spilled from all the roadside stands along the outskirts of town. A smell of woodsmoke and burning leaves hung in the air, and the city fathers had begun the annual downtown cleanup campaign in preparation for the Christmas season.

Soon, Tess knew, Christmas decorations would adorn the lampposts and stoplights lining Main Street, and the huge spruce tree in the middle of Main Street square would be hung with hundreds of lights.

Maple Street, where Tess lived, was now littered with candy wrappers from the previous evening's trick or treaters, and they mingled with the mounds of dead leaves underfoot. Today, over Tess's protests, Hazel had donned her red quilted parka and gone outside to rake the yard. Through the study window, Tess would catch an occasional glimpse of her tall figure working away at her task.

Tess spent the day in a state of agitation. She taught her students, but part of her mind was centered on one thought, and one thought only. At seven o'clock, David would arrive to take her to dinner at the Lodge.

At five o'clock, when the last student left for the day, Tess raced upstairs to begin getting ready. She ran a hot bath and poured bath salts into the steaming water.

At six o'clock she had finished her bath and dried her hair. She then began the arduous task of brushing and braiding. At six-thirty she put the finishing touches to her makeup and walked to the closet to remove the dress she'd decided to wear.

By six forty-five, she stood in front of the cheval glass mirror and took stock. She stared at herself. The same old face stared back. She couldn't help wishing that for one night she could be someone different. Someone vivacious and confident. Someone bright and beautiful. Someone who would captivate David and make him see her as a desirable woman.

Tess smiled wryly. She was who she was. No magic transformation was likely to take place. David would see a pleasant-looking woman wearing a cinnamon wool dress and matching pumps. Nothing flashy. Nothing out of the ordinary. Certainly nothing to compare to Leah.

Remember. Joanne said David was dating someone from his company. Don't get your hopes up.

The doorbell rang promptly at seven. Tess was just coming down the curved stairway into the foyer as Hazel answered the door.

"Hello, Hazel," David said. "How are you?"

"Just fine, David. And you?"

Tess took advantage of the few seconds while David greeted Hazel to study him. He wore a dark gray wool topcoat over an equally dark suit and white shirt. His tie was a paisley print of blues and greens. With his dark hair and shiny black shoes, he looked sophisticated and handsome. Just then he looked up and smiled. "Hi," he said.

"Hi, David," Tess answered. She returned his smile.

"Are you ready to go?"

"Yes. Just let me get my coat." She walked to the hall closet and removed her old brown winter coat. She wished she had a new coat, but hadn't been able to justify spending the money. Not when it was needed for so many other things. When she walked back toward David, he reached out to help her with her coat.

Tess's breath caught as his hands touched her shoulders. Even so slight a touch was enough to set her heart racing, and she was sure her cheeks were flushed. David was close enough so that she could smell his cologne, something that reminded her of forests and mountain streams.

"By the way," he said as he opened the front door, "you look very nice tonight."

Now she *knew* her cheeks were flushed. She could feel their heat. "Thank you. So do you." What was the matter with her? He was just being polite. "Good night, Hazel," she said as she tried to regain her equilibrium.

"Have a good time," Hazel said.

Have a good time. Hazel's words lingered in the air as David, hand on her elbow, guided Tess down the porch steps, along the front walk, and then, more firmly, helped her into the passenger seat of his car. His hair gleamed under the streetlight, and Tess's gaze followed him as he walked around the front of the car. When he opened the door on the driver's side and slid in, her heart pumped harder. She clutched her purse tightly. She knew her reactions were crazy. She knew she should read nothing into this dinner engagement. She knew the only reason she was sitting here next to David was because he looked upon her as his best hope for Francesca's full recovery.

Otherwise, whoever it was he was dating would be here instead.

Despite this knowledge, Tess couldn't seem to help herself. Being with David was thrilling, especially in this venue. She closed her eyes briefly as he turned the key in the ignition. What harm was there in pretending? For just this one night, why was it wrong for her to pretend they were simply a man and a woman going out to dinner?

As long as you realize you're pretending, there's nothing wrong with it.

During the short, fifteen-minute drive to the Collierville Lodge, which was nestled at the edge of a densely wooded area near the western boundary of the town, Tess gave herself up to her fantasy.

"I like this place," David said as they pulled into the circular drive of the Lodge. "We used to come here a lot before Leah died."

Tess nodded, although she didn't come to the Lodge often. She wasn't the kind of woman to indulge in long, gossipy lunches, and since she rarely dated, she also didn't frequent the Lodge much at night. In fact, she hadn't been there since Summer's birthday in the spring when Tess, Sue Dawson and a couple other friends had taken her to dinner.

Tess decided it was far nicer to come to the Lodge with a handsome man as her escort than with a bunch of women. Perhaps it was her imagination, but everyone at the restaurant seemed more solicitous: the valet parking attendant who helped her out of the car, the maître d' who ushered them to their window table, the eagle-eyed waiter who ceremoniously laid their napkins across their laps, then watched as the busboy poured their water and waited patiently while they decided what they wanted to drink.

Finally their drink orders were placed, and the waiter left them. David smiled at Tess across the candlelit table. "Nice, isn't it?" he said.

"Yes."

"I'm glad you could come tonight, Tess."

Tess's chest tightened. *Are you, David?*

"Francesca thinks you're wonderful, you know." His eyes were warm in the soft light. "I'll never be able to thank you for everything you've done for her."

"I don't expect thanks." *Please don't look at me that way. It makes me hope for things that will never be.* "I only wish I could do more."

"I know."

"She *does* seem to be getting better, though, don't you think?"

He nodded. "I just wish . . . I don't know. I guess I'm wishing for the impossible. I want her to be the little girl she used to be. I really thought by now she'd be well on her way toward recovery."

"Be patient, David. It takes time to get over something as traumatic as losing your mother. Believe me, I know."

A slight frown knit his forehead. "What do you mean?"

"Just what I said. I know exactly how she feels."

"But your mother's alive, isn't she?"

Tess smiled wryly. "Yes, she is. But she might as well be dead. I never see her." She hated hearing the bitterness in her voice. She thought she'd gotten over her feelings of betrayal and abandonment long ago.

"Do you want to talk about it?" David asked softly.

His voice was kind, and his eyes said he really cared. Just then the waiter brought their wine, so Tess didn't answer. "Would you like to order now?" he asked.

"Give us a few minutes," David said. When the waiter left, he looked across the table again. "Tell me."

Tess took a sip of her wine. "We're not here to talk about me." She couldn't meet his gaze. She was sorry she'd brought up the subject.

"Come on, Tess. I really want to know."

Tess sighed. "You know who my parents are, don't you?"

Now it was his turn to nod. "Finley and Pauline Collier."

"Yes." Finley Collier was a world-class cellist, Pauline a world-class concert pianist. For the past forty years, they had traveled the world and showed no signs of slowing down.

"According to my Aunt Millicent, neither of them ever wanted a child. They made no secret of their displeasure when they found out my mother was pregnant with me." Tess was amazed that she could still feel the pain. Her gaze met David's over the flickering candles. "But even though they didn't want me, my aunt did. Otherwise," she said dryly, "I'm sure my mother would have figured out a way to get rid of me."

David's mouth tightened, and he shook his head. "That's a big burden for a kid to carry," he finally said.

"I don't want you to feel sorry for me. I had a wonderful childhood. Aunt Millicent was the most loving, caring parent any child could ask for." She twirled her wineglass. The dark liquid glowed a deep ruby. "But still—I can understand Francesca's feelings. I think I experienced some of the same emotions when I realized that my parents threw me away. There's a void inside that will never be filled." Tess wondered if that's why she so desperately wanted a child. In her most introspective moments, she thought that if only she had a child of her own to love, she would no longer feel that void, but she couldn't voice this thought to David. It was too intimate. Too revealing. "Anyway, I've always thought one of the reasons I was so shy and introverted as a child had a lot to do with my abandonment by my parents."

"Do you *ever* see them?"

Tess shrugged. "Occasionally. They used to visit more often than they do now. When Aunt Millicent was alive, they'd usually manage to come once a year, but I think that's because she shamed them into it." She laughed, trying to dispel some of the gloom she knew she'd caused. "It doesn't matter. I don't miss them. How could I miss them? I don't really know them. They've never been a part of my life."

"Maybe this is why Francesca responds to you the way she does. Although she's only a child, she's very perceptive, I think. She probably recognizes a kindred spirit."

Tess smiled. "Yes. I've always thought so myself."

He smiled, that warm smile that always set her stomach to fluttering. Their waiter reappeared again, and this time they placed their orders. After the waiter left, David said, "You mentioned something a week or two ago that I wanted to ask you about."

"What was that?"

"You hinted that you might like to go back to school. I was wondering why. Aren't you happy doing what you're doing?"

"It's not that. I like what I do. It's just…well…" She hesitated. She didn't like talking about money. She'd been raised to believe a person's finances were private.

"What?" he prodded.

Tess looked at him. There was only kindness in David's eyes. She didn't have to fear being honest with him. He was her friend. He might not see her in exactly the way she wished he would, but he did care. "The truth of the matter is, I need money." She grimaced. "The house is badly in need of repair, and there's no money to finance it. If I could figure out a way to get my degree, I could get a full-time teaching job and supplement that income by teaching piano on the side." She laughed. "But going to school costs money, too."

He nodded thoughtfully. "I kind of had an idea that was the way things stood." He drank from his wineglass. "The house means a lot to you, doesn't it?"

Tess didn't answer for a long moment. Finally, deciding that she was tired of pretending to an emotion she didn't feel, she said, "The only reason I care about the house is because of what it meant to Aunt Millicent. Personally, there are times when I wish I could just be rid of the worry and responsibility." She absently played with her napkin. "Sometimes I wish I could chuck everything and start an entirely new life." She looked at him. "Do you ever feel that way?"

He smiled wryly. "Just about every day."

She smiled back. It was one of those rare moments when she felt as if they were in perfect harmony.

"Tess," he said slowly, "I'm thinking of moving back east."

Chapter Five

For the next few days, all Tess could think about was the dismal prospect of David and Francesca leaving Collierville. David's announcement at dinner on Saturday had been a shock. She'd never considered that he might decide to move, although she had to admit his reasoning made sense. Francesca's only relatives lived on the east coast, and Tess knew Francesca was close to both Leah's parents and her sister Rachel. Maybe it really *would* be better for Francesca to be near them.

And away from Collierville, which would probably always be associated in her mind with her mother's death.

Throughout Francesca's lesson on Wednesday, Tess watched her and thought about how much she would miss her. How much she would miss David. She tried to put the thought out of her mind. After all, David had made no decision yet. He was simply considering the idea. But the thought refused to go away. Several times she had to fight against tears.

When the lesson was over, Tess was almost glad. Normally she hated to see the end of Francesca's lesson. But today, Tess couldn't seem to shake her depression, and she was afraid Francesca might realize something was wrong. That was the last thing she wanted.

"You did very well today, honey," she said as the notes from Francesca's final piece died away. Then, even though Tess had told herself she wouldn't mention Francesca's trip, she added, "Your daddy told me about your trip to New York. Did you have fun?"

"Uh-huh."

"I'll bet you enjoyed seeing your grandparents again."

Francesca nodded, her eyes bright. "Uh-huh."

"You miss them, don't you?"

Francesca continued to nod.

Tess swallowed against the lump in her throat. She wanted the best for Francesca. She really did. She wanted the child to get well and be happy. A silent plea ran through her mind. *Please, God, make her be happy here. Don't take her and David away.*

Francesca touched Tess's hand, startling her. "You look sad," she whispered. Her forehead creased into a worried frown.

It took all of Tess's strength, but she managed a reassuring smile. "Oh, no, honey. I'm not sad. I'm...I'm just tired." Her voice sounded fake with forced brightness. Surely Francesca would see right through her.

To Tess's great relief, the sound of footsteps coming up the porch steps drew the child's attention, and she didn't answer. Through the big front bay window, Tess caught a glimpse of David's dark head as he walked across the porch. Her heart leapt. It didn't matter how many times she saw him, each time was thrilling. She wondered if people who had been together a long time still felt that breathless excitement at the sight of their loved one.

A moment later David knocked on the door, and Tess got up to let him in.

He smiled as she opened the door. "Hi."

"Hi. C'mon in."

He followed her into the parlor.

"Good lesson today?" he said, looking at Francesca.

"Uh-huh," Francesca answered. She glanced up at Tess.

"Very good," Tess said. "Francesca gets better and better all the time." Tess smiled. "I've got high hopes for her."

Instead of picking up her books and going outside, the way she usually did, Francesca put on her jacket and hung back, her concerned gaze fastened on Tess's face.

David frowned and looked at Tess. There was a question in his eyes.

Tess bent down and hugged Francesca. "I'm okay. Don't worry," she whispered. Francesca put her arms around Tess's neck and hugged back. Tess closed her eyes and inhaled the fresh scent of Francesca's hair and absorbed the feel of her warm body pressed against her. A moment later Tess gently broke the embrace. They smiled at each other, then Francesca turned and walked outside. Within seconds the creak of the porch swing greeted David and Tess.

"What was that all about?" David asked.

Tess shrugged. "Nothing, really. Francesca was just worried about me, that's all."

Now his frown deepened. "Why? Is something wrong?"

"No, no. I'm just a little tired, but she thought I was sad."

"She actually *said* that?" He sounded amazed.

"Yes. She told me I looked sad."

"She really does respond to you better than anyone else, doesn't she?" he said thoughtfully.

Tess couldn't prevent the spark of hope that flared into life. If David felt that way, he wouldn't go back east, would he? He wouldn't want to remove Francesca from Tess's company.

By now they'd reached the front door. Tess reached for the doorknob, but David stopped her by touching her arm. "Wait," he said.

She looked up.

"There's something I want to discuss with you."

Tess's heart lurched. He looked so serious. "Okay."

"No, not now. Would it be all right if I came over later this evening?"

Oh, no. Please, God, no. Had he decided to leave Collierville? Is that what he planned to tell her tonight? "S-sure," she said, hating the tremor she heard in her voice.

"What time is good for you?"

"We're usually finished with dinner by seven-thirty." Why did he look so serious? He *must* be planning to move.

"I'll come at eight, then." His smile did nothing to reassure Tess.

After he and Francesca left, Tess walked slowly back to the parlor and over to the bay window. She stared outside. Almost all the leaves had fallen now, and the bare branches of the maple trees appeared forlorn. As forlorn as she felt. The lawn looked patchy and ragged, and the roots of the huge elm tree that defined the southern boundary of her lot protruded from the ground like a knobby-legged octopus. The sky was that odd combination of violet and dark blue that signaled the end of the day. Tess always felt melancholy at twilight, and wondered if her melancholy was caused by the knowledge that she had no one with whom to share the night.

What must it be like, she wondered, to look forward each afternoon to the homecoming of the man you loved? To anticipate sharing a good meal and a companionable evening in front of the fireplace? To know that later, when you were both sleepy, you would ward off the chill of the winter's night by snuggling together under soft, down quilts? To savor the delicious knowledge that you would then make love to each other, stroking and touching....

Tess closed her eyes. The picture she'd conjured was so vivid and so compelling, she actually shivered from the imagined caresses. "David," she whispered. Then again, "David." The tears she'd managed to suppress earlier crept from beneath her closed eyes and, swallowing hard, she turned and raced out of the parlor, into the foyer and up the stairs. When she reached the privacy of her bedroom, she closed the door, threw herself across her bed, buried her face in her pillow so Hazel wouldn't hear her, and cried until there were no more tears left.

Although Hazel had fixed chicken and noodles, one of Tess's favorite meals, the food tasted like straw in her mouth. All Tess could think about was David's imminent arrival.

"More cranberry sauce?" Hazel asked. Her bright blue eyes, which always reminded Tess of two shiny marbles, seemed particularly astute tonight.

"No, thanks."

"You've hardly eaten anything. Is something wrong?"

Darn. Hazel was just too perceptive. Way too perceptive. "Nothing's wrong, Hazel." Tess forced a note of impatience in her voice. Better to have Hazel think she was annoyed than have her guess the truth. "Honestly, if I'm not hungry, I'm not hungry."

"Never known you not to be hungry for my chicken and noodles."

Tess made herself finish her plateful of food. She kept her gaze averted from Hazel's the whole time.

Finally the meal was over. Tess helped Hazel clean up and by the time they finished, the clock read seven fifty-five. Tess barely had time to run upstairs, brush her teeth and apply fresh lipstick before she heard the front doorbell ring. She took a couple of shaky breaths, tucked her white blouse more securely into the waistband of her gray wool slacks, then headed for the stairs.

David was already seated in one of the wing-backed chairs that flanked either side of the fireplace in the parlor. He stood when Tess walked in.

Even though she was nearly paralyzed with fright, Tess couldn't help noticing how handsome he looked tonight. He'd changed from his business clothes into a casual outfit of jeans, a red cable-knit sweater and soft-looking brown boots. He smiled in greeting.

She tried to smile back and hoped she succeeded. Her face felt stiff. She prayed she would be able to handle his announcement, whatever it was. She prayed she could be sincerely happy for him, no matter what he had decided to do. She prayed she wouldn't give away her devastation. "Would you like some coffee or maybe a drink?" she asked.

"Hazel's bringing me some coffee," he said. "She said she'd bring you some, too."

"Oh, okay. Good." She sat in the other wing-backed chair. The food she'd forced herself to eat earlier felt like a big lump in her stomach. Her gaze met his.

"Let's wait for our coffee, okay?" he said.

Less than two minutes passed before Hazel entered carrying a tray laden with their coffee, sugar, cream, and a cut-glass plate containing several pieces of narrowly sliced pound cake.

They busied themselves fixing their cups of coffee. Both ignored the cake. Finally, David sat back in his chair and said, "I know you've probably been wondering what was so important that I needed to come by tonight."

Tess shrugged. "Well…" She wondered what he'd say if he had any idea of the agony she'd been through since he'd made his request.

"I'd like to start by saying that I will always be grateful to you for the help you've given Francesca."

Tess's heart sank. He *was* leaving. "Oh, David, I was happy to do what I've done. You know how much I love Francesca. I—I couldn't love her more if she were my own daughter."

His gaze met hers, and there was something about the expression in his eyes that caused Tess's heart to race. He started to say something, then stopped.

Frightened, but knowing she had to know the worst, Tess swallowed hard and said, "What is it?"

"There's something I want to ask you, and I'm not sure just how to say it."

"Y-you can ask me anything. Tell me anything. You know that." She steeled herself for what she knew was coming. *Be strong.*

He looked at her for another long moment, the fire-light reflected in his eyes. "Tess, are you seeing any-one?"

"S-seeing anyone?" she echoed.

He nodded. "Are you involved in a relationship?"

Tess could hardly breathe. She shook her head. "No." A wild hope careened through her.

He took a deep breath. "In that case, would you con-sider marrying me?"

Stunned, Tess stared at him. Her heart beat so hard she was afraid it would burst out of her chest. Was it possible? Did David love her?

He laid his coffee cup down on the small table next to his chair, then leaned forward, resting his elbows on his knees. "I've been thinking about this for some time now. Seeing you with Francesca and seeing how much she loves you and trusts you, and then seeing her go back into her silent world after she leaves here—well, that started me thinking how great it would be if you were around all the time. She needs a woman around, Tess. She needs you. You're good for her. You'd make a great mother to Francesca."

Tess could hardly absorb what he was saying. She felt light-headed and knew if she were standing, she'd have to hold on to something to keep from falling. One thought kept pummeling her. *David wants to marry me.* When would he say he loved her? Why hadn't he given her any warning of his feelings?

"I know this is a shock," he said with a wry smile. "And I realize I'm asking a lot of you." His expression turned serious, his eyes studying her intently. "I've thought it all out carefully, though, and I think—even though we don't have a romantic relationship, or anything like that—we could make a good marriage. We're friends. We like each other, and we're comfortable together. I admire and respect you, and I think you feel the same way about me." He grimaced. "Many marriages have much less. I think we could be reasonably happy together, and I *know* it would be wonderful for Francesca."

Everything else David had said faded. One phrase thrummed through her brain. *Even though we don't have a romantic relationship* . . . So he wasn't saying he loved her. What *was* he saying, then?

"I figured it might seem to you that you would be the one bringing the most to the marriage, without getting much in return, but I feel I have some things to offer you, too."

She didn't answer. She was incapable of saying anything coherent.

"When we talked the other night," he continued earnestly, "you confirmed what I'd suspected for a long time. After our discussion, I realized I could give you the two things you indicated you want—financial security and the opportunity to go back to school." He smiled, obviously pleased with himself. "I know this is an unusual way to go about proposing to a woman, but it just seemed to me that this kind of arrangement would be advantageous to both of us."

The meaning of David's offer finally penetrated. What he was offering her was an arranged marriage. A marriage of convenience. The kind of marriage people made in earlier generations. The giddy hope she'd felt when he'd first mentioned marriage faded, then died. *Oh, God, you're such a fool. You should have known.*

He doesn't love you. Whatever gave you the idea he could?

She felt like crying, her disappointment was so great. Yet... as she absorbed his offer... as she realized exactly what it was he was proposing...it wasn't really that bad, was it? *You'd have what you've always wanted, wouldn't you? A husband and a child. A home and a family.* Just the thought of living with David, being with him all the time, *sharing his bed,* was enough to set her heart to pounding again.

Obviously misinterpreting her silence, David said, "It wouldn't be necessary for us to have a...physical relationship."

Tess stared at him. Just when she thought she understood what he meant, he hit her with something new.

He rushed on. "I know what you're thinking."

You have no earthly idea what I'm thinking. She shook her head. "David, I—"

"I know you probably think my idea is bizarre because I've taken you by surprise, but would you think about it?" he said fast, as if he were afraid she was going to refuse him. "If you think the idea has merit, we can work out the details just the way we'd work out any business contract."

"I see," Tess finally said. She didn't know whether to laugh or cry. In the past ten minutes her emotions had run the gamut—from wild exhilaration to disappointment to cautious optimism to dismay. She wasn't sure what she felt. How ironic that David should think he understood her feelings when he didn't have a clue. She wished she could tell him that he should have quit when he was ahead. That his last words, meant, she knew, to be reassuring, were anything but. A business contract, he had said. Not necessary to have a physical relationship, he had said. What could she say to that? What did she *want* to say to that?

"Tess," David said, "if you'll do this for me...for Francesca...I'll give you everything I have to give in return. You'll never lack for anything."

"Oh, David..." She twisted her hands in her lap. She prayed the right words would come.

"I hope I haven't offended you," he said softly.

Tess sighed deeply. He looked so concerned that he had somehow hurt her feelings. She had to answer him. "I'm not offended. I—I was just so surprised, that's all. You took me completely off guard." She looked at the fire, then back at him. "I can't give you an answer tonight. As you suggested, I'd like to think about this for a few days."

"Of course," he replied, his eyes brightening. "Take more than a few days. Take all the time you need. I'm just grateful you'll consider my proposition at all."

After a few minutes of awkward silence, he stood. "I think I'd better be going."

Tess nodded. As much as she usually loved being with David, her mind was too confused, her brain too cluttered for her to make any sense right now. She stood, too.

They walked out into the foyer together, and he reached for his leather jacket, which was hanging on the clothes tree to the left of the front door. He put the jacket on and zipped it up. "Well...I guess I'll see you at church on Sunday."

"Yes." She looked up.

"Tess..." He reached for her hands, enfolding them in his.

Tess's stupid heart started to gallop again. Her hands tingled from the warmth of David's touch. She couldn't have said anything if her life depended upon it.

"Thanks for not telling me to get lost," he said, smiling down at her. "Thanks for saying you'd think about my offer."

She nodded. "I'll think about it carefully."

"Tess . . ."

Her gaze met his.

"I really value your friendship, and even if you say no, I hope we can continue to be friends."

Tess wet her lips and David's gaze followed her action. For one absurd moment, she thought he was going to kiss her. But the moment passed. He let go of her hands, turned toward the door and opened it. "Good night," he said.

"Good night."

A minute later he was gone.

Tess walked around in a daze for the next few days. Sometimes she couldn't believe David had actually made his offer. Maybe her imagination had conjured the entire scene.

What should she do?

What should she do?

The question repeated itself over and over again.

What should she do?

She listed the factors in favor of accepting David's offer. Most important of all was the fact that she loved David. And she loved Francesca. Although David had made it clear he wasn't in love with her, Tess would be with him. She would be his wife. And she would be Francesca's mother.

Tess smiled. She would have a home and a family. Two things she'd always wanted. She would no longer spend those Saturday nights alone. On Christmas and Thanksgiving and all those other holidays, she would no longer feel like an outsider in the homes of her friends.

As David's wife, she would have her own place in life.

He'd mentioned financial security. Tess couldn't entirely discount that factor, even though it was less important to her than all the other things. Infinitely less important than the way she felt about David.

Yes, there were a lot of reasons—good reasons—for marrying David.

On the other side of the coin was the certain knowledge that it would be hard on her to live with David and not be loved by him. Would she be able to endure it? How would she feel, living in the same house, sharing his table and his bank account and his name, and not sharing his bed? Wouldn't the situation become unbearable after a while?

And even if it didn't, what about later? When Francesca recovered? Got older? Went off to college? Tess had no doubt that eventually Francesca would be well, would be the girl she once had been. What if, once there was no longer a compelling reason for him to stay married to Tess, David wanted out of his businesslike marriage? Tess would once again have nothing. And having nothing after having something would be worse than never having had anything at all, she knew. Did she dare risk it?

Another thing bothered Tess. Even if they *did* remain together, was it reasonable to expect a virile man like David to remain celibate for the rest of his life? Tess knew she was no authority on the subject of men, but this prospect simply didn't seem like one that would work. And if David were to look elsewhere for his physical needs, Tess would not be able to endure it.

If only someone could tell her what to do. If only she could talk the situation over with someone. Someone like Summer. Tess actually considered the idea for about five minutes. Then she knew she could never tell Summer, or anyone, what David had proposed. She would be too embarrassed to have even her closest friend know that her marriage—if she decided to go through with this—wasn't an ordinary marriage. That her husband didn't love her.

No, Tess would have to make her decision on her own. And soon, she knew.

Because David wouldn't wait forever.

"David, you seem so preoccupied. Is something wrong?"

"Hmm?" David looked up from the journal he'd been staring at for the past thirty minutes. Katherine Comstock, his assistant, stood next to his desk. There was a quizzical smile on her face. "Did you say something?"

She chuckled at his obvious confusion. "I said, is there something wrong? You've been off in another world for days."

"No, nothing's wrong. I was just daydreaming."

Katherine's smile became broader, exposing her perfect teeth. She had beautiful teeth, and she liked showing them off. She'd once told David that her parents were too poor to get her fitted with braces as a child, so the minute she'd graduated from college and gotten her first job, she'd had her teeth straightened. "It's not like you to daydream."

"Even workaholics like me occasionally goof off."

"You should goof off more often. You work too hard. You know what they say about all work and no play making dull boys." Her smile turned flirtatious. "I know exactly what you need."

Her last remark irritated David. Sometimes Katherine acted as if she were his wife. David knew she was interested in him. She'd made no secret of her interest. But even if he'd thought it was a good idea to get involved with a co-worker, he wouldn't have returned her interest. Several times, he'd speculated on just why he felt that way. Katherine was beautiful, smart and witty, but he simply didn't feel that spark of awareness necessary for a romantic relationship.

"I have two tickets to the Cleveland symphony for Saturday night. Anton Neuberger is conducting. I thought maybe you'd like to go with me."

"I'm sorry, Katherine. I can't. I already have plans." It wasn't really a lie, he told himself. He *did* have plans. His plans were to rent a children's movie and watch it with Francesca.

She shrugged, but David saw the flicker of anger that crossed her face—anger she quickly disguised. "That's too bad. I know how much you like Neuberger."

"I do. And thanks for asking, Katherine."

"Maybe another time, then."

David smothered a sigh as she walked out of his office. Once Katherine set a goal, she forged ahead doggedly. She wouldn't give up until he was no longer available. Which might be sooner than she or anyone else expected. If Tess agreed to his proposition, that is.

Tess. He had been thinking about her nonstop since Wednesday night. In two days he would see her again. He wondered if she would have an answer for him Sunday. He hoped so. He couldn't wait much longer before making some decisions about his and Francesca's future.

Summer called Tess on Saturday morning.

"Autumn's in town for the weekend," she said. "And she's dying to see you." Autumn was Summer's younger sister and she lived in Chicago. Summer also had a sister named Spring who lived in New York. Tess had once laughingly commented that it was a darned good thing the Clayburghs had stopped at three girls, because Winter would've been a terrible name to stick on a person. "How about coming over for dinner tonight?" Summer continued.

"Did she bring the baby?" Autumn had had her first baby five months earlier.

"Of course."

Tess accepted happily. It would be great to get out of the house and stop thinking about David. It would be equally great not to spend another Saturday night alone. And she'd been dying to see Autumn's baby.

She arrived at Summer's at six-thirty, a gaily wrapped present for the baby clutched under one arm.

"Oh, Tess, it's so good to see you!" Autumn exclaimed, throwing her arms around Tess and giving her a bone-crushing hug.

Tess grinned, returned her hug, then pulled away to look at Autumn. "You look wonderful! You've lost all your weight and then some, haven't you?" Autumn fit her name as exactly as Summer fit hers. Instead of Summer's flaxen-colored hair, Autumn's was red gold, and she had the complexion to go with it—fair and freckled.

"Yes," Autumn crowed. "And it wasn't easy, believe me!"

Summer laughed. "She's been bragging on herself ever since she got here."

"Where's the baby?" Tess said.

"Sitting in her jumper chair in the kitchen."

Tess followed Autumn to the back of the house. The infant seat was sitting in the middle of the kitchen table, and a chubby baby dressed in a pink flannel romper banged away at the toys strung across the front of the seat.

"Meet Sarah," Autumn said proudly.

Tess bent over the baby, who gave her a toothless grin. Something stirred inside Tess. "Can I hold her?" she asked softly.

"Sure," Autumn said. She unfastened the sides of the chair and lifted the baby out. She handed her to Tess.

Tess's arms closed around the little girl. She held her close and buried her face in the baby's sweet-smelling hair. Sarah patted Tess's face, then gave her another big smile.

A great yearning filled Tess, and suddenly, just like that, she knew exactly what she was going to tell David.

Chapter Six

After the service Sunday morning, Tess's departure was delayed by Carla Richardson, the choir director, who had a question about the Christmas music they were planning. As she talked to Carla, Tess kept eyeing the main entrance. Almost all the members had filed outside the church. If she didn't hurry, she would miss David.

But Carla kept talking.

Finally, in desperation, Tess said, "Listen, Carla, I've got to go. Can I call you later today, and we can discuss this then?"

"Oh, sure. No problem."

Tess hurried out. She didn't stop to talk to anyone. She hoped she hadn't missed David. Now that she'd made her decision, she wanted to tell him and get it over with. She was afraid if she didn't, her resolve would desert her. She sighed with relief when she spotted him with Francesca halfway down the front walk.

Just as she opened her mouth to call his name, he turned, and their gazes met. He waved, and she hurried down the steps toward him.

"Hi," she said as she reached his side. Her breath misted in the cold air. The morning was chilly and overcast, and the weather forecasters had predicted rain later in the day.

"Hi." He smiled warmly, and Tess's breath caught at the sudden burst of emotion his smile always produced. Tearing her gaze away, she turned to Francesca.

"Hello, Francesca. My, that's a beautiful coat. Is it new?"

Francesca smiled with pleasure and touched the velvet lapels of the forest green coat. "Uh-huh," she said. Then, surprising Tess, she added, "Daddy bought it for me." As if she'd said more than she'd intended, she suddenly ducked her head.

Tess's startled gaze met David's, and they exchanged a look. She knew he was as surprised and gratified by Francesca's unsolicited comment as she was. Then, quickly, before she lost her nerve, Tess said softly, "David, can we talk privately sometime today?"

His eyes glittered with some emotion she couldn't identify, but he said smoothly, "Of course. Do you want me to come over to your house later?"

Tess wondered what he was thinking. His expression revealed nothing. "If you don't mind."

"Of course, I don't mind. What time?"

"Anytime after two o'clock is fine."

"Shall we say five, then?"

Tess nodded. Her heartbeat suddenly seemed too loud, and she was convinced that David could hear it.

That he would guess exactly how nervous she was now that she'd committed herself to giving him his answer.

She just hoped she didn't lose her nerve between now and five o'clock.

Hazel had gone to play bridge with three of her friends and would be gone until seven or eight that night, so Tess was alone when David arrived at five. She'd dressed very carefully for their meeting. In an effort to feel as much in control of the situation as she possibly could, she'd put on her brightest outfit—a royal blue wool dress trimmed with a wide, white lace collar and cuffs. She'd also added a bit more blush on her cheeks than she would normally wear and rooted around in her cosmetics drawer until she'd unearthed a lipstick that had been given to her as a sample earlier that year. A lipstick in a shade of raspberry she'd never tried before.

As she gazed at herself in the mirror, she had to admit the color suited her. Taking a deep breath for courage, she turned away from her image and slowly went downstairs to wait for David.

Precisely at five o'clock, she saw his car glide to a stop in front of her house, and seconds later he emerged. It was raining, but he had no umbrella. Studying him covertly from behind the filmy curtains stretched over the glass panels on either side of the front door, Tess watched as he dashed up the front sidewalk, mounted the steps, and crossed the porch. Earlier she'd turned on the porch light, so she could see the raindrops glistening on his dark head and his leather jacket.

She wet her lips nervously as she composed herself to answer the door. The chime sounded, and her heart began to beat faster. She grasped the doorknob, but for one long moment, didn't turn it. Instead she sent a silent prayer heavenward. *Please, God, help me say the right thing.* Then, taking a shaky breath and exhaling the air, she yanked the door open. Smiling brightly, she said, "Hello, David. Right on time."

"Hello, Tess." He walked into the foyer, bringing the smell of rain and cold and wet leather with him. She also caught a whiff of his after-shave or cologne—the same outdoorsy scent he'd worn the night they went to dinner. She almost shivered. All of her life she'd been surrounded by the smells and scents of women. She'd never before realized just how different—and erotic—a man's scents could be.

He removed his jacket, and she took it from him, hanging it on the clothes tree. She fought the temptation to let her hand linger on the wet leather. "Let's go into the parlor," she said. "I've got a pot of coffee ready."

She'd also put out some of Hazel's clothespin cookies—a delicacy she'd learned to make from an Italian friend. As they had the other day, Tess and David sat in the same fireside chairs.

Because her heart was beating too hard, and her stomach was quaking with nerves, Tess busied herself pouring coffee and serving the cookies. She evaded David's eyes. Finally, though, she could delay no longer. She settled back into her chair and met his thoughtful gaze. For a long moment, neither spoke. The fire hissed and crackled. The grandfather clock in the foyer ticked. The old house creaked and groaned as the wind buffeted its exterior. The rain fell with a steady, almost mesmerizing rhythm. And Tess's own heart thudded relentlessly.

David broke the silence. Green eyes gleaming in the firelight, he said softly, "You look awfully nice tonight. That's a pretty dress. The color suits you."

Tess knew she was blushing. The compliment had taken her by surprise. She could feel the blood rushing through her veins, heating her with color. "Th-thank you," she stammered, hating herself for betraying her emotions. She'd told herself she would remain cool and businesslike, just as David had been when he'd made his offer. And what happened? At the first words out of David's mouth, she was blushing like a gawky teenager instead of a grown woman.

Come on. Get yourself under control. Mustering all her reserves of strength, she said, "David, before I give you my answer, I've got a question for you."

He smiled—a little half smile that caused her heart to skip a beat. Distractedly, she wondered if he had any idea of the effect he had on her. One tiny smile, and she was in danger of dissolving into jelly. "Ask me anything," he said.

She only hesitated a moment—just long enough to take a deep breath. Then she plunged. "How would you feel about having another child?"

His eyes widened, and he put his coffee cup down— the only physical signs that he was startled by her question. Afraid she would lose her nerve, she rushed on. "I've always wanted a child of my own. And if you'd be willing to give me one, then I'll marry you." She met his gaze, saw the confusion clouding his eyes. He opened his mouth, but she had one more thing to say first. "Just one. We . . . we don't have to . . . to continue a physical relationship once I become pregnant. Although I would expect a permanent commitment."

There. It was out. She'd said it. She held her breath. What would he say in return?

The ticking of the grandfather clock suddenly sounded like a time bomb. The hissing of the fire, the plop of the rain, the groaning of the house—all seemed louder and more ominous as the seconds ticked away.

Tess waited. Her stomach felt as if someone had grabbed it and squeezed. Her heartbeat pounded in her ears. Her throat and lips felt dry. She waited. And waited.

The expression in David's eyes confused her. But the absence of a smile on his face—the complete lack of warmth in his expression—told her everything she needed to know. Her heart plunged. He was going to refuse. She sat straighter in her chair, forced herself to compose her face. She would not let him see that this was the most important moment of her life. She would not let him see how much she wanted him to accept. She would not let him see the disappointment that was, even now, rushing through her.

After agonizing seconds, he finally stirred. Nodding slowly, he said, "All right, Tess. If that's what you want, I'm willing."

Tess nearly fell apart. She had been prepared to lose, but hardly knew how to win. Joy jolted through her, singing in her veins, and she thought her heart might burst with it.

She fought to keep her elation and happiness from showing in her eyes. She couldn't let David see how much she cared.

He doesn't love you. She had to remember that. This was business. To cover her near euphoria, she was almost gruff when she said, "Well, good. I'm glad we've been able to work this out."

She put her coffee cup down, stood, and extended her right hand.

David never even blinked. He stood, too, walked over to her and accepted her hand gravely. But there was just the slightest suspicion of a smile hovering at the corners of his mouth, and his eyes were warm as they gazed down upon her. Where their palms met, her skin tingled and a delicious shiver snaked down her spine. Then, causing her even more confusion than she was already feeling, he raised her hand to his mouth, turned it palm up, and kissed it. His warm lips lingered for one breathless moment, and Tess's heart—which had already had quite a workout that day—went *zing*.

She swallowed, hard.

She couldn't believe this was really happening.

Then he smiled—that wonderful smile that always made Tess want to cry, for some absurd reason. Even now, when she was practically floating with exhilaration, she knew that tears weren't very far from the surface.

Her emotions were so chaotic—they'd fallen into the pits of despair only to be shot straight back up into the heavens. She felt unhinged. Fragile and vulnerable. She knew it wouldn't take much for her to go completely to pieces.

"So where do we go from here?" David said as he released her hand and they sat down again.

Tess managed a casual shrug. "I haven't thought ahead." In a burst of total honesty, she blurted, "I wasn't sure you'd agree to my terms."

He nodded, smiling again. "Well, I'm in a hurry. I think the sooner we're married, the better."

Now it was Tess's turn to nod. The butterflies in her stomach refused to go away.

"Still," he continued thoughtfully, drumming his fingers against the arm of his chair and staring into the fire, "there should be a period of courtship, I think." He turned to face her again, and his eyes—oh, those eyes—glittered with golden lights. "Otherwise, our marriage will come as a shock to Francesca, and Leah's family. Actually, to the entire community."

"Yes, you're right." Even though Tess hadn't thought that far ahead, she saw the logic in his reasoning. Just the fact of their marriage would cause enough gossip. They didn't want to invite even more.

Then he grinned, and there was a little-boy mischievous quality to it—and once again, her silly heart went crazy. "How would a whirlwind courtship suit you?"

For the next two weeks Tess kept pinching herself to remind herself that she hadn't dreamed the whole crazy thing. She really was engaged to David—not officially, because they'd decided to wait a few weeks to announce their engagement formally—but still engaged. She really was going to marry him at the end of December. She really was going to be Mrs. David Bannister.

Mrs. David Bannister. Tess Bannister.

She said the words again and again. To herself, silently. And out loud. Each time she did, she felt like shouting. She felt giddy. Dizzy. Full of elation. And scared. That was half the time.

The other half of the time she was nervous. And scared. So scared. What if David changed his mind? What if he decided he'd made a mistake—a big mistake—and told her he couldn't go through with it?

Doubts plagued her. Doubts and fears. All her old insecurities surfaced. She couldn't eat. She couldn't sleep. She was just plain terrified. She wondered if she should call the marriage off. Back out before David had a chance to. *He doesn't love you. Remember that.*

Then, after she'd run the gamut of doubts, she'd tell herself she was being ridiculous. David certainly didn't act as if he was in any danger of changing his mind. Whether he loved her or not was irrelevant. He needed her. And she needed him.

During those weeks, she spent nearly every evening with David. For many of those evenings, Francesca joined them. And as each day passed, the signs that Francesca was thawing toward her father became more noticeable. One night, in mid-November, the three of them had gone to dinner at a local Chinese restaurant, and afterward, at Tess's suggestion, they went back to her house for a cup of hot chocolate.

"I like it here," Francesca said. She didn't whisper. She said the words clearly and in a normal tone of voice.

Slowly, Tess's gaze moved to meet David's, and in the warmth of his expression, she knew he was thanking her.

"This *is* a great room," he said, looking around.

The three of them were sitting in the big, old-fashioned kitchen. Tess's house had fireplaces in almost all of the rooms, and the kitchen was no exception. Tonight, Hazel had built the fire up before she went to bed, and it burned with a cheerful blaze that warmed the entire room. Budge lay curled on the hearth—as close to the warmth as he could get without burning his fur. The room had always been Tess's favorite, and she could see that Francesca had responded to its homey feel the same way Tess had responded to it when she was a child.

Tess could still see her great-aunt Millicent as she'd looked before she got so sick. She would stand at the big gas stove, a grandma-type apron covering her print housedress, sturdy black oxfords on her feet, and her thick gray hair twisted into a chignon at the back of her head. She'd be stirring a big pot of stew or frying pork chops or potatoes. The smells of the food would permeate the room, and the windows would be steamed up in the wintertime or open to let in the sounds and smells in the summertime.

Tess would miss this house if she ended up giving it to the Collierville Historical Society. There were a lot of good memories here. For a moment, sadness threatened to overcome her, but she quickly shook it off.

Yes, there were good memories here, but she was moving on to a better life. A life with David and Francesca . . . and a baby of her very own.

She smiled at him, then turned back to Francesca. "I like it here, too, honey. But I like being with you and your father even more."

As soon as the words were out of her mouth, Tess wondered where they'd come from and how she'd had the nerve to say them. Then she met David's gaze again, and she saw approval and gratitude and something else. Admiration? Pleasure warmed Tess, and for that moment, anyway, her doubts disappeared. She was doing the right thing, she told herself. It would all work out. She knew it would.

Although no formal announcement of their engagement had been made, word of their involvement began to get around town. After Tess and David had been out together several times, Tess noticed that the phone rang more often.

The first one to call was Summer.

"So how's your job going?" Tess asked.

"I love it. But it certainly keeps me busy!"

"I've noticed," Tess said with a laugh. "I've hardly seen you in the past month."

"But I hear you've been keeping busy yourself," Summer said slyly.

Tess smiled. The old Collierville grapevine was in fine working order, it seemed. "Well, yes, I have been," she hedged, wondering just exactly what Summer had heard.

"How about meeting me for lunch on Friday and telling me all about it?"

"All about what?"

Summer laughed. "Don't give me that Miss Innocent line. You know exactly what I'm talking about. *Who* I'm talking about. Shoot, Tess, the whole town is gossiping about how many times you've been out with David Bannister in the past couple of weeks. I must've heard about it from at least three different sources, including Emma Claridge."

"Oh, Emma Claridge! You know what an old busybody she is, and how she loves to repeat things—true or not."

"Quit dodging the issue. Are you, or are you not, seeing David Bannister? I'm supposed to be your best friend. Am I going to be the last to know?"

Tess chuckled. "All right, already. I've been out with him several times, so I guess you could say I'm seeing him."

"Oh, Tess! That's wonderful!" Summer gushed. "I want to hear every last, juicy detail. Where do you want to have lunch Friday?"

"I'm afraid I can't meet you on Friday," Tess said. "I've started going over to the community center every Friday at noon. The seniors meet for lunch, then have a sing-along, and I've been playing the piano for them."

"Honestly, Tess. Sometimes you make me feel so selfish! Why do you have to be so darned *nice?*"

"I'm not doing this because I'm nice," Tess protested. "I *like* going over there. It's fun."

Summer sighed. "You're hopeless. Well, if we can't meet Friday, how about coming over for lunch on Saturday?"

"Gee, Summer, I'm sorry. I have students all day Saturday."

"Well, when *am* I going to see you?"

"How about Thursday night?"

Tess hadn't lied. She *did* enjoy playing for the seniors. It was fun to play old favorites just for the sheer joy of playing. And the seniors were so appreciative. It made her feel good to see the pleasure they got out of the singalong every week. They all seemed to have such fun together. It got her thinking about Hazel. After her first week at the center, she had tried to persuade Hazel to go along with her.

"No," Hazel said.

"But why? They're such a nice group. You'd make some new friends and have some fun," Tess said.

"I have plenty of friends now."

"A person can never have too many friends," Tess insisted.

"I don't like organized fun," Hazel said. She turned away from Tess and resumed cleaning the stove, which Tess had interrupted. "Bunch of old geezers jumping around and acting like idiots," she muttered under her breath.

Tess smothered a smile. "They're not *old,* Hazel. Some of them are as young as sixty-two! That's not old." Hazel herself was seventy-five, and she'd told Tess at least one hundred times that she did not consider herself old.

"I don't want to go."

"But you don't know how much fun you're missing," Tess said. Then, trying to keep a straight face, she teased, "There are a lot of really nice-looking men in the group. Who knows? You might find yourself a swee-tie."

"I'll give you *sweetie,*" Hazel said, whipping around and glaring at Tess. "Why in the world would I want some smelly old man around, anyway? I don't know what's gotten into you lately!"

Tess wanted to laugh but knew Hazel would be furi-ous if she did. She sighed instead. "Okay, okay, I give up." There was no persuading Hazel once she'd taken a stand.

On the Friday before Thanksgiving, Tess showed up at the center a few minutes before twelve. She had tried again that morning to convince Hazel to come along, with no success.

She immediately noticed the new man in the group. About seventy years old, he was taller than the other men. If she were guessing, she'd say he was about six feet tall. He had a full head of thick gray hair and the softest blue eyes Tess had ever seen. She wondered who he was. She'd never seen him before.

A few minutes after Tess arrived, Gerri Kovach, the activities director at the center, brought the newcomer forward. "I want you to meet Alistair Simpson, Tess," Gerri said. "He just moved to Collierville. He's Norma Simpson's father-in-law. Alistair, this is Tess Collier. She plays the piano for the sing-along."

"It's a pleasure to meet you," Alistair said. He had a British accent, and Tess remembered that Norma Simpson had married an Englishman.

They shook hands, and Tess noticed what a firm grip he had.

Throughout the sing-along, Tess's gaze kept returning to Alistair. There was something about him that she liked a lot. She noticed how gentlemanly he was, how polite and thoughtful. At the end of the session, he lingered at the piano while she gathered up her sheet music.

"I've always wished I could play the piano," he said wistfully.

"It's never too late to learn," Tess said, smiling at him.

"I suppose not." He returned her smile. "You play beautifully."

"Thank you. You know, I teach piano, too."

His eyes lit up. "You do?"

"Yes. And I wouldn't mind taking on a new student." Although David had suggested she might like to begin phasing out some of her piano students, Tess wasn't sure she wanted to do that. Not yet, anyway. Besides, an idea had just struck her.

"You don't think I'm too old to learn to play?"

"Of course not! How old was Grandma Moses when she began to paint? A person's never too old to learn something new." She tucked her sheet music into her tote bag. "I've got an opening on Monday afternoons at two. Are you interested?"

"Yes," he said. "I am."

Tess hummed all the way home. She wondered what starchy old Hazel would think of the courtly Alistair Simpson.

* * *

David chuckled. "You mean, you're planning to fix Hazel up with this old gentleman?"

"Why not? Hazel could use some excitement in her life. She's getting awfully set in her ways."

"What if they don't like each other?"

Tess shrugged. "Then I'll just have a new piano student, and that's all." She took a bite of her ice-cream sundae. It was Saturday evening, and she and David had stopped at Dalrymple's after seeing a movie. Francesca wasn't with them tonight. "But he's such a nice man. I can't imagine why Hazel *wouldn't* like him."

David smiled. "You're a romantic at heart, aren't you?

Tess could feel herself blushing. Once more, she shrugged. "I don't know. I've never thought of myself that way."

For a moment he said nothing. Then, taking her completely off guard, he said, "Why haven't you ever married?"

She met his gaze squarely. "I wasn't free to marry while my aunt was alive. Then, once she was gone, I don't know...I just never met anyone I wanted to marry."

They both fell silent, but David's gaze remained on her face. After a few seconds, Tess looked down at her sundae, but she could feel him studying her. He had done that a lot in the past two weeks, and each time he did, she wondered what he was thinking. Part of her—the insecure, my-own-parents-didn't-want-me part of her—was afraid she knew exactly what he was thinking. He was probably regretting his offer of marriage, wondering how he could extricate himself from the situation, and comparing her, unfavorably, with Leah. The other part of her—the part that knew she had value as a person—hoped he liked her. Hoped he was beginning to see her as more than just a mother to Francesca. Hoped that one day he could love her.

Tess knew that if a fairy godmother were to come to earth and grant her three wishes, she'd only have one.

Chapter Seven

When Alistair Simpson showed up for his first lesson Monday, Tess made sure she was upstairs so Hazel would be forced to answer the door. A few minutes after Tess heard the doorbell chime, Hazel called to her from the foyer.

"Tess! Your student is here."

Tess poked her head around the doorway of her bedroom. "Hazel, could you take Mr. Simpson into the study? I'll be down in a minute." Then she grinned and ducked into the bathroom, where she leaned against the sink and waited a full five minutes.

By the time she reached the downstairs hallway it was a little after two, and Hazel, who had emerged from the study, frowned at her. "What took you so long?" she muttered under her breath.

Tess gave her an innocent smile. "Oh, sorry."

"Who *is* he?" Hazel jerked her head backward toward the study door.

In a spurt of pure deviltry, Tess leaned over and whispered, "A smelly old man, only I think he smells good! Don't you?"

Hazel's indignant "Humph" followed Tess into the study, and she had to fight against dissolving into giggles. Still grinning, she said, "Hi, there, Mr. Simpson. It's good to see you."

It was another cold, blustery day, and he'd been standing by the window, looking out at the rain. He turned at the sound of her voice. "Hello, Miss Collier. But I say, could you please just call me Alistair?"

"Of course. But only if you'll call me Tess." She looked at the rain-swept window. "Miserable day, isn't it?"

He shrugged. "This kind of day reminds me of home."

"Are you homesick?"

"A bit." He smiled. "But I'll get over it. It's always difficult when you make a drastic change in your life."

"Yes, it is." His observation caused her to think of David. Would the coming changes in her own life be difficult, too? She shook off the thought."Well, shall we get started?"

His smile expanded, his eyes crinkling agreeably at the corners. "All right, but I'd better warn you. I'm nervous, so I probably shan't do well."

"Oh, you'll do just fine." Tess thought again how much she liked the older man. And if Hazel's immediate reaction to him was any indication, she wasn't immune to him, either.

The half-hour lesson passed quickly. Tess showed Alistair how the keys were grouped in twos and threes and how his fingers were numbered. She grinned as he clutched the tennis ball she used to demonstrate how his hand should be shaped as he played.

They discussed the shapes of the notes and the difference in the way they looked higher up the scale. Then she instructed him how to position his right hand on the black keys. Fingers one and two—thumb and index finger—on the two black keys and fingers three, four and five—middle, ring and pinky—on the three black keys.

"All right," she said when his right hand was in place, "let's just practice a bit. I'll call out finger numbers, and you play those keys."

They drilled for a few minutes until he got the hang of it, then Tess said, "Now we're ready for you to play your first song. I'm going to play chords down here while you play the melody up there. Okay?"

"Okay," he said doubtfully.

"Ready?"

He nodded.

"Three, three, three, one, two, two, one," she called, playing the accompanying chords as he painstakingly fingered the first notes to "Old MacDonald Had a Farm."

He laughed out loud. "I'm playing!" he said.

"You certainly are. Now—five, five, four, four, three."

"Eee-eye, eee-eye, oh," he sang, and Tess grinned at his unabashed delight.

They continued on for the rest of the song, with Alistair gaining speed and confidence as they progressed. When the song was over, he couldn't stop smiling. "This is great fun, isn't it?" he said.

Tess decided he was one of the sweetest men she'd ever met, young or old. "And it's only begun," she told him.

When the lesson was over, Tess said, "I don't have another student for an hour, and I'm parched. Would you like to have a cup of tea with me?"

"Oh, I hate to keep you—"

"Believe me, you're not keeping me. I'd love some company. Besides, on such a miserable, wet day, you need something warm to fortify you for the trip home."

"You've persuaded me."

"Good. Why don't we go out into the kitchen? I happen to know that Hazel baked an apple pie this morning. I'll bet a piece of pie would taste great with our tea."

The smell of cinnamon and apples grew stronger as they neared the kitchen. When they walked in, Hazel, who had been sitting at the kitchen table making some kind of list, started. The expression on her face was priceless, and Tess wished she had a camera to capture it. If Alistair hadn't been there, Tess would have teased her by saying, "If you don't close your mouth, a bug might fly in!" Instead she said, "I've invited Alistair to stay for a cup of tea. Did you two introduce yourselves?"

Hazel, still open-mouthed, nodded.

"Yes," Alistair said. "Hello, again, Mrs. Wancheck."

"Hello," Hazel said grudgingly.

"Oh, we don't stand on ceremony here," Tess said, looking at Alistair. "I'm sure Hazel would prefer you call her by her first name. Hazel, this is Alistair. He's from England, and he's just moved to Collierville to live with his son and daughter-in-law. You know them—Nigel and Norma Simpson."

"You're Nigel Simpson's father?" Hazel said, her voice just the tiniest bit warmer.

"Yes, I am," Alistair said.

"I told Alistair along with our cup of tea you'd probably give us some of that apple pie," Tess said. "Why don't you sit down, Alistair?"

Once she had served them some pie and fixed their tea, Hazel said, "Well, I think I'll just go on upstairs while you two talk. I've got some things that need doin'."

Tess said, "Oh, Hazel, those things, whatever they are, can wait. Sit down. Since Alistair's new in town, I'm sure there are a lot of things he'd like to ask you about."

"He can ask you," Hazel said. She began to untie her apron.

"But you're his contemporary. I'm not." Hazel was going to get to know Alistair Simpson if it killed Tess.

"Yes, please, Hazel, do sit down," Alistair urged. "I should be glad of any advice you can give me about settling in here in Collierville."

Short of being completely rude and ungracious, Hazel couldn't argue anymore, so she sat.

"So how'd you two meet?" Hazel asked.

"At the center," Tess said. She smiled at Hazel. "I've been telling her she should go," she said to Alistair.

"Friday was my first day," he said, "but it's great fun. You *should* go, Hazel."

"I don't have time for that kind of nonsense," Hazel said. "I've got too much work to do." Her tone was defiant.

Alistair smiled gently. "You work hard."

"Yes, I do." She looked at him suspiciously.

"You deserve some time to yourself, then," he added.

Tess smothered a smile as she watched the struggle going on in Hazel's mind. She knew the older woman so well. Under that gruff exterior was the soul of a kind, caring, wonderful woman who hadn't allowed anyone to get too close in a long time. She even kept Tess at arm's length, and Tess knew Hazel would lay down and die for her. "Well, maybe..." Hazel conceded.

"This pie is delicious," Alistair said a few moments later.

"You ought to taste her pumpkin pie," Tess said. "I can hardly wait for Thanksgiving."

"I've never had pumpkin pie," Alistair said.

Hazel frowned. "Don't you eat pumpkin pie in England?"

"No, as a matter of fact, we don't. Pumpkin is a wholly American food."

"What kinds of pies *do* you eat?" Tess asked.

"Blackberry, gooseberry, mincemeat." He looked at Hazel. "But I'd love to try some pumpkin."

"Norma will have pumpkin pie for Thanksgiving, I'm sure," Hazel said.

"Well, actually, Nigel and Norma and the children are all going to spend Thanksgiving at Norma's parents' home in Columbus."

"But aren't you going, too?" Tess asked.

"No. I didn't want to go."

"You mean, you'll be all by yourself for Thanksgiving!" Tess couldn't believe that Nigel and Norma would leave his father alone over the holiday.

"Since we don't celebrate the holiday in England, I won't mind. It's not like I'm missing anything I was used to."

"That's terrible! Isn't that terrible, Hazel?"

Hazel nodded reluctantly.

"Really, I don't mind at all," Alistair said.

"Well, whether you mind or not, you can't be by yourself for Thanksgiving. You must come here," Tess said. Oh, how perfect. She couldn't have set it up better if she'd tried. She didn't look at Hazel because she was afraid she'd give away her glee. "Hazel and I always cook enough to feed an army, so we'll have plenty of food. And we'd love to have you, wouldn't we, Hazel?"

"Hurry up, Francesca, or we'll be late." David waited impatiently at the front door. What was keeping the child? They'd been all ready to leave for Thanksgiving dinner at Tess's house when Francesca suddenly dashed off to her bedroom. David couldn't imagine what it was she had forgotten to do.

But when she emerged and joined him at the front door, he understood. In her left hand she clutched a gaily colored cardboard turkey cutout she'd obviously made in school.

"And what's this?" he said, smiling.

"For Tess," she whispered.

"May I see it?"

After a second's hesitation, she handed it to him, and for a moment, their eyes met. Hers were solemn, but there was something else in their depths. Something almost fearful. Pain pricked David's heart. God, was Francesca really afraid of him? She certainly acted as if she were. But then, he thought with uncharacteristic bitterness, why shouldn't she be? She was only a child. If she thought he had killed her mother, wouldn't she—with the reasoning of an eight-year-old—be afraid he might harm her, too?

Forcing his black thoughts away, he concentrated on Francesca's artwork. The cutout was cleverly designed so that it would stand up. "Is this for the table?" he asked.

Francesca nodded.

He smiled as gently as he knew how when he handed it back to her. "It's very nice, honey. I think Tess will like it a lot. Now, don't you think we'd better get going?"

They arrived at Tess's house fifteen minutes later. David pulled up into the driveway and parked. As he and Francesca walked from the car to the porch, he took a deep breath of the cold, crisp air. The rain had finally stopped the day before, and today the sun shone brightly in an absolutely perfect sky. Only the tiniest wisp of cloud was visible. So far, Collierville had not had the first snow of the season, but now that the temperature had dropped, David knew it probably wouldn't be long before they did.

David loved winter. Before Leah's death, he and Francesca had gone ice skating together nearly every Saturday. Leah never came with them. She hated skating. He wondered if Tess liked to skate. As he rang the doorbell, he decided she probably did. Somehow he thought Tess would like all the simple pleasures—things like eating cotton candy, or reading *Alice in Wonderland* to a child, or sitting outside on a summer's night and watching the lightning bugs.

Tess answered the door, and David's first thought was how nice she looked. She seemed to grow prettier every day, and he wondered if it was simply his perception of her that was changing or if she really *was* more attractive. He did wish, though, that just once she'd wear her hair down. More than once he'd speculated on its length. He imagined it would look beautiful flowing down her back.

Today Tess wore a soft wool dress the color of cranberries. David smiled. "Did you pick the dress to match the day?"

"What do you mean?" She looked up at him in that shy way of hers. Self-consciously, she fingered the pearls at her throat.

He chuckled. "It's the exact color of cranberries, that's all, a perfect choice for the day. It looks great on you."

"Oh…thank you." She averted her gaze, kneeling to help Francesca unbutton her coat.

David wondered if Tess would ever be comfortable accepting a compliment. His hand itched to touch her cheek where the becoming rose color gave away her embarrassment. If theirs had been a normal courtship, he would have. Because it wasn't, he felt awkward about his instincts. Since the night she'd accepted his proposal, he hadn't touched her in anything except the most casual way. He knew that in this respect, Tess felt awkward, too. He wished he knew how to overcome this problem. He guessed one of these days, when they were alone, he'd be presented with an opportunity. He knew once they were past the first time, things would be okay. At least, he hoped they would.

He wondered what it would be like to make love to Tess. He imagined she would be hesitant and shy. When he had come up with his plan of marrying Tess, he had been thinking strictly about Francesca. He'd never gone further in his thoughts than what it would mean to his daughter to have Tess with them all the time. He'd certainly never considered how unfair his proposition might be to Tess. Or how awkward and potentially uncomfortable. Well, he would have to take care to make her feel at ease. To make her happy. Tess deserved to be happy.

How different she was from Leah, he mused as he watched her with Francesca. Leah had been like a hot-house orchid—vivid and lush and exotic. Tess, on the other hand, reminded him of violets, with their delicacy and subtle beauty. The notion pleased him.

After Tess hung up Francesca's and David's coats, Francesca, face beaming, handed Tess the turkey cut-out.

"Oh, is this for *me?*" Tess's face lit up with delight.

Francesca's eyes sparkled, and she nodded. "It's for the table."

"Did you make this, honey?"

"Uh-huh."

"It's beautiful! Let's go put it on the table right now, shall we?" Tess looked at David, and her soft gray eyes shone with pleasure. "David, why don't you go on into the parlor? Introduce yourself to Alistair. We'll be right there as soon as we put this beautiful turkey on the table." Then she took Francesca's hand and they headed off toward the dining room. For a moment, David stood there and watched, his earlier gloomy thoughts completely forgotten in the wake of Francesca's obvious happiness.

Still smiling, he entered the parlor where a tall, older man stood in front of the fireplace. Like David, the man wore casual slacks and a turtleneck sweater. At David's entrance, he turned and smiled. "Hello. I'm Alistair Simpson."

David walked forward and extended his hand. "It's nice to meet you. I'm David Bannister." He immediately liked the Englishman, who had a friendly face and direct blue eyes. He also had a surprisingly strong grip.

Just then Francesca entered the room.

"And who's this lovely young lady?" Alistair said, looking down at Francesca.

"I'm Francesca," she said, astonishing David. It was the first time since Leah's death that Francesca had spoken directly to a stranger without being prodded by David. She smiled shyly.

"How do you do, Francesca?" Alistair said. He stooped and gravely shook her hand, too. Then he straightened and said to David, "Tess kindly invited me to partake of your holiday meal."

David nodded. "Yes, she told me."

"It will be my very first Thanksgiving."

"You're in for a treat, I understand. Tess says Hazel makes the best bread stuffing to be found anywhere."

"If it's anything like her apple pie," Alistair said, "I can hardly wait."

Soon Tess joined them, and a few minutes later Hazel, who, David was amused to note, seemed far more aware of Alistair Simpson than she pretended to be.

Looking back on the day, David would remember it as one of the nicest holidays he'd ever spent. The food was wonderful, just as Tess had predicted. The turkey was so tender, it nearly fell off its bones. And when David tasted the stuffing, he thought he'd died and gone to heaven. In addition, there were mashed potatoes, sweet potatoes, peas, cranberries, fresh green beans, and assorted raw vegetables and relishes, including Hazel's homemade pickle relish.

"The recipe for it has been handed down for four generations," she told him proudly.

"It's wonderful," David assured her, helping himself to more.

"I'll give you a jar to take home." Then she looked at Alistair. "You can have a jar, too."

Tess met David's gaze, and he fought against the laugh that struggled to erupt. It looked as if Tess's matchmaking might bear fruit, after all.

In addition to the food, the big dining-room table looked festive. It was laid with a beautiful old lace tablecloth, and decorated with a cornucopia centerpiece of fall flowers and Francesca's turkey, flanked by gleaming silver candlesticks holding fat orange candles.

David had provided the wine, a fine Riesling that was one of his favorites, and Tess commented that it was such a special occasion they were using her great-aunt's crystal goblets. "Aunt Millicent's crystal is really old, and they don't make this pattern anymore, so I don't use it often," she explained.

Throughout the meal, the conversation was lively. Alistair Simpson was a delightful guest, and he kept them entertained with stories about his homeland. Before long, even Hazel had loosened up and had a few stories of her own to tell. Francesca didn't say much, but she listened avidly, and several times she giggled—a sound that tugged at David's heart.

And then there was Tess. Tess, who seemed to glow with an inner light. David's gaze kept returning to her. He enjoyed looking at her, he decided. And, as he had been doing more and more often lately, he found himself comparing her to Leah. Inevitably, Leah lost in the comparison. Several times during the day, Tess had caught him watching her, and that charming tint of pink would color her cheeks. David thought it enormously refreshing to see a grown woman blush. He couldn't imagine anything that would have made Leah blush.

After dinner they all gathered around the Steinway in the parlor, and Tess played Christmas carols. David liked to sing, but singing wasn't something he'd had much chance to do in the past. The blend of voices was surprisingly good, he thought. Alistair's strong tenor, Tess's pure contralto, and Hazel's soprano all blended nicely with his baritone. Francesca sat next to Tess on the piano bench, and although she did not join in the singing, she had a happy look on her face that made David feel good.

They sang all the traditional carols, then branched off into other holiday songs. "White Christmas," "Silver Bells" and "Over the River and Through the Woods"— a personal favorite of David's.

When the last notes of the last song died away, darkness had fallen. The parlor, lit by the flames of the fire they'd kept stoked all day, looked like something out of a Currier and Ives painting. David sighed with contentment. He couldn't remember a day that had been filled with so many good things, with nothing to mar his pleasure or to remind him of his daughter's unhappiness and the trauma his family had endured.

He hated for the day to be over. He hated to go back to his empty house where that mocking portrait hung over the mantel. He hated for Francesca's eyes to lose their happy sparkle, for her silence to once again envelope them. But finally he could delay his departure no longer. Alistair was preparing to leave, and David reluctantly said, "I think we'd better be going, too."

Tess didn't protest, as he'd half hoped she might. She yawned and stretched, then laughed softly. "I'm sorry. I guess I'm tired."

"Well, no wonder," Hazel said, "you've been runnin' around all day like a chicken with its head cut off."

"Everything was wonderful, Tess," David said. He felt embarrassed by his selfish thoughts, by his desire to lengthen the day. Of course, she was tired. She'd worked hard to prepare for all of them.

After Alistair said his goodbyes, waving off David's offer of a ride by saying he needed to walk off some of the food he'd eaten, Hazel left David and Francesca alone with Tess. The three of them walked slowly out to the foyer.

"This is the nicest Thanksgiving I've ever had. Thank you," he said, reaching for their coats.

She gave him one of her sweet smiles, and he could see she was pleased. "I'm glad. It's one of the nicest I've ever spent, too."

After he and Francesca had donned their coats and were standing by the front door, David said, "You know, I almost forgot, but Medlock is having their annual Christmas dinner dance a week Saturday, and I'd like you to go with me. I think that might be a good time for our... announcement."

Tess nodded slowly. Then her eyes clouded. "A dinner dance? Is it going to be formal?"

"Yes." He saw her forehead crease into a frown. "Is something wrong?"

She hesitated, then shrugged. "No, nothing's wrong."

David knew something *was* wrong. Didn't she want to go? Why was she frowning? "Look, Tess, I can see something's wrong. Now come on, tell me what it is. Don't you want to go?"

She looked up at him and smiled. "Of course, I want to go. It's just...well, the only evening dress I have is the long black skirt and top I wear for performances. I do have a short black, too, but they both feel like uniforms to me."

"Is that all? That's no problem. I want you to have a new dress. You find what you want, and I'll arrange for payment."

"Oh, David, I couldn't do that!"

"Why not?"

"We're not—" She broke off, looking at Francesca.

He lowered his voice. "Not yet, but we will be."

"But—"

"No buts. Go out this week and find what you want. And don't worry about the price, either. This is a special occasion."

There it was again. That tinge of color in her cheeks. The urge to touch her, which had recurred several times throughout the day, came back even stronger. They stood there for a long moment, not saying anything. Then, slowly, he raised his right hand and softly brushed her cheek, reveling in its softness. She didn't move, but he saw her throat work as she swallowed, and he could see the pulse beating in her throat and the soft rise and fall of her breasts. Her lips parted, and his gaze was drawn to them. He realized he wanted to kiss her, and the realization jolted him. He also realized that if Francesca hadn't been there, he would have kissed her.

Maybe more than once.

Reluctantly, David withdrew his hand. "Good night, Tess," he said softly. "It was a wonderful day."

All the way home he kept remembering the way she'd looked at him when she'd said goodbye. It was a look he hoped she'd never lose.

"I'll go with you to find a dress," Summer said.

"Oh, would you?" Tess trusted Summer's judgment more than she trusted her own. Summer always looked so stylish, and Tess knew she managed the look without spending a fortune on her clothes.

"Absolutely. It'll be fun!" Summer declared with enthusiasm. "We'll go to Brigitte's," she added, naming a popular and trendy boutique that had opened the previous year.

"Oh, I don't know," Tess demurred. "I'm not sure Brigitte's is my style."

"I think it's time to change your style a bit," Summer said, grimacing at Tess's navy blue skirt and white blouse with its Peter Pan collar.

Tess let herself be persuaded, and the following Saturday found herself at Brigitte's Boutique.

"We want something sexy yet ladylike," Summer said. "Don't say a word!" she added when Tess opened her mouth to say she didn't think she was the sexy type.

Brigitte, a bubbly redhead with an infectious smile, said, "I have several outfits that would work beautifully."

Five minutes later, Summer carefully inspected Brigitte's offerings. "No, not this one. Too bright. And this one's too fussy for Tess. These two are great, though. Here, Tess, try these." She handed Tess a peach silk evening suit and a long, claret, silk crepe dress.

Tess eyed the silk crepe doubtfully. The skirt was slit two-thirds of the way up in front and plunged to the waist in the back. She thought it looked way too daring for her. But she had a feeling Summer wouldn't listen to her argument, so she accepted both outfits and went into the dressing room.

She tried on the peach silk suit first. She loved it. The skirt was just the right length, hitting her mid-knee, and the jacket—embroidered with tiny seed pearls—fit perfectly. Tess felt elegant and sophisticated when she looked at herself in the mirror. She could even wear Aunt Millicent's pearls.

"Come on out here," Summer said, "where we can see you."

Tess, preening a bit, exited the dressing room. "Well, what do you think?"

Summer nodded. "That's nice." She looked at Brigitte. "Don't you think so?"

"Yes, I do. But I'd like to see the claret evening dress on her, too."

Tess had hoped they'd forget about the other dress. She took a last look at herself in the three-way mirror, then returned to the dressing room and carefully removed the suit. When she put on the claret silk and looked at herself in the dressing-room mirror, she almost took it off again, but Summer poked her head in just as Tess was about to strip it off. "Do you need help zipping that dress up?" she said.

Tess sighed. "Yes."

Two minutes later, at Summer's urging, Tess walked outside the dressing room.

"Wow!" Brigitte said. She grinned at Summer.

Summer nodded. "Oh, yes," she said.

"Oh, no," Tess said. "I like the suit much better. Besides, Summer, this dress just isn't my style."

"I told you, kiddo. We're going to change your style."

"I feel self-conscious." Tess looked down. "Look how high up this slit is." She stuck her leg out.

Summer grinned. "Hey, you've got gorgeous legs. It's about time you showed them off."

"Summer... I don't know..."

"Trust me," Summer said. She turned to Brigitte. "She's taking this one. Wrap it up."

NO RISK, NO OBLIGATION TO BUY ... NOW OR EVER!

CASINO JUBILEE
"Scratch'n Match" Game

Here's how to play:

1. Peel off label from front cover. Place it in space provided at right. With a coin, carefully scratch off the silver box. Then check the claim chart to see what we have for you – FREE BOOKS and a gift – ALL YOURS! ALL FREE!

2. Send back this card and you'll receive brand-new Silhouette Special Edition® novels. These books have a cover price of $3.50 each, but they are yours to keep absolutely free.

3. There's no catch. You're under no obligation to buy anything. We charge nothing – ZERO – for your first shipment. And you don't have to make any minimum number of purchases – not even one!

4. The fact is thousands of readers enjoy receiving books by mail from the Silhouette Reader Service™ months before they're available in stores. They like the convenience of home delivery and they love our discount prices!

5. We hope that after receiving your free books you'll want to remain a subscriber. But the choice is yours – to continue or cancel, anytime at all! So why not take us up on our invitation, with no risk of any kind. You'll be glad you did!

YOURS FREE!

This lovely Victorian pewter-finish miniature is perfect for displaying a treasured photograph – and it's yours absolutely free – when you accept our no-risk offer.

CASINO JUBILEE
"Scratch'n Match" Game

SCRATCH HERE

PLACE LABEL HERE

CHECK CLAIM CHART BELOW FOR YOUR FREE GIFTS!

YES! I have placed my label from the front cover in the space provided above and scratched off the silver box. Please send me all the gifts for which I qualify. I understand that I am under no obligation to purchase any books, as explained on the back and on the opposite page.

235 CIS ANFA (U-SIL-SE-03/94)

Name _____

Address _____ Apt. _____

City _____ State _____ Zip _____

CASINO JUBILEE CLAIM CHART

	WORTH 4 FREE BOOKS AND A FREE VICTORIAN PICTURE FRAME	
	WORTH 4 FREE BOOKS	
	WORTH 3 FREE BOOKS	CLAIM N° 1528

Chapter Eight

"Summer, I've got something to tell you."

"Oh?" Summer turned toward Tess. They were driving home after their shopping expedition, and had stopped for a red light. When Tess hesitated, Summer said, "Well, *what?*"

"At the Medlock dinner dance..."

"Yes?"

"Uh, well..." Tess took a deep breath, then said in a rush, "David and I are going to announce our engagement."

"*What!*" Summer's face broke into a wide grin. "Tess! You stinker! That's *wonderful!* When did *this* happen?"

The car behind them honked. "The light's green," Tess said.

Summer grinned sheepishly. After they were once more on their way, she said, "Well? How long have you been keeping this secret from your *very best friend?*"

Tess laughed at Summer's outraged tone. "He asked me a while back, but we decided to wait before making any announcement."

"And you couldn't even tell *me?*" Summer made a sound like a huff. "My feelings are hurt."

Tess grimaced. "I'm sorry. I wanted to tell you, but we both thought it was better to wait."

Summer frowned as she navigated a turn. "I guess I don't understand why. Is there some kind of problem?"

"No. It's just that... well, we weren't sure how Francesca would react, and...after all...it's not even a year since... Leah died."

Summer nodded, slanting a sideways look at Tess. "Yeah, I see what you mean. I guess it *is* a touchy situation. But, *Tess*... I'm your best friend! Couldn't you have at least told me? I can keep a secret. I wouldn't have blabbed it all over. You know that."

"I'm sorry." Tess could never explain the real reason she'd held off telling Summer—the fact that Tess hadn't been sure David wouldn't change his mind. Tess swallowed. Sometimes it was hard to be really happy about marrying David—even though she wanted the marriage with all of her heart. If only David loved her...

Summer's excited words cut through Tess's thoughts. "Well, I guess I forgive you. And Tess, this really is wonderful. I'm so happy for you. In fact, I'm going to give you an engagement party!"

"Oh, no, that's not necessary," Tess protested.

"Listen, when my very best friend snags the most eligible bachelor in town, the very *least* I can do for her is have a party."

"Summer, really, I don't want a fuss. Because of Leah's death and all, I just want to get married quietly." What if someone were to guess that she and David were not the usual engaged pair? Didn't most engaged couples hang all over each other? No, she couldn't place David in that uncomfortable position. The less fuss made about this engagement, the better.

"Nonsense. No one's going to think less of you or David because his wife died and he's marrying again. I mean, it's not like the two of you were carrying on while Leah was alive or anything." Summer's voice had fallen into its I-won't-listen-to-any-argument tone she adopted when dealing with her children. "You're doing nothing wrong. Now I'm going to have a party for you, and that's that."

Tess felt as if an avalanche had begun, and no matter what she did, it would be impossible to stop.

The feeling persisted, gaining momentum as the night of the Medlock dinner dance approached. Summer insisted on coming to the house to help Tess get ready. Tess didn't even try to protest when Summer said, "I'm going to do your makeup and hair. I think you need a more festive look."

And as Tess looked at her emerging self under the skillful hands of her friend, she knew Summer had been right. About the hair and the makeup and even the dress.

Summer gave Tess a quick kiss on the cheek when she was finished. "You look terrific," she said. "Have a great time, and call me the instant you wake up in the morning. I want to hear all about it."

Tess promised. After Summer was gone, Tess took one last look at herself in the mirror. She saw a woman who looked better than she'd ever looked. She wasn't vividly beautiful, as Leah Bannister had been, but she wouldn't shame David. She touched her hand to her hair. Summer had fashioned it into a Gibson girl style— loosely upswept, with soft tendrils falling around her face.

What would David think? she wondered. She was nervous about tonight. All of his colleagues would be at the dinner dance, and she wanted David to be proud of her.

Taking a deep breath, she turned away from the mirror. She picked up her evening bag and walked slowly downstairs to wait for his arrival. She could hear Hazel in the parlor, and from the sounds, she was stoking the fire.

Self-consciously, Tess walked in. Hazel straightened, her eyes widening as she took in Tess's appearance. She looked her up and down, but all she said was, "New dress?"

Tess nodded. She fingered the pearls at her throat. "D-do you like it?"

"Looks nice."

Coming from Hazel, that was a high compliment. Tess smiled, her gaze meeting the older woman's. "Thanks."

When the doorbell announced David's arrival about five minutes later, Tess's heart pumped faster. She walked slowly to the door, her high-heeled evening pumps tapping against the wooden floors. She said a quick, *Please, God, let everything go well tonight,* then opened the door.

Oh, my, she thought. David in a tuxedo was something to behold. "Hello, David," she said.

His gaze swept her from head to toe as he stepped into the foyer. For a moment he seemed taken aback, and Tess had an uncomfortable few seconds of uncertainty.

Maybe he didn't like her dress. Maybe he thought she looked ridiculous, like a little girl trying to play dress-up.

But then he smiled. "You look beautiful, Tess."

She knew he was exaggerating, being gallant, being David, but his comment made her happy, anyway. She was grateful to him for trying to put her at ease.

Tess had borrowed Summer's fur-lined velvet cape, and she reached for it. David helped her put it on, and as his hands lingered for a moment on her shoulders, Tess's heart skipped alarmingly. His masculine scent drifted around her. She breathed it in, thinking he smelled wonderful. As wonderful as he looked. Suddenly the full realization hit her. This man—this handsome, successful, *sexy* man—was going to be her husband. They were going to live together and . . . sleep together. She closed her eyes, feeling her heart pounding away. *Oh, please, God, I want to make David happy. I want to make him love me.*

Gently, he turned her to face him. A strange expression hovered in the depths of his green eyes as her gaze met his. Did he somehow know what she'd been thinking? Her throat suddenly felt dry.

Then, with a crooked little smile, he dropped his hands and reached into the right pocket of his overcoat. He withdrew a small, gray velvet jeweler's box and held it out to her. With trembling fingers, Tess took it. "Now that we're officially engaged, I thought you should have this," he said softly.

When Tess, with fingers that suddenly refused to work properly, managed to snap open the box, she stopped breathing. Inside, gleaming from soft folds of satin, lay a stunning emerald-cut diamond ring. Under the chandelier, it sparkled brilliantly. "Oh, David," she said. The ring must have cost him a fortune. Tess wasn't knowledgeable about gems, but she knew enough to know a diamond this large and perfect-looking wasn't exactly inexpensive.

Smiling at her obvious astonishment, he removed the ring from the box and slipped it onto the ring finger of her left hand. It was a bit loose. "Sorry about the way it fits. We'll take it back to Royer's on Monday and get it sized properly."

Tess looked down at her hand. The diamond blazed with fiery brilliance. Oh, she loved it! She had never expected a ring, even though—now that she thought about it—Leah had had a gorgeous engagement ring. Tess remembered admiring it once and Leah's offhanded thank-you.

Of course, David would want his wife to wear a nice ring. And even if the reason he'd given this to her was more a matter of pride than an indication of his feelings for her, she wanted to keep it. She swallowed hard, then slowly lifted her face to meet his gaze once more. "Thank you, David. I love it." *And I love you, too.* The thought was so strong, for one horrified instant, she thought she'd said it aloud. *I must never say it aloud. I must never back him into a corner. That wouldn't be fair,* she admonished herself.

His smile was gentle as his gaze swept her face. Then, to Tess's complete amazement, he bent his head and his lips brushed hers in a feather-light kiss. The kiss lasted only a heartbeat in time, but it was enough to leave her lips tingling and her heart racing. Then he took her arm, smiled down into her eyes, and said, "Ready?"

As they walked outside into the starry night, Tess's thoughts whirled. Why had David kissed her? Did the kiss mean anything? *No, of course not. Don't be ridiculous. Don't read something into his actions that isn't there*. The kiss hadn't meant a thing. In kissing her, David was just being David. A perfect gentleman who always did the proper thing. He'd just presented her with an engagement ring, and the proper thing to do afterward was kiss her. At most, the kiss was intended to show her he liked her and had some affection for her.

So don't make a big deal out of it.

But, oh, it had been wonderful. Thrilling. And no matter what she told herself, Tess wanted more.

Much more.

The evening had started off even better than he'd expected, David thought as he introduced Tess to his co-workers during the pre-dinner cocktail hour. He was very proud of her. She acted so much more self-assured than he'd expected her to.

And she knew so many of the people there. That surprised him, although once he thought about it, he realized it shouldn't have. After all, Tess was not only the great-great-granddaughter of the founder of their town, she was also the music director at the largest church in Collierville, a respected piano teacher with more than forty students, she sang with the Collierville choral group, and she volunteered at the community center. Why *wouldn't* she know practically everyone?

But what was particularly gratifying to David was how obvious it was—to him, at least—that these people admired and respected Tess. It didn't surprise him. Not really. After all, Tess was worthy of admiration and respect. But still…sometimes quiet people who didn't toot their own horns didn't get noticed. Because not everyone was as discerning as he was.

She looked so lovely tonight, he thought. Her hairstyle, while still retaining the old-fashioned look of her normal braids, looked elegant and sophisticated. It was also sexy, he thought with a flicker of surprise. He grinned. So was her dress, with its plunging back and that slit skirt that revealed tantalizing glimpses of long and beautiful legs.

Funny how he'd never thought of Tess as sexy. Tonight, in that stunning wine-colored dress, it was hard to think of her in any other way. Sexy and classy.

And she would soon belong to him, he thought with a sudden burst of possessiveness. A little bemused by his train of thought, he studied her while she talked with Julia Medlock, the wife of Walter Medlock, owner of David's company.

"My dear, it's been such a pleasure talking to you," Julia was saying. "I hope we'll see a lot of each other in the future."

"I'd enjoy that," Tess said. She touched the pearls at her throat in an unconsciously graceful gesture, and the diamond David had placed there earlier sparkled brilliantly.

David noticed how Julia eyed the ring. He smiled to himself. He was sure a lot of tongues were wagging. Maybe it was time to make his official announcement. He turned to Walter Medlock and quietly told him what he wanted to do.

Walter nodded, then walked up to the bandstand, where a small combo played softly. He motioned to the bandleader. After the song was over, the bandleader conferred with Walter for a few minutes. Then Walter walked to the microphone and said, "Ladies and gentlemen, I think most of you know David Bannister, the head of our advanced research team. Well, David wants to say a few words."

A few people clapped, and David, reaching for Tess's hand, led her up front with him. She gave him a questioning look, and he smiled reassuringly.

"Hi," David said into the mike. "Great party, isn't it?"

There was a much larger burst of applause, and David waited until it died down. Then, leading Tess forward to stand next to him, he slipped an arm around her waist and said, "I have an announcement to make. It gives me great pleasure to tell all of you that this lovely lady—Tess Collier—has consented to be my wife."

A murmur of ohs and aahs rippled through the crowd along with a few gasps of surprise. David smiled down at Tess, then spoke into the microphone again. "We're going to be married the Saturday after Christmas. I'd like to say you're all invited, but we're planning a very small, very quiet ceremony." Everyone there knew about Leah, so David figured they'd understand.

After the announcement, people crowded around them. Once again, he was enormously proud of Tess, for she fielded all the questions and congratulations as if she'd been doing this kind of thing for years.

"Congratulations, David," said the marketing manager, Steve MacAllister. "You're a lucky man."

"Yes, I am." And for the first time since entering into his unconventional marriage plan, David really *did* feel lucky. Not just because he'd found a solution to his problem with Francesca, but personally, as well.

Yes, he thought, Tess was going to be an asset to him in more ways than just as a surrogate mother to Francesca. It was obvious his co-workers thought David had done well for himself. But David knew he had to be careful not to overwhelm Tess or place demands on her she was reluctant to meet. He had to remember they had an agreement, and the lines of that agreement had been clearly drawn. Unless and until Tess gave him some indication she wanted to change the agreement, David needed to be cautious and not overstep those lines.

As the crowd of well-wishers thinned out, Katherine Comstock approached, looking extraordinarily beautiful in a sleek, blue cocktail dress. He hadn't seen her earlier, and he wondered if she'd just arrived. He also wondered if she was alone. She'd hinted, for the past week, that they might come to the party together, and he'd pretended not to understand. He hadn't wanted to come right out and tell her he already had a date for the dinner dance, because knowing Katherine, she wouldn't have been satisfied until she'd pried Tess's name, as well as their relationship, out of him.

David hadn't felt ready to answer questions about Tess. He'd purposely wanted to announce his engagement in this public forum because he figured it was the best way to avoid personal questions. Still, he'd felt sneaky about his evasiveness, and he wondered now about Katherine's reaction to his announcement. He was sure she'd heard it, because her blue eyes glittered as she walked up to them.

Resting his hand against Tess's waist, he said warmly, "Well, hello, Katherine. I wondered where you were." He turned to Tess. "Tess, this is my assistant, Katherine Comstock. Katherine, my fiancée, Tess Collier."

"Hello, Miss Comstock. It's nice to meet you," Tess said.

"Hello," Katherine answered, casting a haughty glance at Tess, then turning away and locking gazes with David. "Well, this...development...was quite a surprise. How long have you two known each other?"

David really couldn't blame her for her anger. He realized suddenly that he *should* have told her about Tess before tonight. As he strove to find an answer, Tess forestalled him.

"David and I have been friends for a long time," she said softly. She smiled at Katherine. "His daughter takes piano lessons from me."

"I see." Katherine eyed Tess speculatively. "So you knew David even before Leah—"

David's hand tightened around Tess's waist. "It looks as if it's time to be seated for dinner," he said, interrupting Katherine. "Shall we look for our table?"

Katherine Comstock hated her. Tess could feel the woman's malevolent gaze from across the round table where Tess, David, Katherine, the Medlocks, and five other senior Medlock people were seated together for dinner.

Tess tried to ignore the woman's icy stare, but it was difficult. Tess figured she understood what was behind it. Obviously, Katherine was in love with David. Uneasily, Tess wondered how David felt about the beautiful blonde. His assistant, he'd said. That meant they worked together all day, every day. She thought about Katherine's beautiful figure, shown to advantage in a short, royal blue, strapless cocktail dress. She thought about her self-assurance, her blatant sexuality. Was Katherine the one he'd been dating? The one Sue Dawson had mentioned that night?

No wonder she hates me. I don't blame her. In her shoes, I'd hate me, too. What would Katherine think if she knew the whole story behind David's and Tess's engagement? Suddenly Tess knew she would do anything to prevent that ever happening.

When dinner was over, Tess said, "David, I'm going to go look for the ladies' room."

He smiled at her. "Okay. I'll be around here."

As Tess headed off in the direction she thought was the right one, Katherine Comstock fell into place beside her. "So you're Francesca's piano teacher," she said. "Is that how you and David met?"

"Yes, it is."

"You must have known Leah, too."

"Yes, I knew Leah."

"Fabulous woman, wasn't she? Beautiful *and* brilliant."

Tess nodded. Why didn't the woman go away? Tess needed no reminders of Leah's brilliance or her beauty.

"Rotten shame about her, isn't it?" Katherine persisted, lowering her voice as if confiding a great confidence. "David was so torn up after the accident. Those of us who are close to him were afraid he'd *never* get over it."

By now they'd reached the ladies' room, and Tess was relieved not to have to comment on Katherine's remark. She escaped into an empty stall and hoped that by the time she emerged, Katherine might be gone.

No such luck.

When Tess walked out, Katherine stood in front of the big mirror in the outer powder room. She was touching up her lipstick—a glossy shade of bright red that Tess would never have been able to pull off. Her reflective gaze met Tess's in the mirror. She reminded Tess of the way Budge looked right before he pounced on an unsuspecting bug.

"It's terrible about Francesca, isn't it? David and I were *so* worried about her in Switzerland."

Tess had primed herself for a zinger. But the revelation that Katherine Comstock had been in Switzerland with David rocked Tess—primed or not. He'd never mentioned it. But why should he? she thought with a rare touch of bitterness. It wasn't as if they were *really* close enough to talk about his personal life. Keeping her face impassive and her voice just as casual as Katherine's had been, Tess nodded and answered, "Yes, I'm sure you were. She's getting better, though. I can see improvement almost every day."

Katherine cocked one perfect eyebrow. "Oh? That's not what David says."

Tess swallowed, fighting to keep her self-confidence from eroding. *The woman's trying to intimidate you, you know that. Don't let her.* "David and I are both pleased by her progress," she said lightly, "and speaking of my fiancé, I'm sure he's looking for me by now."

Without waiting to see if Katherine was coming or not, Tess headed out the door. She walked straight over to David, who stood where she'd left him—talking to Walter Medlock. The two men were only a couple of feet away from the table where they'd eaten dinner. Waiters were clearing the table behind them, and at the front of ballroom, the band tuned up in preparation for the dancing that would begin shortly.

"So when did you and David begin dating?" Katherine asked from directly behind her, and Tess nearly jumped.

"Oh, a while back," Tess said vaguely. What would David want her to say? Why hadn't he prepared her for Katherine? Surely, as smart as he was, he knew how Katherine felt about him. He'd have to. No man, and especially a man as perceptive as David, could work with a woman on a daily basis and not know she was in love with him. Besides, Katherine wasn't exactly trying to hide her feelings. For the second time that evening Tess couldn't help thinking of Budge. When he got mad he acted just like Katherine and bared his claws. If the situation hadn't been so serious, Tess might have laughed at the comparison.

"Funny," Katherine said, her eyes narrowing, "that David has never mentioned you. Not once. Why is that, do you think?"

Tess gritted her teeth. She knew Katherine's rudeness was born of desperation. And if she *was* the woman David had been dating, she probably felt deceived. Still, the woman's attempts to make Tess feel as if she were somehow doing something wrong, rankled. Sighing, she met Katherine's antagonistic gaze. "Well, obviously he doesn't tell you everything, Miss Comstock." Then she turned her back and, head held high, walked over to David, slipping her hand through his arm.

Immediately, he turned to her and smiled. "You're back. Good. I'm ready to dance. Will you excuse us, Walter?"

Walter Medlock's jovial face creased into a grin. "Certainly. In fact, I think I'll find my better half and join you on the dance floor."

As David led her to the dance floor, Tess caught a glimpse of Katherine standing a few feet away. The expression on the woman's face told Tess that she would need to be very careful in the months and years ahead. For if there were to be the slightest rip in the fabric of her marriage to David, Katherine Comstock would be there—waiting to pick up the threads.

Later, in David's arms, Tess almost forgot Katherine. She almost forgot everything but David and how he made her feel. A bittersweet happiness filled her as he held her close and they danced to a slow ballad. David was a good dancer—firm and masterful as he led her around the floor. With his arms around her, and the smell of him filling her, she could almost forget that theirs wasn't going to be a normal marriage. She could almost forget the only reason he'd asked her to marry him was his daughter's problems. She could almost forget David didn't love her.

Almost, but not entirely.

Oh, if only he *did* love her. If only theirs was going to be a *real* marriage. If only she felt secure about their relationship. Then she would never have to care about women like Katherine Comstock.

She sighed softly, and David tugged her closer. "What's wrong?" he murmured into her ear. "Aren't you having a good time?" His warm breath feathered her neck.

She closed her eyes. "I'm having a wonderful time."

"Good." He shifted, and as he did, his right hand moved up from her waist and rested against her bare back. His thumb slowly, almost absently, stroked her skin. Something elemental and painful stirred deep inside her—a yearning as old as time itself. She shivered, and David's hold tightened. Now as their bodies moved, she could feel every hard line of his. Her heart began to beat harder, and she wondered if David had any idea how she felt. What he was doing to her. How much she wanted him.

The thought shocked her.

She'd known for a long time that she loved David. But now she admitted that the thought of making love with him excited her unbearably.

For the rest of the evening, Tess could hardly think about anything else. Every time David looked at her, she

imagined his hands on her instead of his eyes. Every time
he touched her, she imagined his touch without the bar-
rier of clothes. And every time they danced together, she
could imagine another dance—a dance of intimacy and
passion—and her blood raced from the images.

By the time the evening was over, she felt too hot and
she was convinced David knew exactly what she'd been
thinking. He kept looking at her in an odd way, and she
was sure she'd betrayed herself. Embarrassment flooded
her. She must never let David know how she felt about
him. The knowledge would place an impossible burden
on him, because they had a covenant. And if the terms
of that covenant were to change, David would have to
initiate the changes just as he had initiated the original
agreement. No, he must never know.

All the way home, Tess worried. Had she given herself away? Oh, she wished she knew how to act. If
only— She abruptly cut off the thought. It was no use
wishing for the impossible. Her impending marriage was
a business arrangement. No, that wasn't exactly right. It
was an emotional compromise. Yes, that's what it was,
and she'd better not forget it. Just because David had
been attentive tonight didn't mean he was falling in love
with her. After all, he'd had to pretend in front of his
colleagues.

And David seemed to reinforce that theory by the way
he acted when they reached her house. All the intimacy
and closeness she'd felt with him earlier in the evening
vanished as he matter-of-factly said, "Well, Tess, I think
our announcement went over well, don't you?"

"Yes. It seemed to."

"I hope you had a good time." He shoved his hands
into his pockets. They were standing on the porch, and
it was cold.

"I had a wonderful time." She placed her hand on the doorknob. "Would you like to come in for some coffee or something?"

He hesitated for just a second, then said, "I'd better not. It's late."

"Oh, okay." The faint hope she'd cherished that he might kiss her again disappeared.

"Well, I'll see you tomorrow, then." Earlier they'd decided that the two of them would take Francesca out for brunch after church the following morning and they would tell her, together, about their plans to marry.

"Yes, tomorrow," Tess echoed, swallowing her disappointment. It was ridiculous to be disappointed. Hadn't she *told* herself David's behavior tonight meant nothing? But everything in her cried out in protest. She didn't want David to leave. She especially didn't want him to leave in this impersonal way, as if they were no more than friends.

She wanted him to pull her into his arms and kiss her.

Kiss her thoroughly.

Kiss her until her blood heated to that impossible pitch she'd felt when they were dancing. Even thinking about it, her heart thundered in her chest and her knees felt weak. Her desire was so strong, she was sure David could sense it. The very air seemed to throb with her need.

He reached out, and for one impossibly long moment, Tess thought he was actually going to fulfill her wish. But his fingers just brushed her cheek, and he said gently, "It's cold. You'd better go on in."

Long after he was gone, Tess lay in bed and wondered if the bargain she'd struck would turn out to have too high a price tag after all.

She had once thought not being married to the man you loved would be the most devastating thing that could happen to a woman. But now she wondered if that was true.

Perhaps being married to the man you loved and having him not love you was even worse.

Chapter Nine

"And so, Francesca, Tess and I are going to be married, and Tess will be moving into our house and living with us," David said.

Francesca, eyes wide, stared at him. Then, slowly, her gaze turned to Tess. "M-married?" she finally said.

Tess nodded.

David held his breath. What was his daughter thinking? He darted a quick glance at Tess, who sat very still, her only sign of nervousness the restless pleating of her gray wool skirt where it lay against her thigh. The three of them were sitting in the parlor of Tess's home. They had gone out to brunch after the morning church service, but by unspoken agreement had waited until arriving here before broaching the subject of their marriage.

The ticking of the grandfather clock suddenly sounded too loud in the tense silence. Then, as if guided by a hidden director, Budge padded into the room and emitted a loud "Meow," then sidled up to Francesca and rubbed her leg.

Like players on a stage, David, Tess and Francesca all laughed. Then Francesca, who was sitting next to Tess on the love seat, threw her arms around Tess's neck. "I'm glad," she said.

Tess's gaze, suspiciously shiny, met David's over Francesca's head. They exchanged a wordless communication. In Tess's soft gray eyes he saw thankfulness and hope and something else—something he couldn't define—yet something that made him feel happy and optimistic about the future.

"Well," David said, forcing a lightness to his voice to cover the emotion welling inside, "I think this calls for a toast, don't you? How about some hot chocolate to celebrate?"

Hazel took the news stoically. Tess knew the older woman must be happy for her, but she didn't say so. All she said, in her gruff way, was, "Well, this is going to mean a lot of changes for both of us, isn't it?" It was Monday, the day after Tess and David had told Francesca of their plans, and Tess felt it was only fair to talk to Hazel next.

"Yes, it will," Tess said.

Hazel's bright blue eyes studied Tess for a long moment. Tess squirmed under Hazel's penetrating gaze. Why did she always make Tess feel as if she could look inside her and see her darkest secrets?

"Are you planning to live here?" Hazel finally asked. She walked to the stove and lifted the kettle. "Do you want a cup of tea?"

"No, thanks." Tess hesitated. This was the hard part. "No," she said softly, "we're not planning to live here.

We both felt it would be too traumatic on Francesca to move her out of the home she shared with her mother. I—I'm planning to move into David's home.'' Tess was a bit worried about this decision. She had only been inside David's home once—when Leah was still alive—and she remembered how much the house had reflected Leah's personality.

Hazel nodded. "Makes sense to me. That child doesn't need anything else to upset her. She's got enough on her plate."

Tess flinched. What was Hazel saying? That her marriage to David was going to upset Francesca? No, she was just being paranoid. But if Hazel knew the real reasons behind the marriage . . . what would she say then? Tess wondered if the older woman would approve. It hadn't been so long ago that the majority of marriages had been arranged in just such a fashion.

"But you don't need to worry, Hazel," she said. "David and I both want you to come and live with us."

"No, ma'am. I don't think so," Hazel said.

"But why not? Why does anything have to change? We'd love to have you, and I'm sure Francesca would, too."

Hazel continued to shake her head, her lips pinched together in stubborn refusal.

Tess got up and walked over to the other side of the big kitchen table. She sat down next to Hazel and touched her hand. The skin felt dry and paper-thin, and a sudden spurt of sadness gripped Tess. Hazel was getting older. Everyone was getting older. As the old cliché went, time was marching on. Things were changing, and Tess felt powerless to stop them. "Please, Hazel," she said softly. "I need you."

Hazel turned toward her. Her mouth softened and her blue eyes no longer blazed. Instead they were gentle as they rested on Tess's face. She didn't move her hand from Tess's, and when she spoke, her voice was warm. "You did need me, and I was glad to step in. But you're movin' on to a different life now, and I'm glad for you. I hope you'll be happy. You just think you need me, Tess. But I've done my job, and now I can think about myself."

"Oh, Hazel..." This wasn't what Tess had wanted to happen. She couldn't bear the thought that she was hurting Hazel. Hazel had been there for her for so many years.

Now Hazel smiled, and her eyes brightened with enthusiasm. "Edith Shoemaker's been tellin' me about that new apartment building—you know the one, I think they call it the Great Lakes Apartments—where a lot of women my age have moved. She took one of them efficiencies, and she's been braggin' about how nice it is not to have to worry about housework. She says all she has to do is tidy up once in a while." Hazel pursed her lips. "Maybe that's what I'll do. Move in there. Take life easy." Edith Shoemaker was one of Hazel's bridge cronies and a lifelong friend.

"Oh, Hazel, you'd hate living in a tiny apartment!"

Hazel frowned. Now she did withdraw her hand. "How do you know that? Maybe I'm tired of keeping a big house, of killing myself day in and day out. Maybe I'd *like* takin' it easy for a change. Who knows? I might even start going to the center, like you and that Alistair Simpson have been pesterin' me to do."

Tess opened her mouth to retort, then closed it again. Maybe Hazel really was tired of working so hard. Who was Tess to try to tell her how to live her life? Hazel had been independent for most of her seventy-five years, and she'd lived alone before moving into Tess's house. Maybe Hazel was being truthful in her suggestion that she'd moved in to help Tess, not the other way around.

"The question is, what do you plan to do with this house?" Hazel said. She looked around the kitchen, and suddenly Tess saw all the things wrong with the room. The peeling paint on the ceiling, the faded wallpaper that should have been replaced years ago, the scarred old sink, the vinyl flooring that had seen much better days, and the inadequate plumbing—something Tess had promised herself she would attend to the moment she had any spare cash.

She thought about the rest of the house. The threadbare drapes. The equally threadbare carpets. The antiquated furnace. The gutters that needed to be replaced. The roof that had been repaired and repaired and now needed replacing. The cellar that flooded. The driveway that needed repaving. The trees that should be pruned by a professional.

The house needed money. Lots of it. It was an albatross around Tess's neck, and she was tired of worrying about it.

She met Hazel's eyes. "I'm thinking of giving the house to the Collierville Historical Society."

Hazel's eyes widened in momentary shock. But the shock was quickly replaced by a gleam of approval. "That's a grand idea!"

"You *approve?*" Tess could now admit to herself that she had been afraid Hazel would hate the idea. That she might somehow think it a betrayal of Tess's Aunt Millicent.

"Yep. And I think Milly would have approved, too."
Hazel drummed her fingers against the maple table. "In
fact, it's a *brilliant* idea!"

"Oh, do you really think so?"

"I know so. Think about it, Tess. The historical society will put money into this old place, fix it all up, and
it'll become a landmark in Collierville. Why, I can just
see the ladies during the Summer Festival. They'll get all
dressed up in Victorian dresses and serve tea and punch
and cookies in the parlor. It'll be the nicest house on the
tour." Her face shone proudly, as if she were responsible for the changes she'd described.

Sometimes things really *do* work out, Tess thought.

Tess and Hazel talked for a long time, and that night,
when Tess relayed most of their conversation to David,
he smiled at her obvious relief.

"You were worried about her, weren't you?"

Tess nodded. "But I think everything is going to be
okay now. In fact, in some ways, I think she might be
relieved to get out from under. Maybe she felt obligated
to stay with me."

"Could be. Things are not always the way they ap-
pear on the surface, you know." His green eyes seemed
reflective as they gazed into space.

Tess briefly wondered if he was thinking about something other than the situation with Hazel, but forgot
about it when David added, "Perhaps we should consider keeping Peggy Kaminski on if Hazel isn't going to
live with us."

"Why, David? I'll be there. We won't need Peggy."

"But what if you decide you want to go back to
school? I want you to be free to do whatever you like.
You're not to think of yourself as Francesca's nurse-
maid. Just the fact that you'll be part of our family is

enough. You don't have to watch her every hour of the day." He smiled. "I want you to be happy, Tess. That's important to me."

Tess felt a warm glow surround her heart, yet it was tempered by a twinge of sadness. *I'd be the happiest woman in the world if you'd say you love me, David.* She looked into the green gold depths of his eyes, wondering if he had any idea of her thoughts. Wondering what he'd say if she ever drummed up the courage to speak them aloud. Wondering what he *really* thought about their impending union.

"You're not having regrets, are you, Tess?"

His soft question jolted Tess. "No, of course not," she said quickly.

"You'd tell me if you were, wouldn't you?"

"Of course." Was *he* having doubts? Is that what had prompted his question? Fear, cold and bitter, flooded her.

He smiled. "Good. Now, let's talk about the wedding. Have you heard from your parents?"

Josie Yarberry, president of the Collierville Historical Society, was ecstatic. "Oh, Tess! I can't believe it! This is wonderful!" She continued in that vein for more than ten minutes, gushing and laughing and punctuating her remarks with a giddy fluttering of her beringed hands. "The Collier home! What a coup! Oh, I can't wait until the board finds out! Oh, thank you, thank you."

Josie threw her plump arms around Tess, standing on tiptoe to do so—Josie was only five feet two—and hugged.

Tess grinned. She'd known Josie for years. Both Wendy and Caroline, Josie's teenage daughters, had been piano students. Ed, Josie's equally plump husband, owned a butcher shop on Main Street. Tess finally extricated herself from Josie's grip.

For the next hour, they discussed how the transition could take place. Then Tess said, "I'll have Mike O'Neill call you." Mike was the lawyer David had insisted on retaining to represent Tess in the transaction with the historical society.

After Tess left Josie's home, she drove straight to Summer's house. Although Summer had protested that Tess was going to be the guest of honor and shouldn't be expected to do any work at all, Tess was equally determined to help Summer prepare for that evening's engagement party. First she'd tried to talk Summer out of the party, saying, "But, Summer, the wedding is only three weeks away. It seems kind of silly to have a party to announce an engagement everyone knows about, anyway."

"It's not to announce the engagement. It's to celebrate it. Those are two very different things," Summer said.

Tess stayed at Summer's for three hours. Then Summer, glancing up at her kitchen clock, said, "It's four o'clock. Go home. I'll expect you and David back here at seven."

The party was a great success. Even Tess enjoyed herself and had to admit she was glad Summer had insisted on having it. They'd agreed on a guest list of twenty people—mostly young couples their age.

Tess wore a winter-white wool dress trimmed in black velvet. Standing beside David, resplendent in a dark gray suit, she felt like someone other than herself. It was the strangest feeling. She was the same person she'd always been, yet she knew, in the eyes of the young marrieds at the party, she had gained stature because of her engagement to David.

The thought should have angered her, but it didn't. She knew she had been just as guilty of similar thoughts all of her life.

Only two episodes jarred the otherwise perfect evening. The first occurred early in the evening when Summer made the first toast. Grinning at David and Tess, Summer said, "Here's to the future Mr. and Mrs. David Bannister. Best wishes for a long and happy life together." Then she giggled. "And let's hope there are lots of little Bannisters!"

Everyone laughed, and Tess could feel her cheeks heating. She couldn't look at David. They all drank from their champagne glasses, then someone yelled, "Kiss her. Kiss her."

Tess wanted to die. She certainly did not want her first kiss from David to come in front of all these people.

But soon they were all shouting and laughing, and David, good-naturedly laughing along with them, drew Tess into his arms. Tess's heart began to beat too fast as his lips descended. The kiss didn't last a particularly long time, nor was it particularly sensual. Still, its impact left Tess feeling as if she'd received a knockout punch. Her lips felt branded, and she wondered what it would be like to receive a *real* kiss from David.

The second episode was just as disturbing, but in a different way. Toward the end of the evening, Kelsey Arnold, an old high-school friend who now worked as a lab assistant at Medlock Chemical, took Tess aside.

"Tess," Kelsey said, "I hope you won't think I'm speaking out of turn, but…" She hesitated. "Well, I've always liked you a lot."

Tess smiled quizzically.

Kelsey put her hand on Tess's forearm and drew her closer. She also dropped her voice so that no one around them could hear. "You know I work out at Medlock."

Tess nodded.

"Well, I know David's assistant pretty well. Have you met her? Katherine Comstock?"

Tess sighed. "Yes, I've met her."

"Listen, Tess, I'm not a troublemaker or a gossip. You know that, don't you?"

"Yes."

"All I wanted to say was, watch your back. Katherine Comstock has been after David for years." Kelsey's dark eyes glittered as her gaze met Tess's. "Even before Leah died."

A chill snaked down Tess's spine, and Aunt Millicent's voice, as clear as if she were standing next to her, said, *Someone is walking on your grave.*

"Anyway," Kelsey continued, "just be careful. Katherine's a real bitch. And she's obsessed by David Bannister."

For the rest of the evening, Tess tried to put Kelsey's warning out of her mind. Kelsey really hadn't told her anything she hadn't pretty much figured out herself, anyway. Still…hearing about Katherine's obsession with David from someone who knew the woman was far more ominous than suspecting it.

Especially since Katherine would be there, day after day. Especially since Tess's coming marriage to David was so unconventional. And most especially because David didn't love Tess.

The last two weeks before the wedding flew by. There seemed to be a million things to do, and Tess wasn't sure they'd all get done in time. She had to make arrangements to have a mover come and move the pieces of furniture she wanted to take to her new home. The rest of the furniture would be divided between the pieces that would stay with the house and the pieces Tess wanted to store for the future.

The decisions about furniture necessitated a visit to David's house—a visit that he had seemed reluctant to have take place. At first, Tess worried about his reluctance. Then she realized that David, with his sensitivity and concern for her feelings, was probably just worried that this first visit would be hard on Tess.

Finally, a couple of days before she had to make her final decision on furniture, Tess called David at his office and said, "David, I can't decide which pieces I want to take until I see the house."

"All right," he said. "How about tomorrow night? I'll swing by after work and pick you up."

"Okay."

The next night David arrived at six o'clock, and within minutes they were on their way. Tess wondered if he was still worried about her feelings. Something was bothering him, because he was awfully quiet and preoccupied. She started to say something to reassure him when he said, "Look, Tess, there's something I have to tell you."

Tess stared at him. She'd been right. Something *was* bothering him.

"I should have talked to you about this before, but I, well, I've been putting it off."

What is it, David? She held her breath.

He slanted a glance at her before returning his gaze to the road. "I guess, like everyone else, I try to avoid unpleasant subjects."

Tess clenched her hands in her lap. If he didn't tell her soon, she was going to scream.

"A few weeks before Leah died, she wanted us to have a family portrait taken."

Tess wasn't sure what she'd expected, but this wasn't it.

"We did, and now that portrait hangs over the fireplace. I wanted to take it down before bringing you to the house, but Francesca is obsessed with the portrait. She got hysterical the one time I tried to remove it, and the other day, when I suggested again that she might like to have it in her bedroom, she started to cry. She's too young to realize that having the portrait hang in the living room where everyone entering the house can see it will be uncomfortable and awkward for both of us." He grimaced. "I'm sorry, Tess."

"I don't mind, David."

He looked at her. "You don't *mind?*"

Tess shrugged. She couldn't explain that there were so many more serious things he could have told her, like he felt they'd made a mistake and he wanted to call off their wedding, that a little thing like a portrait didn't seem important at all. "I know I can never take Leah's place in Francesca's heart." *Or yours, either.* "I don't ever want Francesca to think I'm trying to usurp her mother's place."

He exhaled noisily, and she realized he'd been really nervous about telling her. She smiled and reached over to touch his arm. "Don't worry, David. It's okay. I can handle the portrait."

Saying she could handle the portrait and actually seeing it for the first time were two very different things, Tess realized as she stood in the living room and tried to keep from staring at it. It was so huge. And Leah dominated the portrait. Everywhere Tess stood she could feel Leah's eyes on her back. She knew her reaction was crazy. A portrait was just an inanimate object. Leah wasn't alive, and she wasn't staring at Tess.

Still, Tess hurriedly took inventory in the living room. She breathed more easily as she looked over the furnishings in the rest of the house.

"You can get rid of anything you like," David said.

Unfortunately, the sleek modern lines of David's house didn't really lend itself to the mostly antique pieces Tess owned. Plus, she didn't want to change David's house too drastically. She had no idea how much importance Francesca might attach to familiar things.

When she was finished, she and David had decided that the master bedroom would be completely redone with Tess's furniture, as would the dining room. She would also move the Steinway and the spinet as well as the spool bed from her aunt's bedroom. A few of the better pieces from her parlor would go into the small upstairs room that David had designated as Tess's sitting room.

As they left the house to go back to Tess's home, Tess averted her eyes as they passed the living room. She did not want the portrait to be the last thing she saw before leaving. And in the next few days, she tried to forget about it completely—just as David had tried to forget about it.

For the most part, she was successful, because she was so busy with the wedding preparations. Hazel and Summer both helped her, but Tess still wondered how she would get everything done in time. Then there was Christmas, as well as her work with the church. She canceled all her piano lessons for the month of December except for Francesca and Alistair.

Up until three days before the wedding, Tess still didn't know if her parents were planning to be there.

Then, Christmas morning, early, while Hazel and Tess were drinking their first cup of coffee before leaving for the morning service at church, her parents called from Vienna.

"Merry Christmas, Tess," her father said.

"Merry Christmas, Tess," her mother said. Then finally, after going on for long minutes about the success of their current tour and the beauty of Vienna during the Christmas season, her mother offhandedly added, "Your father and I both wish you every happiness in your marriage. We've shipped our gift off, and you should have it within a week."

"You're not coming, then?" Tess kept her own voice as casual as her mother's had been.

"No, we can't make it. I know you understand."

"Of course." Although Tess had told herself not to care, and especially not to show her mother that she could still wound her, she couldn't resist adding, "Haven't I always understood that nothing—especially not your only child—is more important than your career?"

If Tess had hoped she might make her mother feel guilty, that hope was soon dashed. Her mother acted as if what Tess had said was perfectly normal and acceptable by saying, "Yes, well, that's the way it is with *serious* musicians." And a few minutes later, she said, "Well, Tess, I'd better go. Your father is waiting to take me to an early supper, and you know how impatient he is!"

After Tess replaced the receiver, she stared at it for a long moment.

"They won't be here, will they?" Hazel said.

Tess looked around. She'd forgotten Hazel was in the kitchen. "No."

"Does that surprise you?"

"No."

Hazel walked over to where Tess still stood by the wall phone, and in a totally uncharacteristic gesture of love, put her arms around her and hugged her. "Don't you care, Tess," she whispered fiercely. "Don't you care! I love you, and now you're going to have a husband and child to love you. You don't need them."

A long time later Tess thought about how ironic it was that Hazel—a woman who was not related to her and who was intensely private—could say she loved her, and her own mother couldn't.

The night before the wedding, it took Tess a long time to fall asleep. Uncertainty about her future, fear of the unknown, and doubts about whether she could make David happy all plagued her. And when she finally did fall asleep about three in the morning, she had disturbing dreams with dark images. She saw the shadowy face of Leah—a Leah with glittering eyes that were very like Katherine Comstock's eyes.

In the dream, Leah said, "You'll never take my place with David. How could he possibly love *you* after having me for a wife?" Her face twisted into hard, cruel lines. "After all, your own parents don't love you." Then she laughed—a mocking laugh that made Tess cringe. "You think you're going to finally be happy, don't you? Well, you won't be. You'll be miserable. And so will David. He'll never be able to forget me."

The next morning, even though Tess told herself it had only been a dream, she couldn't shake the fear that it might be a portent of things to come.

* * *

David wondered if Tess felt cheated by the absence of pomp and spectacle at their quiet wedding ceremony. He watched as she walked slowly up the short aisle in the small chapel to the strains of Air with Variations from Handel's water music. He searched her face as they stood before the Reverend Humble and said their vows in front of Francesca, Hazel, Tess's best friend, Summer McKee—her only attendant—and the Medlocks. David had asked Walter Medlock to be his best man.

David and Tess had discussed inviting a few other friends but had decided that it was impossible to draw the line. If they just asked a few, there would be hurt feelings. In the end, they'd decided to limit the guests to Francesca and Hazel and their attendants.

"People will understand," Tess assured him. "It's less than a year since Leah died, so a more extravagant wedding wouldn't seem right."

"It doesn't seem fair to you, though," David said.

"Really, I don't mind."

David had also called Leah's parents and sister and invited them, but they declined to come, which didn't surprise David. He'd known his second marriage would be a bitter pill for his former in-laws to swallow. They had adored Leah and thought she was perfect. They wouldn't be happy about David marrying someone else, and especially so soon. He grimaced, remembering the conversation he'd had with them.

"I just don't understand how you can do this," Lenore Parrish had said, sniffling. "If nothing else, you should think about Francesca and her feelings."

"Lenore," he'd said patiently, "believe me, I *am* thinking about Francesca. She loves Tess." He knew he could have explained just why he was marrying and maybe made himself look better in his ex-mother-in-law's eyes, but he could never do that to Tess. As it was, Tess would have to be around the Parrishes from time to time—after all, they were Francesca's grandparents and always would be. He didn't want Tess to have the added burden of their knowledge of the kind of marriage she and David had. No, he owed Tess his loyalty, and that meant taking his lumps with Leah's parents.

Arthur Parrish, Leah's father, did tell David that he and his wife would come to Collierville the day of the wedding, stay overnight with Francesca, and be there when he and Tess came home the following day. "Then we'll take Francesca somewhere nice and bring her back in a couple of days. That'll give you and your new wife some time alone."

David had reluctantly agreed, even though he and Tess weren't taking a wedding trip and had planned to spend the week at home with Francesca.

David sighed, thinking about that conversation. Why did life have to be so complicated?

He looked down at Tess. She looked very lovely today, he thought. She had chosen to be married in a off-white wool suit, and she carried a small bouquet of white and pink flowers. On her head she wore a filmy chin-length veil decorated with a small nosegay of the same flowers.

He hoped he could make her happy in their unusual marriage. It suddenly seemed very important to him that Tess be happy.

"I now pronounce you husband and wife," Reverend Humble said. He looked at David. His dark eyes twinkled behind his wire-rimmed glasses. "You may kiss your bride."

David pushed aside his worries as he gently lifted Tess's veil, smiled down into her trusting eyes, and bent to kiss her. The shy sweetness of her soft, warm lips meeting his filled him with determination. He *would* make her happy. She had agreed to marry him, and even though they weren't passionately in love the way he and Leah had been, maybe in the end they could build something even better because it would be a union based on friendship and trust instead of a fleeting physical attraction.

As he lifted his head and smiled down into her eyes, he vowed he would do his best to make their marriage work.

When he and Tess turned around to face their guests, Walter Medlock said, "Congratulations. You're a lucky man." He pumped David's hand.

"I know it," David said. He looked at Tess, who blushed becomingly. Then Summer hugged her and the rest of their guests rose from their seats and gathered around them. For the next ten minutes, David and Tess accepted the best wishes and hugs and kisses that were bestowed.

Later, as the ten of them sat around a big round corner table at the Collierville Lodge and were served a lavish lunch complete with champagne and a beautiful wedding cake, David looked around. He saw how Francesca's eyes shone as she looked at her new stepmother and the good wishes on the faces of the others.

Once again, he repeated his vow. This time, he would not fail. He *would* make this marriage work. No matter what it took.

Tess told herself to take deep breaths. She told herself to calm down. She told herself everything would be all right. *Just go out there. He's waiting for you.*

She took one last glimpse at herself in the bathroom mirror. A flushed, nervous-looking woman looked back. A woman dressed in a mauve satin nightgown and matching peignoir. A woman who was getting ready to face her new husband for their first night together.

All day, in the back of her mind, had been the realization that this moment would come. Throughout the short ceremony, as she and David exchanged their vows, the awareness of what would happen tonight hovered. Even the realization that she really was Mrs. David Bannister failed to banish her jitters.

Then during the lovely wedding lunch at the Collierville Lodge, thoughts of tonight tormented her. When it was time for David and Tess to say their goodbyes, Tess's stomach started to quiver.

And then, during the two-hour drive to this remote and beautiful country inn where she and David would spend their wedding night, her nerves had gotten the best of her. So much so that she was unable to carry on an intelligent conversation with her new husband.

David had tried to put her at ease. When they'd arrived at the hotel, he'd done everything he could to make her feel comfortable. Tess had been afraid he might suggest dinner in their room, but instead he'd arranged for a leisurely dinner in the firelit dining room. He'd seemed perfectly content to stay there for hours and hadn't try to rush her. He'd ordered a bottle of wine, which they'd shared, and after her second glass, Tess had begun to loosen up. But her pleasantly relaxed state hadn't lasted.

As soon as they'd climbed the stairs to their second-story room, the buzz from the wine disappeared, and her butterflies and fears returned.

She sighed, pressing her hands against her stomach. Her heart was beating too fast. She was scared to go out there. What would David think when he saw her? Would he be disappointed? Tess looked down at herself. She was too thin. She could feel her hipbones. *Oh, God.* She touched her breasts. They were too small. What if she didn't please David?

Taking two more deep breaths, she snapped off the bathroom light and placed her hand on the doorknob. A short prayer ran through her mind. *Don't let me disappoint David. I know I'm not Leah, but let me please him.*

She opened the door.

David's breath caught as he looked at Tess standing in the open doorway of the bathroom. Shimmering folds of satin gently caressed her slender figure, and her hair—that glorious hair!—cascaded down her back and over her shoulders. She looked beautiful, he thought as she walked slowly toward him. She also looked uncertain...almost frightened...as she drew closer to the bed.

Be patient. Go slow.

He smiled as gently as he knew how and held out his hand. When she shyly placed her hand in his, he reached up and slowly untied the narrow satin ribbons that closed her peignoir. As it fell to the floor in a gleaming pool, he was suddenly very glad Tess had insisted on her terms for their marriage.

Because he could now admit to himself that he wanted to make love to Tess.

He wanted that very much.

Chapter Ten

As her peignoir cascaded to her feet, Tess was very glad the only light in the room came from the fireplace. Her gaze met David's—who sat propped against a pillow in the big four-poster bed—and she prayed he wouldn't see how nervous she was. In those first seconds, her brain quickly assimilated the information that David's chest was beautiful and more muscled than she had imagined. Dark, curly hair was dusted across the top and tapered down into a V that disappeared beneath the covers.

For a long moment, they just looked at one another. He shifted slightly, and Tess realized that under the comforter that covered him to the waist, he was probably naked.

Now her heart raced so fast, she felt dizzy.

And then David smiled. His green eyes smoldered in the flickering light as he drew back the comforter and beckoned her in. Tess swallowed hard, then slipped into the bed beside him.

Immediately, he turned on his side and folded her into his arms. Tess's heart pounded furiously as David, holding her loosely, looked into her eyes.

"Don't be frightened," he whispered.

"I—I'm not," she lied.

His smile was so gentle, yet so knowing. "Yes, you are. But it's okay, Tess. I won't hurt you, and I won't do anything you don't want me to do."

Oh, David, I'm not frightened of you! I'm scared you won't like me. I'm scared I'll disappoint you. I'm scared you'll think you've gotten the worst end of our bargain. If only she could say what she was thinking aloud. But all she could do was whisper back, "I know that, David. I trust you."

His right hand tightened, bringing her closer. With his left hand, he delved into her hair. She wondered what he was thinking as he touched it. She wondered if he was comparing her hair to Leah's. She wished he would say something.

Instead, his hand moved to her face. With his fingertips, he stroked her skin. His touch was feather-light, no more than the kiss of a spring breeze, yet as his fingers traced her eyebrows, her cheekbones, the outline of her lips and chin, then trailed softly over her ear, Tess shuddered. Without conscious thought, her body arched.

He continued his exploration, allowing his fingers to tiptoe over her collarbone, then glide over the satin nightgown to linger with tantalizing accuracy over the sensitive tips of her breasts. Tess closed her eyes against the onslaught of sensations.

Continuing its journey down her body, his hand stroked and caressed. Everywhere he touched, Tess's body tingled and cried out for more. And when he finally, finally, touched her in that most intimate of all places, she moaned.

"Shh," he said. "It's okay."

It's more than okay. It's wonderful. I love it. I love it. And I love you.

She never would have dreamed that such a tender touch could cause such turmoil in her body—such excruciating pleasure and the buildup of such unbearable excitement and need.

Shyly, with hands that trembled, she placed her palms against his chest. Oh, he felt so good! She could feel his heart beating beneath her fingers and, emulating him, she traced the contours and curves of his body.

Suddenly, with a sound halfway between a grunt and a moan, David crushed her to him and captured her mouth under his for their first kiss since the wedding ceremony. Their first real kiss, was Tess's last coherent thought. Because as David parted her lips, thrusting his tongue inside her mouth, she stopped thinking at all.

Now there was only sensation. The feel of his body as he held her tightly against him. The feel of his tongue and lips as she met their eager quest with a quest of her own. The ripple of his muscles under her hands as she gripped his back. The heat of his hands as they stroked her back, then cupped her bottom to hold her fast against his arousal.

Tess's heart thundered in her ears as David's gentleness disappeared. As the deep kiss ended, he groaned and none too gently yanked her nightgown up. Shakily, she helped him get it over her head, and he tossed it to the floor.

Then he raised himself up and looked down at her. "Are you still afraid?" he murmured, his voice thick.

His eyes glittered in the firelight, and sweat glistened on his skin as he ran his hand down her body. She trembled.

"No," she said. "I'm not afraid." *Only that you'll hate my skinny body.*

But he didn't seem to hate it. He bent over her and kissed her again. Another deep, searching kiss. And then his mouth moved down. He kissed all the places he'd touched before: her collarbone, her breasts—paying loving attention to each one—her stomach, her thighs, and then...the place that throbbed with a need that was almost painful. The sensations that rocketed Tess were so intense, she gasped.

"You're beautiful," he murmured.

"I'm not." But she loved him for saying so.

"You are." He drew her into his arms again, and they kissed. With each kiss, Tess's need grew. Soon the kisses became more demanding.

"Touch me," he whispered.

When she did, he made a gutteral sound that thrilled her because she knew he liked her touch. More boldly, she closed her palm around him, and he groaned. Then his mouth clamped over hers greedily, his tongue hot and hard as it pushed inside.

She'd never felt this way with Glenn. Tess was shocked that she could feel the way she did. Shocked that she could be so abandoned, could crave David's kisses and touches. Yet she reveled in the feelings and welcomed every new sensation.

And when, finally, he parted her thighs and entered her, she was more than ready. She tried to hold off, tried to wait until he, too, could feel the pleasure that began to ripple through her in wave after wave, building in intensity as they began that dance she had dreamed of. But she couldn't stop the momentum. David had been too thorough a lover. Instead, she wrapped her legs around him and allowed herself to feel his heat and strength as her body gave itself up to the glorious fulfillment it craved.

And as his life force spilled inside her, and he cried out, Tess closed her eyes. *I love you, David. I love you even more than I thought it was possible to love you.*

Afterward, tucked under the comforter, safe in the warmth of David's arms, Tess watched the shadowy images dance across the ceiling from the dying fire. David was asleep. His even breathing, his lack of movement, told her so. But she didn't fall asleep for a long time. And when she did, her last thought was, *Please, God, let David love me.*

David awoke to bright sunshine and a very cold room. He knew it was cold because his nose felt frozen. Trying not to disturb Tess, who slept in his arms, he very gently extricated his right arm from under her back. She sighed once, then turned over and slept on.

He smiled. Good. He wanted to turn the heat on and build another fire in the fireplace before she woke up. He also wanted to order a room-service breakfast.

He did all those things as well as shaving and taking a fast, hot shower. Dressed in his thick navy robe, he reentered the bedroom. Tess still slept soundly.

He walked to the window and looked outside. No wonder it seemed so bright. It had snowed in the night and a blanket of white covered everything as far as the eye could see. David always thought it amazing that snow had the ability to make even the most barren landscape look beautiful. *Because it camouflages the flaws.* The snowfall seemed suddenly symbolic to him.

As if, by snowing in the night, he had received a sign that the flaws of his past could be forgotten. That he had a bright, new future ahead of him.

He turned away from the window and walked to the bed. For a long moment he stood at the bedside and watched Tess. She looked sweet and lovely and vulnerable as she lay there, unaware of his gaze. Her beautiful hair—even more beautiful loose than David had imagined it to be—lay across the pillow in shining masses. Her skin, creamy and soft, had felt like silk under his hands. David wondered if Tess realized how lucky she was to have such skin. Her breathing remained even and quiet as David watched her.

Making love to Tess had been an incredibly satisfying experience, he thought as he walked to the small table near the fireplace. He opened the newspaper that had been slipped under their door earlier that morning, but he couldn't concentrate on the paper. His mind kept returning to the previous day and night. Especially the night.

He couldn't get over how much he'd enjoyed it. He had known lovemaking with Tess would be pleasant, but he hadn't expected to feel the passion and desire she'd awakened in him. Or the tenderness and deep emotion.

He looked at her again. His wife. A curious elation coursed through him. Life with Tess would hold more in the way of rewards than he had ever imagined.

He wet his lips, remembering the sweet curve of her hip under his hands. Remembering her soft moans and cries. Remembering how good it had felt to kiss her and touch her. Remembering how she had welcomed him in…how warm and sleek and ready she had been…. He squirmed in the chair.

He eyed the door. Their breakfast would come soon. Too bad, he thought ruefully. He shouldn't have been so hasty in ordering it. If he hadn't, he could crawl back into that warm bed and slip his arms around his wife—who he knew would smell and feel wonderful this morning—and make love to her again.

Of course, after breakfast, he still could. He smiled. His former in-laws didn't expect them home until this evening. They had the rest of the day if they wanted it.

And David knew, with a certainty he hadn't felt about anything in a long time, that he wanted it. And before he was through, Tess would want it, too.

Tess knew she would never forget this day. When she finally woke up about nine o'clock, David was leaning over her and smiling.

"It's about time, sleepyhead," he said. "I ordered breakfast an hour ago."

"Oh," she said, and yawned. "Why didn't you wake me?" She knuckled her eyes and wished she could get out of bed without him watching her. She felt shy this morning and unable to meet his gaze.

When he showed no signs of moving, she tossed back the covers. Her peignoir lay neatly folded at the bottom of the bed, and she reached for it. David took it out of her hand and held it up. Still shy about looking at him, Tess allowed him to put it on her. When it fell into place on her shoulders, his hands lingered there, then slid down her arms and around.

Tess's heart galloped as his hands slowly moved to cup her breasts and draw her back against him. She closed her eyes as he nuzzled her hair away and kissed her neck. And when his mouth moved up to her ear and he whispered, "Last night was wonderful," she shivered violently.

Before she knew what was happening, he had turned her around, and his mouth captured hers. And then she forgot everything but David.

Much later, after David had ordered a second breakfast, Tess drew a steaming bath that she liberally laced with bath salts. Her body felt sore from the unaccustomed lovemaking, but happiness filled her.

All her worrying had been for nothing. Instead of disappointed, David had seemed to love making love with her. *Last night was wonderful,* he had said. She closed her eyes and leaned back in the tub. Oh, it had been wonderful. More wonderful than she'd ever dreamed. She'd always known David would be a good lover. He was too considerate, too gentlemanly, not to be. But he was more than good. He had a passion and fire under that considerate, gentlemanly exterior—something Tess hadn't expected. And she loved it. Oh, yes, she loved it!

Dreamily, she thought it might be a very good thing if she didn't get pregnant right away.

After breakfast, they decided to get dressed in warm clothes and go outside for a walk. Their breath misted in the air as they tramped through the snow, hand in hand. The sky looked like a piece of blue parchment paper, and the snow glistened under the sun's rays.

They walked for a long time, stopping from time to time to make snowballs and pelt one another. They laughed and frolicked like two kids, and Tess thought she'd never been so happy.

Later, after they returned to their room, Tess thought they'd pack and get ready for the drive home, but David had other ideas. Minutes later Tess found herself burrowed under the comforter with David, and soon his hands and lips were working their magic again.

Arthur and Lenore Parrish were at the house when David and Tess arrived. From the moment Tess was introduced to Leah's parents, she could feel the animosity in Lenore. Even though Tess wished the older woman could put aside her grief and unhappiness over Leah's death and accept Tess, she understood how Lenore must feel.

How heart-wrenching to lose your beloved daughter, she thought. It was no wonder Lenore saw Tess as a threat to Leah's memory.

Tess was never sure how she managed to get through the evening. Somehow she sat at the dinner table and ate the food Lenore Parrish had prepared. Somehow she endured the rest of the evening after Francesca had gone up to bed. And somehow she found the reserves of strength to be as nice as she could possibly be.

But she was tremendously relieved when Lenore, with a yawn, said, "Arthur, we'd better go to bed if we're leaving early in the morning."

David, with a sensitivity that made Tess love him all the more, kissed her gently when they finally got into bed together. Then he murmured, "You must be very tired. Why don't you try to go to sleep?"

Tess gratefully closed her eyes. She was exhausted. And even if she hadn't been, she could not have made love with David while Lenore and Arthur Parrish were under the same roof.

The next morning, Tess arose early. David was still asleep, and she took care not to wake him. After showering and dressing in black slacks and a thick, powder blue sweater, she braided her hair and put on her makeup. Then she quietly walked downstairs. Someone was up, she knew, because she could smell freshly brewed coffee.

As she reached the bottom of the stairs, she glanced into the living room. Lenore Parrish, dressed in a red wool pantsuit, stood in front of the fireplace and stared up at the portrait.

Tess wanted to walk on by. But Lenore turned and saw her. Slowly, Tess advanced into the room. As Lenore's gaze once more rose to study the portrait, Tess's own gaze was drawn in the same direction.

For several moments, only the sound of the mantel clock broke the silence. How perfect the three of them looked, Tess thought. The perfect family. David— handsome and serious. Francesca—sweet and shy.

And Leah. Tess's heart beat in slow thuds as she studied Leah's face. The bright, dark eyes. The insolent tilt to her head. The laughing lips and beautiful smile.

"It's a beautiful portrait, isn't it?" Lenore said. Despite her reluctance to do so, Tess turned and looked at Leah's mother.

Lenore's cool blue eyes settled on Tess's face. She didn't smile. "David adored my daughter, you know."

Tess swallowed. *Yes, I know.* "Mrs. Parrish, I know this is hard for you—"

Lenore's face tightened. "You don't know anything about the way I feel."

Tess knew that no matter what she said, it wouldn't be right. But this was Francesca's grandmother. This was a woman who would be a part of their lives, whether Tess liked it or not. "You're right. I don't. But I want you to know I'm not trying to take Leah's place—"

"As if you could!" Lenore cried. "No one will *ever* be able to take her place!"

Chapter Eleven

For the next couple of weeks, Tess found herself in front of the portrait more and more often. In the mornings, after David left for work and she'd watched Francesca board the school bus, Tess would tell herself she was not going to detour into the living room.

But her feet seemed to have a mind of their own. Before Francesca had been out the door ten minutes, Tess, coffee cup in hand, stood in the living room.

Looking up at the portrait.

Looking at Leah. At the sultry eyes and the supple body and the radiant smile. At the perfect self-confidence.

And why shouldn't she be self-confident? Tess thought. Leah had had everything. The perfect child. The perfect husband. The perfect marriage. Until fate had taken those things away from her. Fate and an eighteen-wheeler.

Leah had been so beautiful. No wonder David had loved her so much. No wonder he probably still did.

Lenore Parrish's anguished words played endlessly in Tess's mind. *David adored my daughter, you know.... No one will* ever *be able to take her place!*

Tess knew she was torturing herself needlessly. She knew no purpose was served by constantly reminding herself of what David had lost when he'd lost Leah.

But, like Francesca, the portrait mesmerized Tess. Her fascination with it was almost mystical. The portrait became a symbol of everything the Bannisters had been and would be no more. No matter how momentarily happy Tess might feel, when she looked at the portrait, her happiness faded. She feared that even if David were to someday tell her he loved her, she would never feel completely secure.

The portrait caused horrified gasps from Tess's friends. She grimaced, remembering Summer's reaction. About a week after the wedding, Tess had invited Summer for lunch.

"Oh, I'm dying to see you and the house and everything," Summer said. "Let me see if I can wangle a longer lunch hour on Friday."

Looking fresh and lovely in a black wool suit topped by a gray fox jacket, she showed up on the front doorstep at eleven-thirty that Friday. After stamping the snow from her snug leather boots, Summer grinned, and they hugged several times. Then Tess took Summer's coat, hung it up, and began to show her around.

She started with the dining room, which was to the right of the foyer. Tess had been afraid that Aunt Millicent's antique dining-room furniture would look out of place in the ultra-modern, high-ceilinged room with its large expanse of glass, but it didn't. The beautifully carved mahogany pieces lent balance to the otherwise stark lines of the room, softening it and giving it a subtle beauty it had lacked before.

"Your aunt's things look great," Summer said.

Tess nodded happily. "I think so, too. And David likes them, as well. I was a little worried about that," she admitted. "Leah's things were so modern." She was very proud of herself. Her voice hadn't changed by even the slightest inflection when she'd said Leah's name.

From there they toured the combination kitchen/family room and the huge pantry and utility room.

"Heavens, what a kitchen!" Summer said. "I'd kill for space like this."

"It's a bit intimidating, though, don't you think?" Tess said. She looked at the proliferation of gadgets. "All these things make me feel as if I should be out here whipping up gourmet meals every night."

Instead of the commiserating chuckle Tess had expected, Summer gave her an odd look. "Tess..." she said slowly, "if I'm out of line, just say so, but... isn't it kind of *weird* to be living in another woman's house?"

Tess shrugged. She tried to keep her face impassive, even though she was sorely tempted to confide in Summer. Only loyalty to David kept her from spilling her frustration and uncertainty. "It can't be helped. I told you. David and I discussed the problem. He knew it might be hard on me, but both of us feel Francesca's mental health is more important than any discomfort either of us might feel."

Summer nodded, but her blue eyes were filled with concern. "It's very like you to think of Francesca first. I've always admired that selfless quality in you."

Embarrassed, Tess said, "Please don't put me on a pedestal. I'm not a saint. Besides, you'd do the same thing. I know you would."

"I'd like to think I would," Summer said thoughtfully. "But I don't know.... I'm not sure I could take living in the same house my husband had lived in with someone else."

"Leah will always be a part of David's life. I accept that," Tess said quietly. "Even if he wanted to remove her memory, how could he? Francesca is Leah's daughter."

"You're right, of course." But Summer's normally clear eyes were shadowed by doubt. And concern.

For just a moment, Tess wanted to throw her arms around her friend, voice every insecurity and fear she had, but the moment passed and Tess continued with the tour.

All the while Tess showed Summer the small downstairs office that was David's domain and which Tess had left unchanged, she wondered what Summer would say when they reached the living room. But reaching the living room might take a while, because Summer was nosy. She poked her nose into every crevice, nodding her approval as she went.

"Nice half bath. That's good."

"Hmm, I wish I had a coat closet this big."

"Boy, I *love* this telephone nook. How clever!"

Finally, they reached the formal living room. The only piece of furniture in the room that belonged to Tess was the Steinway, standing proudly in the far corner. It was positioned so that when Tess played she could look out the floor-to-ceiling windows to the woods beyond.

"Wow!" Summer said, looking slowly around.

Tess knew the exact moment Summer spied the portrait.

"Ohmigod," she said, bringing her hand to her mouth. She stared at it for a long moment, then, eyes wide, she turned to Tess. "Tess, *why* is that . . . that *picture* hanging there?"

"Because Francesca got hysterical the last time David tried to take it down."

"But, *Tess!* How can you stand it?" Summer glanced up again. "How can you stand having *her* there? Good grief, it's bad *enough* you're living in her house with a lot of her furniture around, but *this!*" Summer shuddered.

Tess knew Summer had never liked Leah. She wasn't sure exactly why, and Summer had been unable to explain her feelings. All she'd said the one time the two had discussed Leah, shortly after the Bannisters had moved to Collierville, was, "It's hard to say what it is about the woman that bothers me. She just seems so damned smug and superior to the rest of us small-town hicks." Although Tess hadn't agreed, she hadn't argued the point, either. Now, though, she felt compelled to defend Leah.

"Look, Summer, I know this is hard for you to understand, but believe me, the picture doesn't bother me."

Summer didn't look convinced, but like the good friend she was, she said, "I'm sorry. It's none of my business. It's just that I care about *you*. But if it doesn't bother you, well, you're a better woman than I am!" She laughed, and Tess forced herself to laugh with her.

Hazel's reaction was no less troubled. She showed up two days after New Year's in her still-mint-condition fifteen-year-old Cadillac that she refused to consider replacing. After greeting Tess with a warm-from-the-oven pound cake and a bag of peanut-butter cookies for Francesca, she said, "Well, show me around!"

Tess, grinning, did just that. Only this time she thought she might as well get the bad part over with first, so instead of starting Hazel's tour with the dining room, Tess took Hazel's elbow and propelled her into the living room.

Hazel looked around slowly, taking in the nubby oatmeal sectional sofa, the teak coffee table with its smoked-glass top, the teak side tables, the teal fireside chairs, the ice blue and teal ottomans, the Steinway, the huge windows with their sweeping views, and then...the mantel . . . and the portrait.

Hazel gazed at the portrait for what seemed an eternity to Tess. Tess nervously pleated her corduroy slacks as she waited for Hazel's reaction.

When Hazel finally turned, her bright blue eyes pierced Tess. "Suppose that picture's got to stay because of the child."

Tess nodded.

Hazel glanced up one more time. Her voice softened. "Well, Tess, the sooner that thing comes down, the better for all concerned." Then she walked over to Tess and put her arms around her, giving her a quick hug.

Tess's eyes misted. A gruff, no-nonsense Hazel was much easier to take than a kind, comforting Hazel. Sadly, she wondered why this should be so.

After Hazel left, Tess thought about her words. *The sooner the picture comes down, the better for all concerned.* If only she could get up the nerve to talk to Francesca about it. If only she thought the removal of the portrait was all it would take to normalize her marriage. If only she wasn't afraid that her marriage was like a house of cards—one that the least bit of wind would knock over in an instant.

Unfortunately, Francesca's obsession with the portrait remained the one constant in her life, and Tess feared it would be a long time—if ever—that the portrait could be removed.

Yet Tess also knew it wasn't healthy for Francesca to spend so much time looking at the picture. For David had been right. Each day when Francesca came home from school, she would take off her coat and boots, hug Tess, then head for the living room. She would look up at the portrait for a long time—sometimes as long as five minutes—and only then would she come out into the kitchen to share a cup of hot chocolate or a glass of orange juice with Tess.

No, it wasn't likely the portrait would come down anytime soon.

Tess decided that—portrait or no portrait—she would be the kind of wife David deserved. In fact, she would be such a perfect wife and she would make his life so much more pleasant than it had been, he would not be able to get along without her.

He might not love her.

But she would make sure he needed her.

And not just for Francesca's sake, either.

After much thought, Tess cut her piano students from forty plus to just twelve. From Monday through Thursday, starting at three-thirty and ending at five o'clock, she taught piano. Fridays she liked to have completely free to shop and cook, because it wasn't long after their wedding that David mentioned how much he liked staying home on Friday evenings.

"After the pressure of the week, it's great to just relax at home, don't you think?" he said.

He didn't say so, but Tess got the idea that Leah had liked to go out on Friday evenings. So Tess tried to make their Friday evenings as stress-free and relaxed as she could.

She also thought about the rest of her commitments. She knew David must admire women who accomplished a lot. Why else would he have married someone like Leah? So she had no qualms over continuing to volunteer at the center or her work as music director at the church.

She did worry about being gone two evenings a week, though—Wednesday nights for choir practice and Thursday nights for the Collierville choral group. Sometimes that entailed getting a baby-sitter for Francesca because David's hours tended to be long.

But when she asked him if he minded, he gave her an odd look and said, "Good heavens, Tess, I don't expect you to give up your activities. Of course, I don't mind. In fact, I'll make a point of getting home early those two nights."

Because David was so well-read, Tess decided she would also try to enlarge her own sphere of knowledge. She spent long hours reading, both books and magazines. She made a point of discussing the topics with David.

One night, David gave her a quizzical look after she commented on an article about a congressional bill coming up for a vote. "I didn't know you were interested in environmental issues," he said.

"Well, I know *you* are, so I—" She broke off abruptly, realizing she'd been about to confess something she wasn't sure she wanted him to know.

He laid down his newspaper. His eyes were thoughtful as he looked at her. "Tess, I want you to enjoy yourself. I think it's great you have more free time, but do the things that make you happy." He smiled. "Frankly, I'd rather talk about your interests than mine. Mine are boring."

Since her foray into world events hadn't yielded the reaction she'd hoped for, she decided she should improve her homemaking skills. So she spent long hours sewing, and even though the kitchen still intimidated her, she experimented with cooking and baking her own bread.

She *did* take time for her friends, though. She visited Hazel at her new apartment. She went downtown and had lunch with Summer at least once a week. She even—feeling deliciously guilty—went to see an occasional afternoon movie.

At least once a week she visited her old home and watched the repairs in progress. At times during these visits she'd be seized by melancholy. But mostly she just felt tremendously satisfied that her family's homestead would be a town treasure for many years to come.

Tess liked the weekends best. On the weekends, she and David and Francesca did things together. They went ice skating, which Tess hadn't done much of since her childhood days, but she found she loved it. It was exhilarating to skim over the ice at Yellow Creek Pond and then toast her fingers and toes in front of the barrel containing glowing charcoal. And sharing this delightful activity with a laughing David and giggling Francesca doubled her enjoyment.

Afterward, they always ended up at Dalrymple's for hot chocolate and a cheeseburger. On days like this, Tess could almost believe they were a normal family. On days like this, Tess could almost believe David loved her.

Other Saturdays David puttered around the house, and Tess helped Francesca with school projects or worked in the kitchen while Budge sat on the window ledge over the gleaming double sink and watched them.

On Saturday nights, Tess and David did some quiet entertaining or accepted dinner invitations from other couples. Occasionally they asked Hazel to baby-sit with Francesca, and the two of them went out to dinner. Tess cherished these evenings and told herself that David, too, appeared to be content. But tiny slivers of doubt crept in when Tess least expected them—times when David would gaze off into space or seem preoccupied. Then Tess would wonder if he were thinking of similar evenings with Leah and comparing Tess to his dead wife.

And then there were the nights together in their bed. David was a wonderful lover, Tess thought. She gloried in the feelings he had aroused in her, the sensual nature he had uncovered. Although he never said he loved her, he was considerate, thoughtful, and oh, so delightfully thorough in his attentions to her. She told herself this was enough.

They made love often. Three or four times a week. Only on the nights David worked late and came home exhausted did they skip their pleasurable prelude to sleep. Tess knew David was simply keeping to his end of their bargain, but that knowledge didn't prevent her from reveling in his attentions.

As January gave way to February, and February gave way to March, Tess actually began to hope she wouldn't get pregnant soon. She still wanted a baby of her own with the same intensity as always, but she didn't want to lose the part of David she had.

Because she was desperately afraid that once she got pregnant, David would no longer make love to her. She felt torn by her opposing needs.

Throughout the winter months Tess's relationship with Francesca deepened and became richer. Francesca seemed to trust Tess, and she gradually communicated more and more. Tess had always loved Francesca, but now there were times when Tess could almost forget that Francesca wasn't her child. One of those times would always remain crystal clear in her mind.

It was a Friday afternoon at the end of March, and Tess stood scraping carrots at the kitchen sink. Budge sat up on the windowsill in a weak patch of sunlight. It was a cold, blustery day and traces of snow still dusted the hard ground. Tess had wondered if spring would ever come. Just as she'd begun to wonder if she would ever get pregnant. She sighed.

What if she didn't get pregnant? What if years went by and no pregnancy occurred? How would she feel about that? She no longer knew. If David loved her, she thought she could be content just to be a family with him and Francesca.

But he doesn't love you.

She wondered if she should make an appointment to see her gynecologist.

Suddenly melancholy, she turned from the sink and walked over to the stove where she began to cut up the carrots and drop them into the stew she was preparing for dinner. She glanced up at the wall clock. Nearly three. Francesca should be home soon.

Sure enough, a couple of minutes later, Tess heard the grinding creak and whoosh of the brakes signaling the arrival of the school bus. And then the running footsteps down the driveway and around to the back door.

The back door burst open, and Francesca erupted into the room, bringing a whirlwind of cold air with her. Her cheeks were red, and her green eyes sparkled with excitement. The hood of her navy blue quilted coat barely covered her dark curls.

"Tess!" she said. "Guess what?"

Shaking off her melancholy, Tess smiled. "What, honey?"

Francesca started unbuttoning her coat. "Miss Wilson picked me to play Mother Nature at the Spring Fling!" Her voice vibrated with happiness.

"Oh, honey, that's *wonderful!*" Actually, it was amazing, Tess thought. Who would have ever imagined, just six short months ago, that this day would come?

"Will you make my costume? I told Miss Wilson that you would. All the other mothers are doing things for their kids."

Tess's heart nearly stopped. *All the other mothers are doing things for their kids.* Had Francesca realized what she'd said? A lump the size of a tennis ball formed in Tess's throat. For a moment, she couldn't speak. *All the other mothers . . . all the other mothers.* She managed a tremulous smile. "Sweetheart, nothing would make me happier than to make your costume." She opened her arms.

Francesca never hesitated. She propelled herself into Tess's arms, and they hugged. Tess closed her eyes, taking in the little-girl smells, feeling the slender little body. A fierce love pulsated through her. At that moment she realized that even if she were never to become pregnant, the love of this child would be enough.

Even later, when Francesca made her inevitable trek to the living room and the portrait, the glow of happiness that the child's inadvertent use of the term "mother" had engendered hadn't faded.

"You know, David, I'd say marriage agrees with you." Walter Medlock smiled. "You look happier and more rested than you've looked in a long time."

David returned his smile. The two men were sitting in Walter's office. It was the first week of April, and they were discussing a new project that David hoped Medlock would adopt. "I feel better than I've felt in a long time," he admitted.

Walter leaned back in his swivel chair. "Julia really likes that wife of yours. Just last night she said we ought to get together for dinner."

"We'd enjoy that, too."

"Shall we nail down a date right now?" Walter said.

That evening, when David arrived home, he thought how different his marriage to Tess was from his marriage to Leah. Although he'd entered this second marriage for reasons that most people would consider not conducive to his own personal happiness or contentment, in actuality, he had never been so contented.

Or happy. For just a moment, the thought stunned him. He couldn't remember ever feeling really happy during his marriage to Leah. Even in the beginning, when they'd been so hot for each other, he wasn't really *happy*. No one could be happy in a state of perpetual turmoil, which was the best way he could describe those early days of their marriage. Leah was too much a chameleon—too highly charged and volatile, too emotionally taxing and demanding—for anything as relaxing as happiness.

Yes, he thought—entering the house from the front door because the garage door was blocked, and immediately feeling Tess's soothing influence everywhere—he was happy in this second marriage. Very happy. Happier than he'd ever imagined he could be. Not only had his daughter blossomed and benefitted by Tess's presence in their home, but he, too, had reaped unexpected rewards.

Shedding his coat in the foyer and hanging it in the coat closet, he glanced into the living room. Immediately, his good spirits faded. That damned portrait! If only he could get rid of it. He walked into the living room and stared at it.

He hated it. He hated it more now than ever before. The portrait was an absolute lie, and somehow he would figure out a way to banish it from this house.

As he headed toward the kitchen, where he could hear Tess and Francesca talking, he thought that except for that portrait there was only one other disturbing aspect of his life that he'd like to change.

He wished now that he and Tess had not placed conditions and terms on their marriage. He hated the idea that when Tess became pregnant she might no longer want him to make love to her. Making love with Tess had brought them close in a way David had never expected, and he liked the feeling. He didn't want to lose it.

But he knew he couldn't change the terms of their agreement just because he now felt differently. That would be taking advantage and completely unfair to Tess. She was honoring her end of their bargain, and he had to continue to honor his.

Whether he liked it or not.

Chapter Twelve

By the second week of April, spring finally visited Collierville. The temperature crept up, and tender shoots of green poked through the ground. The birds magically reappeared in the budding branches of the maple trees, and Tess knew it wouldn't be long before the tulips, narcissi and forsythias made their appearance.

As she gazed out the kitchen window, she spied a cardinal perched on the lip of the birdbath in the backyard. For a long moment she watched him—the way his proud head moved slowly to survey his world, the way his feathers twitched as something startled him, the way he lifted up and flew away.

She smiled, glad spring had come.

The third week of April, Tess missed her period.

Every day she waited and wondered. She was afraid to believe she might be pregnant, not only because she didn't want to get her hopes up in case the missed period was just a freak of nature, but because she was afraid of what the news might mean in terms of her physical relationship with David.

In May, when she missed her second period, she bought a home pregnancy test. She hid it in her underwear drawer, and the next day, the minute David left for work, she used it.

It came out positive.

She wasn't surprised. Not really. Her breasts were tender, and she felt nauseated most of the time.

A curious mix of elation and fear nearly drove her crazy during the next few days. Tess wondered if David would notice the physical differences in her. Part of her wanted him to notice.

The other part of her—the cowardly part—couldn't bear the thought that once he knew about the baby, there would be no reason for him to continue to make love to her. And even if he *did* continue, how could she be sure it wasn't just because he didn't want to hurt her feelings by stopping? She wouldn't be able to bear that, either.

What was she going to do? Down deep, she knew what she must do. It would be far, far worse to have David pull away from her than it would be to pull away herself. At least then she'd have her pride. At least then she could look David in the eye. At least then he wouldn't pity her.

She couldn't stand for him to pity her.

So she put off telling him. And she put off going to the doctor.

One night, toward the middle of May, she had a couple of heart-stopping moments when she thought David might suspect the truth. He had worked very late on an exciting new project that had consumed much of his time recently, and he came home looking exhausted. Tess warmed up the chicken casserole and sat down to share the meal with him. They ate, and after Tess cleaned up the kitchen, she followed David up to bed. Tess required a lot of sleep now—another telling physical change—so it was no hardship for her to retire early.

David was already half asleep when Tess joined him in their bed. She snapped off the bedside lamp and turned on her side—facing away from him. To her surprise, a few seconds later his warm hand touched her hip and gently tugged her around to face him.

"I—I thought you'd be too tired," she said.

"You thought wrong," he said softly, gathering her close. He buried his hands in her hair and kissed her—a slow, deep kiss. Tess closed her eyes and gave herself up to the complex emotions his touch and his kisses always kindled. Sometimes she loved David so profoundly, it almost hurt to give way to her feelings, especially because she knew he did not return them. Tonight was one of those nights. Their lovemaking, while still deeply sensual, seemed almost mystical in its quality. There wasn't one moment during their shared passion that Tess wasn't aware of her feelings for this man.

Later, when he turned her and held her close—spoon-fashion—his hands gently cupped her breasts. "You feel different, somehow," he whispered, and Tess's heart began to beat in heavy, slow thuds.

He knows, she told herself. She waited for him to say something more, but his breathing evened out and his hands became slack, and she knew he'd fallen asleep.

She lay there for a long time, awake and staring into the darkness. It wasn't fair to keep David uninformed about her condition. She was being selfish and a coward. It also wasn't wise to put off going to the doctor any longer. That, too, was selfish and potentially dangerous. She needed to be examined and make sure everything was proceeding normally.

She would have to do both. And soon.

The very next morning, Tess called and made an appointment with her gynecologist/obstetrician. To her chagrin, there had been a cancellation for that very afternoon. Obviously, the fates had decided Tess had stalled long enough.

"If you can come in at one o'clock, Mrs. Bannister, Dr. Ellis can see you then," the receptionist said.

One o'clock. She would still have time to make it back for her three-thirty piano student. "All right," Tess said. "I'll be there." So she would not have the luxury of even a few days' reprieve.

She tried to keep her mind free of worry the rest of the morning. She tried not to think about the upcoming appointment or telling David or anything. It wasn't easy.

One o'clock came all too soon. Tess had a thirty-minute wait before Dr. Ellis, a motherly type woman who Tess had always liked, entered the examining room.

Later, when Dr. Ellis and Tess were sitting across from each other in the doctor's office, Tess wasn't at all surprised to hear Dr. Ellis say, "Well, Tess, according to my calculations, you're about seven weeks pregnant."

Joy—pure, sweet, and untempered with any regrets, rushed through Tess's veins. She realized that she thought she'd been prepared for this announcement, but she really hadn't been. It was one thing to suspect she was carrying David's child. It was quite another to have her suspicion confirmed. Heart almost too full to speak, she said, "That's wonderful."

Dr. Ellis's round face creased into a smile. "Yes, it is, isn't it? This is one of my favorite times. Giving a mother happy news."

For a few minutes they discussed what Tess should do in the coming months. Dr. Ellis gave her some tips on how to try to alleviate her nausea. "Because of your age, I recommend amniocentesis, just to be sure everything's okay." Tess nodded.

Then the doctor continued, "And if you like, we can tell you the sex of the baby."

"I don't think I want to know," Tess said. It would be more fun to speculate, she thought.

"That's entirely up to you. Some mothers do. Some don't."

Tess left Dr. Ellis's office in a daze. But by the time she'd driven to the pharmacy and filled her vitamin prescription, stopped at the supermarket to pick up a couple of things she needed, and driven home, some of her glowing happiness had been replaced by gnawing uncertainty.

For the rest of the afternoon she thought about how and when she should break the news to David. At dinner? Maybe she should make a production of it. Run out and buy some flowers and wine...no, she couldn't drink wine...but he could...no, she didn't want to make a formal announcement. Besides, Francesca would be at dinner with them. Tess knew she had to tell David first. They should tell Francesca together.

Francesca. That was another niggling worry. How would Francesca react to this news? Would she be happy? Oh, Tess hoped so.

When David came in a little after six, Tess was so keyed up she felt sick to her stomach.

"Is something wrong?" David asked during dinner. He looked at her plate. "You've hardly touched your food."

Tess looked down. She'd barely eaten half of her portion. She met David's gaze across the table. His forehead was knitted in concern. She forced a smile. "No, nothing's wrong. I guess I was just daydreaming...."

His eyes—so clear, so compelling, so astute—studied her face for a long moment. Then he nodded and smiled. "I do that myself once in a while."

To divert his attention, Tess turned to Francesca. "Francesca, tell your father what happened at rehearsal today." The Spring Fling, the annual school pageant, would take place that weekend. Francesca could talk of nothing else lately.

Later, after Tess had cleaned up the kitchen and Francesca had gone upstairs to her room, David sat in his favorite chair in the family room and picked up the book he was reading. Tess knew she could not settle down to her embroidery or a book. Not while her emotions were so chaotic. Not when she had something so important on her mind.

She wanted to get it over with—tell David her news, but she couldn't just blurt it out. Maybe she should wait and tell him after they were in bed. At least then it would be dark. He wouldn't be able to see her expression if she wasn't able to hide the way she felt.

"I think I'm going to go in and play the piano for a while," she said. "You don't think it'll bother Francesca, do you?"

David looked up from his book. "I don't think so. She probably enjoys listening to you play as much as I do."

Something painful welled into Tess's throat as she met his gaze. Oh, she loved him so much. Did he have any

idea of the strength of her feelings? Of course, he didn't.
And it was a good thing because then he'd feel uncomfortable around her. She could feel tears welling in her
eyes, and she hurriedly looked away. Fighting hard to
keep from crying, she headed blindly toward the living
room.

She sat at the piano. Why couldn't she be happy with
what she had? She'd desperately wanted a baby, and now
she was going to have one. *Quit wishing for more.* After
a few minutes, she had gained control of herself again,
and she sat at the piano and began to play. Music had
always been an outlet for her emotions, especially the
ones she couldn't voice.

First she played Chopin—the études and the preludes. Her melancholy deepened as the music claimed
her, yet in some way she almost welcomed the catharsis
of allowing those feelings free rein. Closing her eyes, she
drifted into more contemporary music, playing from
memory.

As "Claire de Lune," then "Moonlight Sonata"
flowed from her fingers, she thought about the past
months. She thought about how much she loved David
and Francesca. She thought about the baby she carried
inside her. A baby she and David had created. No matter what else she didn't have, she would always have
that—a part of him.

She knew she had more than many women ever have.
But would it be enough?

"That's a beautiful song," David said, and Tess
looked up. She hadn't heard him come into the room,
but he stood about three feet away. "It sounds familiar.
What is it?"

"It's called 'I Will Wait for You,' from *The Umbrellas of Cherbourg*," she said.

He walked closer. "Do you mind if I watch you play?"

I don't mind anything you do. "No." She segued from the end of the song into another. It wasn't until she was part of the way through the new piece that she realized how her subconscious had worked. Her gaze met David's as she poured her heart into her playing. The hauntingly lovely melody floated around them.

"What's the name of that one?" he asked softly, leaning against the piano as he watched.

"'I Can't Make You Love Me.'" She wanted to look away from his eyes, but she couldn't. *I can't make you love me, David, I know that. But, oh, how I wish you did. If only you'd say you love me, David. How different things could be.*

When the last notes echoed in the room, David stirred, then smiled. "That was beautiful."

Suddenly exhausted, Tess slid off the bench and stood. Out of the corner of her eye, she caught the gleam of the gilt edge of the frame containing the portrait. Pulled by forces she couldn't control, her gaze turned unerringly, and Tess stared at the picture.

Leah's eyes mocked her.

Leah's smile mocked her.

Even the way Leah held her head and body mocked her.

He'll never love you, Leah seemed to say. *How could he—after me?*

The overwhelming futility of her hopeless love for David was all too clear. She'd been a fool to ever think she had a chance to *really* be his wife. The only reason he'd married her was because of Francesca. Just because he seemed to enjoy making love to her meant nothing. And, after all, what did she know about men and making love, anyway? Maybe they all acted the way David acted. Maybe, to a man, making love had nothing to do with emotional commitment but was a purely physical thing.

Oh, yes, you're a fool.

Tess straightened her shoulders and without looking back at David, said, "I'm really tired tonight. I think I'll go up to bed."

"I'll be up soon, too," he said.

When she emerged from the bathroom fifteen minutes later, David was undressing. He looked up. "You needn't have worried. Your playing didn't bother Francesca at all. She's already asleep."

"I know. I looked in on her."

"She's so excited about the pageant, isn't she?" He smiled.

"Yes." His smile tore at her heart. Why did she love him so? What was it about human nature that made her want what she could never have?

"I can't believe how much she's changed since we've been married. At times, she almost seems normal. It gives me real hope for an eventual recovery."

Something tightened in Tess's chest. *Almost seems normal. Is he trying to tell me my usefulness will soon be over?* In some part of herself, she knew she was being paranoid, but she couldn't seem to help it. That futile feeling had her in its grip, and she couldn't shake it loose.

Tess walked to the bed and sat on the side. She removed her slippers, then swung her legs up and settled herself under the cool sheet and summer-weight blanket. She picked up the book on her bedside table and pretended to read, but her gaze kept returning to David as he finished undressing.

Despite her unhappiness, she loved looking at him. His strong, firm back and broad shoulders. His dark hair, a little messy from pulling his undershirt off. His neat, narrow waist. Mesmerized, she watched as he removed his briefs and pulled on his silk pajama bottoms. They settled low on his hips.

She shivered. There was something so sexy about David in those gray pajama bottoms. Even if she hadn't had such deep feelings for him, she knew he would still have excited her physically. If only he felt the same way... *Stop that! Stop this endless moaning. Get a grip on yourself.*

She watched as he strode to the bathroom, listened as he brushed his teeth and splashed water on his face. But when he snapped off the bathroom light and reentered the bedroom, she hurriedly bent her head to her book and continued her pretense of reading.

Her heart began to thud harder as David turned off his bedside lamp, then climbed into bed. She kept her gaze glued to her page. Her heart went *bang, bang, bang.* She knew she could no longer put off the inevitable. *Tell him now. Put your book down. Turn and look at him. Now.*

She closed her book. She reached over and turned off the bedside lamp.

The room settled into darkness. *Now. Tell him now.*

"Tess." His hand touched her bare shoulder, and her tenuous hold on control began to slip. She knew if she didn't get this over with, do what she had to do, she would shatter inside.

"David, there's something I have to tell you." Her voice sounded like someone else's—strained and oddly pitched.

"What is it?" He slipped one arm around her and tried to draw her close.

Desperate, Tess pulled away. "I went to the doctor today," she blurted out. "I'm seven weeks pregnant."

She felt him stiffen beside her. He said nothing for agonizing seconds. Then, in a quiet voice, he said, "That's wonderful. I know this is what you wanted."

"Yes." She lay very still. She could hardly breathe. Outside, somewhere in the distance, a car backfired. The sound felt like a pistol shot through her heart.

"So are you saying it's not necessary for us to make love anymore?"

Tess closed her eyes. What did he want her to say? If only he'd give her some indication of how he felt. But his voice was unemotional, matter-of-fact. "No, it's not necessary." The tears that had hovered under the surface all evening long pooled in her eyes. She willed herself not to cry. Not to give away her hopeless yearning.

The bed creaked as David leaned over and brushed his lips across her cheek. Tess's heart stood still as she breathed in the fresh scent of his toothpaste mingled with the deeper essence that was uniquely David.

Then the bed creaked again as she felt then heard him leave the bed. Now that her eyes had adjusted to the night, she could see his silhouette as he walked to the foot of the bed. Very softly, he said, "I'll move into the bedroom across the hall. You'll rest better that way." He waited, then added, "Don't you think that's best?"

The quiet question reverberated in the room.

No, no, no! Tess's heart cried. *No, David, please don't go. Please stay here with me. Please come back into our bed and hold me and say you love me.* "Yes, I suppose so." Her chest ached, and she could feel tears trickling down her cheeks. She was powerless to stop them.

"Yes, I think so, too. Good night, then."

She managed a strangled "Good night" before he opened the bedroom door. For just a second, his beloved body was outlined in the light spilling in from the hall.

David, David, I love you. If only she could say the words. If only she wasn't trapped by their agreement. If only he loved her.

Two seconds later, he was gone.

Chapter Thirteen

David couldn't sleep.

For hours, he lay awake and tried to make sense out of what had happened between him and Tess tonight. He had, foolishly perhaps, begun to think they had built something good between them.

Sure, maybe they weren't in love, but . . . damn it, he *cared* about Tess. She was very important to him. Why, she was almost . . . no, damn it . . . she wasn't *almost*, she *was* as important to him as Francesca!

Stunned, David sat up in bed and ran his fingers through his hair. *As important to him as Francesca.* It was the first time he'd ever admitted to himself that his new wife—the woman he'd married because of his daughter—had somehow burrowed her way into his heart.

Did he love Tess, then?

He didn't know if what he felt for her was love. It was certainly a very different emotion from what he'd felt for Leah, and that was the only yardstick he had to go by.

Maybe he did love Tess.

He thought about her—all the things she did to make his home warm and peaceful and a place he looked forward to coming to each night. Tess, who would soon give birth to his child. *His child.* A child they had created together.

He got out of bed and walked to the window. Parting the drapes, he peered into the street. Moonlight silvered the road, and the only sign of movement was the slight swaying of the branches of the big elm tree in the front yard.

God, he wanted to be happy about the baby. If theirs were a normal marriage, he *would* be happy. He'd be delirious, in fact. But now…especially after the way Tess had acted tonight when she'd told him about her pregnancy, he was suddenly afraid.

Afraid Tess no longer wanted to be married to him. Afraid that once Francesca was completely well and the baby was born, Tess would want out of their marriage. And he would have no choice but to allow her her freedom. After all, he couldn't force her to remain married to him. Just as, tonight, he couldn't force her to let him hold her or make love to her.

The thought of losing Tess hurt. It hurt in ways he had never imagined he would feel again. It was really funny. Nothing about his marriage was the way he'd thought it would be. This was especially true of Tess. He'd always known she was a gentle person and had figured she'd be easy to live with. And she was. But there were also dimensions to Tess he would have never dreamed existed. He reflected on their lovemaking over the past four and a half months. How surprised and pleased he had been by her eager response to him. How close he had felt to her. How he had looked forward to the nights. How his desire for her—rather than diminishing as time went on—had increased and deepened.

What a fool he was. Why hadn't he realized what was happening to him?

How...*when* had his feelings for Tess changed? When had he gone from respect and liking to this new emotion, which if it wasn't love, was awfully damn close? Did it really matter, though? The question now was, what did Tess feel for him?

He didn't know.

He also didn't know what to do next. The only thing he *did* know was that he was in the spare bedroom, alone and lonely, and his pregnant wife was across the hall.

And it damn sure looked as if that was exactly the way she wanted it.

The next morning, when the alarm went off at six-thirty, Tess felt as if someone had taken a vise and tightened it on her head. She'd never had a hangover in her life, but she imagined that this horrible feeling of heaviness accompanied by a dull throbbing in her temples, was what one felt like.

As she emerged from the master bedroom, she glanced across the hall. The door to the spare bedroom was closed. David must still be asleep. But when she walked downstairs, the smell of freshly brewed coffee drifted from the kitchen, and she knew he was already up.

She put her hand to her forehead and massaged her temples. She hadn't heard him get up. Had he come into their bathroom? Had he watched her as she slept? She hadn't heard a thing. Of course, that was hardly surprising. She'd lain awake until well after 3:00 a.m. No wonder she'd slept so soundly when she finally did fall asleep.

Feeling brittle and vulnerable, she tightened the sash on her cotton robe and took a deep breath before entering the kitchen. Facing David this morning would be the hardest thing she'd had to do in a long time—right up there with telling him he didn't have to make love to her anymore. She hoped she could pull it off without giving away her feelings.

He stood with his back to her, and for a long moment, she silently drank him in. A lump formed in her throat as her gaze traveled from the top of his neatly combed hair to the tips of his shining black loafers. He was already dressed for work in a pale blue shirt and dark blue pants. His suit jacket lay draped over one of the kitchen chairs. In his right hand he held a cup of coffee. With his left hand, he was scratching Budge's head—Budge, who sat on top of the kitchen table—a place Tess had tried, without success, to keep him off. At her entrance, Budge's amber eyes swiveled her way.

"Good morning," she said.

There was an almost imperceptible stiffening to David's shoulders, then he turned. His expression was enigmatic as his green eyes—glinting under the fluorescent lights—met hers. "Good morning," he said quietly.

Tess struggled to act as normal as possible. She knew these first few days would be the hardest to get through. Once she was past them, she imagined she would be okay. She would *have* to be okay. To be this miserable forever would be intolerable. *Time heals all wounds, child,* her Aunt Millicent had been fond of saying. Pray God, her aunt had been right.

"You're up early," Tess said as she advanced into the room. "And *you*..." She gave Budge a mock glare. "What are you doing up on that table? How many times do I have to tell you?" She gave the cat a playful swat, all the time avoiding David's gaze.

"I didn't sleep well," he said.

Her heart turned over. What did that mean? Did that mean he was as unhappy as she was over the turn of events? She darted a glance his way, but he, too, looked at Budge, who had now jumped up to the countertop and stood eyeing the top of the refrigerator. "I'm sorry," she finally answered. "It... it was probably because you were in a strange bed."

"Yes, probably..." David inclined his head toward the coffeemaker. "Coffee's ready." He drained his cup and walked to the sink where he rinsed it and put it in the dishwasher. Then he turned and faced her squarely.

Tess's heart thudded as their gazes locked. She swallowed and wondered if he could hear her heart beating. It suddenly seemed so quiet in the kitchen. Only the hum of the refrigerator and the ticking of the wall clock broke the silence.

What was he thinking? What was that odd expression in the depths of his eyes? Why didn't he say something?

As if he had heard her unspoken thoughts, he cleared his throat and said, "Look, Tess, if I didn't say so last night, I'm happy about the baby. Tonight, when I come home, I want to hear what the doctor had to say. Also, I think we should tell Francesca tonight, don't you?"

"Y-yes." Her throat felt as dry as stale bread.

He nodded, and she thought he sighed, but the sound was so faint she couldn't be certain. Reaching for his suit coat, he said, "I need to get to work early today, so I guess I'll be going."

Tess finally found her voice. "Don't you want any breakfast?"

He shook his head. "I'll pick up something on the way. A biscuit and sausage, maybe." Then, with an almost normal-sounding chuckle, he added, "Cholesterol be damned."

After he was gone, Tess walked around in a fog. A miserable, headachy fog. She awakened Francesca, fixed her breakfast, packed her lunch, dealt with her own nausea, and tried not to think about David.

All through that long day, Tess felt as if she might burst into tears at any moment. Why was it that things were never the way you thought they'd be? Here she was, carrying David's child—a child she'd wanted more than anything in the world—and she wasn't happy. She'd thought she would be ecstatic. Instead, she was wretched.

That afternoon was her day to volunteer at the center. She thought about calling to say she wasn't feeling well and wouldn't be there. Then she changed her mind. It would be good for her to get out of the house, forget about her problems for a while. Besides, she didn't want to disappoint the seniors.

When she walked into the center the first person she saw was Hazel. For a moment, she was speechless. Then, forgetting her own misery, she grinned. "Hazel! You finally came!"

Hazel, who looked great in tailored black slacks and a pretty black and white silk blouse, walked over. Tess could tell she was fighting a smile because her eyes gave her away. They twinkled as she said in that dry way of hers, "Well, I'm gonna give this group a chance. Just one, mind you."

Tess laughed, and Hazel finally succumbed and chuckled, too. Then her face turned serious. "You look a little under the weather." She peered at Tess, her blue eyes much too sharp for Tess's peace of mind.

Tess shrugged. "It's nothing. I didn't sleep well, that's all."

Hazel nodded, but her eyes remained thoughtful, and throughout the sing-along, she watched Tess more closely than Tess would have liked.

After the hour was up, a beaming Alistair, who, to Tess's astonishment and amusement, held fast to Hazel's hand, walked to Tess's side.

"Hazel and I would like to take you and David out to dinner one night," he said without preamble.

Delighted, Tess grinned. "Oh, that would be great!"

"Shall we settle on a date right now?" Alistair said. "How about next Saturday evening? Is that all right with you, Hazel?"

"I think I'm free next Saturday," Hazel said.

Tess laughed. "I think we're free next Saturday, too." Then she said, "Hazel, will you be home later today?"

"Yes."

"Good. I'll call you. There's something I want to tell you."

As Tess drove home she thought again how seldom it was that things worked out the way you wanted them to. This was one time they had. It actually looked as if Hazel and Alistair were hitting it off. *And it's all your doing.* Wouldn't it be wonderful if Hazel and Alistair were to fall in love? The happy thought made her smile. But the closer she got to the house, the faster her good feeling faded. And by the time six o'clock came—

bringing David's imminent arrival—she was once more solidly mired in unhappiness and uncertainty over the future. Even her telephone call to Hazel and telling her about the baby wasn't enough to keep her spirits up.

When David walked in, Tess's heart leapt. She wondered if she'd ever get over this feeling when she saw him after an absence of any duration. He looked tired, she thought, looking at him closely. Tired and . . . unhappy. The thought gave her pause. If only she knew what he was thinking. If only she could believe his imagined unhappiness had something to do with her. *If only wishes were gold bars, you'd be a millionaire.*

Somehow Tess got through dinner.

Somehow she smiled and listened to Francesca and even managed to make conversation with David—all the while avoiding his gaze whenever possible.

Somehow she pretended today was just an ordinary day.

When dinner was over, David said, "Francesca, let's you and I both help Tess clean up tonight."

Francesca smiled. "Okay." She was such an agreeable child, Tess thought. So sweet and good.

As the three of them worked, Tess wondered what a stranger would think if he happened to glance into their windows. He would see a man and his wife and child quietly working side by side. He would see the lovely home with its lovely furnishings. He would see an outward harmony and tranquility. He would probably think they were a perfect family.

Tess blinked back sudden tears. Appearances could certainly be deceiving.

When they finished their cleanup, David said, "Francesca, Tess and I have something we'd like to talk to you about. Let's go sit down, okay?" He motioned to the family room.

When they were all seated, David, after exchanging a glance with Tess, said, "Tess and I were wondering..." He stopped. *Help me,* his eyes implored as they met Tess's gaze.

Tess took Francesca's hand. "Honey, what your daddy is trying to say is that a week or two before Christmas, you're going to have a little brother or a little sister." She smiled. "What do you think about that?"

Francesca's eyes widened, and for one heart-stopping moment, Tess thought everything would be fine. But then Francesca's lower lip quivered, and her throat worked, and she yanked her hand from Tess's grasp. She glared at Tess as if Tess had somehow betrayed her. "I don't want a little brother or sister!" she cried. Then she jumped up, whirled around, raced out of the room, down the hall and up the uncarpeted stairs—the sound of her pounding feet like cannon booms in the shocked silence she'd left behind.

When Francesca's bedroom door slammed, Tess, clasping her trembling hands together, met David's stricken gaze.

He started to rise.

"No. Please, David, let me go and talk to her."

He nodded, and Tess saw the relief that slid across his face. Even though Francesca was greatly improved, and her attitude toward her father warmed more and more each day, Tess still shared a closer relationship with his daughter than he did.

Praying she would find the right words, Tess climbed the stairs to Francesca's room. When she reached it, she knocked softly. "Francesca, honey...it's Tess. May I come in?"

"Go away," came the muffled reply.

"Honey, please. Please let me come in. I just want to talk to you for a minute."

No answer.

"Francesca?" Tess turned the doorknob and opened the door a crack.

Francesca lay face down in a tangled heap in the middle of her bed. Her body shook, and Tess forgot her own unhappiness in the face of Francesca's misery. She walked over to the bed and sat on the edge. She laid her hand on top of Francesca's dark curls.

After a moment, Francesca lifted her head, and they stared at each other.

Please, God, help me say the right thing. "Honey, your daddy and I love you, you know that, don't you?"

Francesca, eyes downcast, said nothing.

"And we want you to be happy." Tess slipped her arm around the trembling child and pulled her close.

Francesca still said nothing, but she didn't pull away.

Encouraged, Tess said, "We thought you'd love having a sister or brother of your very own. Someone to take care of and play with. Someone you can help with schoolwork and teach all the things you've learned." What was the child thinking? Her body still trembled as if she were struggling with emotions too complex to articulate.

Tess closed her eyes. *Please, God.* "Francesca, honey, I love you so much," she murmured. She kissed the top of Francesca's head, drinking in the familiar, little-girl smell. "I want you to be happy about the baby."

Francesca sobbed aloud, then clutched at Tess. Tess held her tightly. "I love you," she whispered again. "I can't stand to see you unhappy."

"W-will you s-still love me when the baby's born?"
Francesca said.

"Oh, Francesca, sweetheart, of course, I will."

Francesca finally looked up. Her green eyes swam with
tears. "I—I thought you wouldn't love me anymore if
you had a baby of your own."

"Oh, honey!" Tess's own eyes filled with tears, and
she crushed Francesca to her. "Don't ever think things
like that! Of course, I'll love you. I'll always love you.
Always," she vowed fiercely.

A long time later, Tess went downstairs. She hoped she
had reassured Francesca, and she thought she had, but
she wasn't completely sure. Only time would tell.

"Is she all right?" David said. He stood where she'd
left him, and Tess wondered if he'd remained in that spot
the whole time she was upstairs.

"I hope so."

David looked in the direction of the stairs. "Should I
go up, do you think?"

"Not now. Why don't you wait until you're ready to
go to bed, then look in on her?"

"What did she say to you?"

Tess explained, ending with, "I think she just needs
reassurance, David. Losing her mother the way she
did...maybe she's afraid she'll lose everyone's love." She
sighed heavily. "Who knows what goes on in a child's
mind?"

On the surface, the next weeks passed uneventfully.
Tess and David settled back into their daily routines, and
that mythical stranger, looking on, would have said
nothing was amiss in the Bannister household.

But the reality was very different from the outer picture. At least it was on Tess's part—she had no idea how

David felt. She missed David's presence in her bed unbearably. She had never realized just how much their physical intimacy had contributed to her feelings of well-being. Sleeping alone had changed the dynamics of their relationship in ways she had never expected. Gone was all feeling of closeness. And the little bit of security she'd managed to build disappeared as surely as if it had never existed.

She told herself, over and over again, that she was going to have a baby. His baby. The baby she'd always wanted. She told herself to be satisfied. She told herself to be content. She touched her stomach constantly—just to remind herself that she really was going to be a mother. She really was going to have someone who would love her and whom she could love unconditionally. She would never be alone again—no matter what happened between her and David in the future.

But it wasn't enough. Maybe if she hadn't been living in the same house with David, maybe if she'd never known what it was like to share his bed—maybe then she could have better adjusted to this change.

But she was here. And she did know.

Every day, in every way, she was reminded of just how much she *didn't* have. And the fact that David treated her with kindness and thoughtfulness at all times, that he couldn't have asked for a more considerate husband, somehow made it all seem even worse.

One thing made Tess feel good, though. And that was Francesca's behavior. After her outburst the night they'd told her about the baby, she had gradually seemed to accept the coming changes in their family.

In June, David had to go to Switzerland for two weeks. Tess missed David, but she had to admit that life was a lot easier with him gone because she didn't have to be constantly on her guard. Without the ever-present reminder of what she could never have, she was almost happy. Without his physical presence, she could lose herself in a fantasy world where she was a normal wife with a normal marriage.

But the fantasy had to end sometime. The night before David's return, Tess played the piano for hours. And afterward, she looked at the portrait.

This time, instead of Leah's, she studied David's face. If possible, she loved him even more now than she had loved him before. She wished she could tell him so. She wished that when he came home tomorrow she could throw herself into his arms and tell him everything that was in her heart. But she knew that would be the worst thing she could ever do. It wouldn't be fair to burden him in this way. David had lived up to his end of their bargain. She must live up to hers.

David couldn't wait to get home. Hardly daring to admit it, he hoped that maybe, just maybe, his absence would have made a difference in how Tess felt. After all, didn't absence make the heart grow fonder?

What an idiot you are. What do you think? Just because you were gone a couple of weeks, she's going to throw herself into your arms?

But that was exactly what he hoped.

When he walked in the door later that day, the only thing that happened was that Tess looked up and smiled. "Hi," she said. "You're right on time. Did you have a good trip home?"

Disappointment welled in his throat, a disappointment he fought to overcome. All right, fine, nothing had changed between them. He'd be just as impersonal and casual as she'd been. "It was long, but not too bad." He looked around. "Where's Francesca?"

"She'll be here any minute. Summer picked her up to spend the day with Lisa."

Although he continued to tell himself he was a fool, he couldn't keep his eyes off Tess. Throughout the evening, he watched her surreptitiously. She was about three and a half months pregnant now, and had just begun wearing maternity clothes. Even though he knew she was happy about the baby, she looked tired and pale. "Aren't you feeling well?" he asked.

"I'm okay. Dr. Ellis said some women just don't have easy pregnancies. I guess I'm one of them."

Concern for her wiped out his other thoughts. "What's happening? Has your nausea gotten worse?"

"No. It's just constant."

"Well, can't that doctor do something about it? Give you something to take?"

Tess shook her head. "Not really. She told me the best thing I could do is keep something in my stomach at all times." She smiled. "I'm supposed to carry crackers and fruit with me wherever I go."

He nodded. "I think we should hire someone to come in and clean."

"Oh, that's not necessary, David. I'm not an invalid."

"I know that. But I don't want you doing heavy work."

She didn't argue with him, and he was glad. He might not be able to be a husband to her in one sense of the word, but he certainly could protect her and make sure she didn't overtax herself.

A few minutes later she said, "Summer has invited us to their Fourth of July party next weekend. I told her I'd ask you if you wanted to go."

He sighed. "Tess, how many times have I told you to go ahead and accept any invitations you want to accept? You don't have to ask me about every one of them." He was immediately sorry for the note of exasperation that had crept into his voice, especially when he saw the wounded look she gave him.

"I'm sorry. I—I thought you might have made other plans." She touched her stomach in an unconsciously defensive gesture.

Oh, God. He couldn't seem to do anything right. The last thing he wanted to do was hurt Tess's feelings. "No, I'm sorry. It was thoughtful of you to ask me. And yes, I'd love to go. But are you sure you feel up to it?"

"I'll be fine."

During the rest of the evening he noticed how she constantly touched her stomach. Each time she did, something painful welled in his chest. Painful and poignant. That was his child growing inside Tess. His child.

He wondered what she would say if, when it was time for bed, he simply followed her into the master bedroom and said, "Listen, this has gone far enough. We're husband and wife, and I intend to sleep in the same bed with you." As quickly as the thought formed, David knew he couldn't do that. Maybe if she wasn't pregnant, maybe if she were feeling better, but he couldn't force himself on her in her condition. He couldn't put that added pressure on her. She had enough to worry about with her pregnancy and Francesca.

And so, when she said good-night, he just glanced up from the newspaper and said, "Sleep well."

Later, as he climbed into his solitary bed, he said softly, "Welcome home, David. Welcome home."

The summer turned out to be the hottest one Collierville had seen in years. Everywhere Tess went, people talked about the weather. The heat and humidity were particularly hard on her as her pregnancy advanced. By mid-August, when she was five months along, she felt swollen, miserable and cranky. Even the thoughts of the baby's arrival failed to make her feel better.

Her feet swelled, too, and she had to spend more and more of her time with them propped up. Regretfully, she relinquished her piano students. She even stopped Alistair's lessons. "I'm sorry," she said. "I'm just too tired and miserable to teach."

Alistair gave her an understanding smile and a fond kiss on the cheek. "After that little one's born, I'll be back. You'll take me back, won't you?"

"Absolutely," she promised.

The last two weeks of August were filled with thunderstorms. Tess loved the gentle rain of spring. She didn't even mind the bleak rain of early winter. But she hated the lightning storms of late summer. Ever since she'd been a child, she'd been scared to death of lightning. Her heart pounded, and her hands became clammy, and she tried to pretend she wasn't scared to death.

David, on the other hand, seemed to revel in nature's show. He would stand on the back patio and watch the fireworks display as lightning streaked the sky and thunder boomed around them.

During one storm, when Tess jumped at a particularly loud crash of lightning, he walked over to where she was standing at the kitchen sink. He slipped his arm

around her waist. "It's okay. The storm is almost over."
Tess's heart jumped the same way her body had jumped
earlier, and she trembled. A great yearning filled her. She
closed her eyes and fought the urge to turn in David's
arms, put her own arms around his waist and never let
go.

After a moment, he squeezed her waist in reassurance and went back to the book he'd been reading.

By the first of September, the weather cooled down a
little, especially in the evenings, and the storms passed.
One night, when Tess was almost five and a half months
pregnant, she and David and Francesca sat on lawn
chairs in the backyard. They'd barbecued chicken and
had finished eating an hour earlier. They watched the
sun set, and just as the last rays of orange turned to the
violet of early nightfall, the baby kicked.

"Oh," Tess gasped, touching her stomach.

"What is it?" David said, sitting up.

Francesca got up and walked over to Tess. "What's
wrong?" she said, frowning.

Tess couldn't speak. A rush of emotion so powerful
she would not have been able to put it into words nearly
overwhelmed her. Then the baby kicked again—a
strong, pay-attention-to-me kick. Still almost too choked
up to speak, Tess said, "The baby kicked. I felt the baby
kick."

"You did?" Francesca squealed.

Tess looked at David. He smiled crookedly.

For one fleeting moment, she wished they were alone.
Maybe if they had been, she would have been able to
bridge the gap between them. But they weren't, and after returning his smile, she turned to Francesca. "Would
you like to feel?"

Francesca nodded, her eyes gleaming in the twilight.

Tess took Francesca's hand and placed in over the spot.

"I don't feel anything."

"Wait," Tess said. "The baby will kick again." Sure enough, a few moments later, she felt the lurch. She looked at Francesca. "Did you feel that, honey?"

Francesca nodded slowly, her eyes wide with wonder. Then, as Tess watched, her face crumpled and tears filled her eyes. Stunning Tess, Francesca threw her arms around Tess and sobbed, "I don't want the baby to die! I don't want the baby to die! It won't die, will it?"

Chapter Fourteen

"Of course, the baby won't die!" Tess exclaimed. Totally bewildered, she looked up at David, who had walked over to where she was sitting.

"I didn't mean it!" Francesca cried. "I didn't mean it! I didn't *really* want Mommy to die!" She clutched at Tess.

"Francesca, honey…" David squatted beside them and stroked Francesca's back. He looked as shocked as Tess felt. "We know you didn't want Mommy to die."

"I don't want the baby to die, either."

Tess smoothed Francesca's hair and stared at David. What was going on?

He shook his head as if to say, *I have no idea what's going through her mind.*

Francesca's sobs finally subsided. Slowly she raised her head, exposing her tear-streaked face. "Are you s-sure the baby won't die?"

"I'm positive," Tess said. "Why would you ever think so?"

"Because I..." She looked first at Tess, then at her father.

"Come on, honey. Tell us," David said.

She stared at David. "Y-you'll be mad," she finally said.

"I promise you, we won't be mad," Tess said.

"Are you sure?"

"Yes, we're sure," David said.

Francesca ducked her head. "'C-cause I...I wished it would die." She raised her face. "But I didn't mean it. I really didn't mean it. I was...I was mad at you."

"But, honey, why did you think the baby would die?" Tess asked.

"I thought...I thought it would be just like when Mommy died." Francesca looked at David.

"But why?" David asked.

"'Cause I...I didn't want to go to New York. And Mommy said I had to. And then you and Mommy were fighting about it. You were yelling at each other. I heard you."

David's face looked strained, and he avoided Tess's gaze. For a fleeting moment she wondered why Leah and David had been fighting, but she had no time to explore the thought because Francesca continued talking.

"And I got so mad at Mommy. I hated her, and I...I wished she was dead. And then...and then..."

Tess sucked in her breath. *Oh, dear heaven.*

"And then she died!" Tears poured down Francesca's cheeks. "I'm sorry, Daddy. I'm sorry! It was all my fault!"

Tess felt like crying herself. What a terrible burden for a child to carry. All this time, David had thought that

Francesca blamed him for her mother's death, and she'd been blaming herself. No wonder she'd spent so much time in front of Leah's picture. No wonder she'd retreated into her silent world. No wonder she'd been so traumatized.

David got up and walked to Francesca's side. He lifted her and cradled her in his arms. His eyes looked suspiciously bright as he stroked her and murmured to her. "It wasn't your fault, sweetheart. It wasn't anyone's fault. It was an accident. And you didn't cause it."

"But I w-wanted her to go away."

"Shh," he said. "Shh." He extended a hand to Tess, helping her up. He inclined his head toward the house, and Tess followed him in.

Later, when Francesca was calmer, and they were all settled into the family room together, David said, "Honey, why did you wish the baby would die?"

"She doesn't have to talk about—" Tess began.

"She does," David said, silencing Tess with a look.

Francesca sighed. "Y-you didn't blame me anymore after Tess came here, Daddy. You were happy, and I was happy. And then...and then..." Her face twisted. "I... I was so scared that...that once Tess had the...the new baby, no one would love me anymore...s-so I wished the baby would die." Her eyes reminded Tess of a mouse she'd once trapped behind the furnace. He'd looked just as cornered. Just as frightened.

"And all this time, I thought..." David let the sentence trail away, but Tess knew what he'd thought.

Much later, after Francesca had gone to bed, and David had retired to his room and Tess to hers, Tess thought about the events of the evening.

Now that Francesca had been able to talk about her fears and feelings, Tess knew the child would finally be able to heal. One day she would be completely well. The thought should have made Tess happy. And it did.

But it also frightened her, because when that day came, David wouldn't need Tess for anything.

Two days after Francesca broke down and told David and Tess about her feelings, David signed her up for psychiatric counseling. She started going to counseling sessions three times a week. There was no overnight cure, but after each session with Dr. Hawthorne, Tess noticed subtle changes in Francesca.

She became more confident. More carefree. More assertive. And she slowly transferred her dependence on Tess to her psychiatrist. Francesca's speech became peppered with references to Dr. Hawthorne.

David laughed about it one night. "Looks like Dr. Hawthorne is Francesca's new idol."

Tess forced herself to laugh, too, but the thought that she no longer occupied that place in Francesca's heart stung. Did no one need her? She touched her stomach and felt the soothing flutter of the baby's movements under her hand. The baby would need her.

One day, when Francesca wanted to sleep over at a girlfriend's house, and Tess said she didn't think it was a good idea because it was a school night, Francesca threw her an angry look and said, "Dr. Hawthorne told me I'm old enough to make my own decisions about things."

"I'm sure she wasn't talking about everything," Tess said quietly. She rubbed her stomach and told herself Francesca was just trying her wings. Testing the waters. *What did you think? She'd never disagree with you? Never act bratty or selfish? She's just a child, and you should be glad she's finally acting like a normal child.*

Then, one Wednesday, when it was time for Francesca's piano lesson—which Tess still taught—Francesca pouted and said, "I don't want to take lessons anymore." She leveled a calculating look at Tess. "Dr. Hawthorne said I didn't have to if I didn't want to."

Tess couldn't stop herself from saying, "But, honey, I thought you *loved* playing the piano."

Francesca's lower lip protruded and she didn't answer.

Tess knew it was silly for her to take these gestures of independence so personally.

One change didn't bother Tess at all. Francesca's obsession with the portrait seemed over. Although she still occasionally looked at the picture, the times became farther and farther apart.

It was ironic, Tess thought. Now maybe the portrait could come down. But what difference would that make? Her marriage was doomed. The portrait might just as well stay where it was.

David began to hope that soon he could remove the portrait entirely, even though he realized it was probably too late to help his marriage. Just as Francesca seemed to be, he was trying to pull away from his need for Tess. He figured that once the baby was born, Tess would probably want her own independence. He knew he had to be ready for that day, no matter how much he wished things could be different.

He sighed and laid down his pen. He'd been sitting writing checks in his study, but now he stood and wandered out of the room and down the hallway toward the living room. It was a Saturday afternoon nearly a month after Francesca's catharsis, as he'd begun to think of that evening. She'd gone roller skating with two school friends, and Tess was somewhere upstairs. He had heard her earlier, and from the noises, it had sounded as if she were taking a shower.

He walked into the living room. He felt lonely. He remembered all the Saturdays this past winter when the three of them had done so many things together. Even though he was happy Francesca was on the road to recovery, he wished they could recapture those days. He wished he and Tess could recapture that feeling of closeness that had all but disappeared.

He turned and his eyes settled on the portrait. He stared at it for a long time. He wondered if he would ever be happy again.

Tess paused halfway down the stairs. David stood in the living room, his gaze on the portrait. There was an expression of longing on his face that tore at Tess's heart. Even if she hadn't seen the expression, she would have known he was unhappy. The slump of his shoulders, his utter stillness, would have told her so.

She turned silently, taking one last look at David's forlorn stance. She tiptoed back upstairs. Above all, she didn't want David to know she had seen him. Obviously she had caught him in a moment he'd thought to be private. Obviously he would not want her to know how much he still missed Leah. How much he still loved Leah.

Tess walked into the bedroom and shut the door. She leaned against it and closed her eyes. For a few days after Francesca's emotional confession, Tess had thought maybe she'd been mistaken about David's feelings for Leah. She kept thinking about what Francesca had said—about him and Leah and their fighting. But gradually Tess had realized that Francesca's disclosure meant nothing. Of course, David and Leah had fought. He hadn't wanted her to go to New York. If he hadn't loved her, he wouldn't have cared. And even if they'd been fighting about something else, that also meant nothing. People who loved passionately *did* fight. It was only people who did not have strong feelings for each other who didn't. People like her and David, for example. People like her and David were excruciatingly polite at all times.

Wearily, Tess walked over to the full-length mirror on the outside of the bathroom door. She looked at herself. She looked at her pale face, her swollen ankles and her puffy body. She looked at the circles under her eyes. She looked at her hair—plain light brown, long and straight and old-fashioned. She looked at her clothes. A pink maternity top and gray cotton pants.

Hopelessness, desolation, an impossible yearning filled her.

She thought about Leah. Her dark flashing eyes. Her sleek dark hair. Her bright, stylish clothes. Her bright personality and brilliant mind. And even though Tess could never know for sure, she could just imagine what kind of lover Leah had been to David.

Tess swallowed. No wonder David couldn't forget Leah. No wonder he had been so quick to move out of Tess's bed. No wonder he became more remote every day.

No wonder he didn't love her.

The following Saturday was the Medlock company picnic. It was a bright, beautiful October day with just a nip of fall in the air. Tess listlessly prepared to go. She hadn't wanted to, but she hadn't quite had nerve enough to tell David so.

She felt so sluggish lately. She knew most of it was physical. But a lot of it was mental, as well. She and David had lost all of the feelings of camaraderie and friendship they had once had. Although he was unfailingly considerate, kind and attentive, he had distanced himself from her. His solicitousness reminded her of the way you would treat a frail, old person. With impersonal concern. When she looked at David, when she talked to him, and especially when he talked to her—she always knew he was holding part of himself back. So many times she wanted to cry out, *David, where are you? Please, please come back to me.*

Some days despair nearly overwhelmed her, and she knew she had to fight against it. She knew that negative feelings could be self-fulfilling. So she tried hard to hold on to the hope that somehow, miraculously, everything might still work out for them. But keeping a positive outlook was getting harder and harder every day. Today, for some reason, she felt particularly vulnerable to her insecurities and fears. For that reason alone, she wished she could have stayed home and away from curious eyes. How could she talk and laugh and pretend all day long in front of David's co-workers?

When they arrived at the picnic site—a big state park about forty-five minutes from Collierville—Tess found herself a comfortable lawn chair and sank down gratefully. David carried the small stool they'd brought along and positioned it under her feet.

"You going to be all right?" he said.

Tess nodded.

"Do you mind if I join the softball game?"

"No. Of course not."

Francesca, who had been allowed to bring a friend with her, ran off to join the other children in their games, and David, after bringing Tess a cold drink, escaped to the softball game. Tess tried not to think he'd been relieved to get away from her.

Julia Medlock walked over and sat with Tess for a while, and Tess—to her surprise—enjoyed chatting with the older woman. But then Julia left, and Tess found herself alone. She was glad. She felt too tired to try to make idle conversation with anyone else. She preferred to just sit quietly and watch.

A few minutes later she heard a familiar voice coming from somewhere behind her. She listened for a minute, then identified the speaker. Katherine Comstock. Tess wanted to turn around. But she didn't want Katherine to catch her looking. She turned very slowly and just glanced in the direction of Katherine's voice. Sure enough, there she was, standing with two other young women.

Katherine looked just as beautiful as Tess remembered her. Her blond hair was tied up in a ponytail, and she wore tight black shorts and a black and white striped T-shirt. Tess thought about how David spent every day in Katherine's company. Katherine—who was so much more like Leah than Tess could ever hope to be.

Tess hurriedly turned back around, but the image of Katherine—tanned and sexy—was firmly stamped in her mind. Tess looked down at her own loose-fitting flowered maternity outfit. Why couldn't she have been one of those women who glow with good health during their pregnancy? *Oh, for pity sake! Quit feeling sorry for yourself. That's the most negative emotion of all!*

Snatches of Katherine's conversation drifted over. "Oh, yes, David said..."

Katherine was talking about David. Tess leaned back, trying to catch the rest of what the woman was saying, but she couldn't make it out.

One of the women laughed.

Tess strained to hear. She knew the conversation was probably completely innocuous, but she couldn't seem to help herself.

Then, as clear as if Katherine were standing right behind them, her voice floated over. "Look at her sitting over there like a blob. My God, she's so *dull* compared to Leah. I can't imagine what David sees in her."

Tess went perfectly still. There was a roaring in her ears, and she felt faint. She gripped the arms of her lawn chair. She closed her eyes and willed herself to be all right. *Don't faint. Don't faint.* Oh, God. If she fainted, people would crowd around. David would come. The last thing she wanted was to call attention to herself, to let Katherine know her words had affected her so strongly. She knew Katherine had said what she'd said deliberately. Tess willed her dizziness away, and gradually, she felt better.

For the rest of the day, Tess forced herself not to think about the hurtful words. She forced herself to laugh and talk to other people. To eat hot dogs and potato salad and coleslaw. To pretend she was happy. To pretend she and David were a happy couple. To pretend life was wonderful.

It doesn't matter, she told herself. *It doesn't matter. Katherine Comstock is not important in your life. Nothing matters except David and Francesca and the baby. That's all.*

But down deep, she kept thinking of what Katherine had said. *She's so dull...I can't imagine what David sees in her.* Unfortunately, no matter what Kelsey had said at the engagement party, and no matter what Tess told herself, Katherine was right. Tess *was* dull. And if she wanted to have a prayer of keeping David, she had better do something about it.

And quickly, because time was running out on her.

On Monday, Tess called the salon where she got her manicures. She made an appointment for the following day. On Tuesday, telling herself she was doing the right thing, the only thing she could do, she walked into the salon at eleven in the morning.

"Hi, Tess," said Pepper Whelan, the owner. "I'm ready for you. Come on back."

Tess followed Pepper into the back room.

"Well, what are we having done today? You said you wanted a haircut? A trim, or what?" Pepper said brightly.

Tess took a deep breath. "I want more than a trim. I want a complete overhaul. I want you to cut my hair chin-length, dye it black, and perm it."

Pepper stared at her. "Dye it black?" she said weakly. "I don't think that's a good idea."

"It's what I want," Tess said stubbornly. If David wanted Leah, Tess would just have to do whatever she could to make herself like Leah.

"But, Tess, you're so fair. Dying your hair black... it'll completely overwhelm you."

"Black." *Stop arguing with me. It's hard enough to do this.*

"I don't think you're going to like it."

"Pepper..."

"Okay, okay. Sit down."

She began to remove the pins in Tess's hair. Then she led her back to the shampoo station and shampooed her.

When Tess was settled into the chair at Pepper's workstation, Pepper combed her hair, then swiveled Tess's chair so they were both looking at Tess in the mirror.

"Are you sure, Tess?" Pepper said quietly. "Your hair is really lovely."

"I'm sure."

Pepper began to cut. With the first snip, Tess felt a moment of panic. *Oh, God, what am I doing?*

The haircut didn't take as long as Tess had imagined it would. Twenty-some years of hair hit the salon floor in less than twenty minutes. Tess only looked down once, and then she swallowed hard and watched her new self emerging.

When Pepper was finished, she said, "You know, short hair might be better than I thought. Why don't we cut it even shorter, and add some soft bangs here?" She lifted the top of Tess's hair.

Tess shook her head. "No." Leah hadn't worn bangs. Her hair had been parted on the side and allowed to billow out naturally. Tess described what she wanted.

"I don't really think that style will suit you," Pepper said. She continued to play with Tess's hair. "See? Your face is fairly long and narrow, and if I cut more here—"

"No," Tess said.

Pepper sighed. "Okay. Let's do the perm first. Then I'll color it."

Tess nodded.

Two hours later, Pepper took the curlers out of Tess's hair and rinsed off the setting solution. Then she applied the color. When all the steps were completed, she blew Tess's hair dry, fluffing it as she went. When she was finished, Tess stared at herself in the mirror.

She touched her hair. It felt so strange. She felt light-headed. And she looked...ridiculous.

Pepper had been right. Black looked atrocious on her. It made her skin look anemic. She looked like a caricature of a vampire, or something.

She certainly didn't look even remotely like Leah.

Oh, God, what have I done? Her heart began to pound. *Dear God, what have I done?* She wasn't Leah. She would never be Leah.

"What do you think?" Pepper said. Her eyes looked concerned.

Tess wet her lips. "I...you were right. It looks awful."

"I knew you wouldn't like it."

What was wrong with her? Why had she thought cutting and dyeing and styling her hair like Leah's was going to make her over into a new person? And why had she thought she wanted to be a new person?

Suddenly, like the proverbial lightbulb going off, everything became clear in Tess's mind. She met Pepper's gaze in the mirror. "Pepper, is it possible to get rid of this color?"

Pepper grinned. "Well, I have a confession to make." Her grin got wider. "I used a color shampoo. Some of it will wash out today, the rest after two or three more shampoos."

While Pepper worked on her, Tess had plenty of time to think. Why had she ever imagined she wanted to be Leah? If she had to become Leah for David to love her, did she really want his love? If he couldn't love her for herself, was his love worth having?

You're a worthwhile person. There's nothing wrong with you the way you are.

"Now, like I said, not all the color will come out today," Pepper said, "but after you wash your hair a couple of times, it'll all be gone."

Tess smiled. She looked at Pepper. "About those bangs...and that shorter style you mentioned..."

When Tess finally emerged from the salon at four o'clock that afternoon, she walked with a lighter step than she'd had in weeks. For the first time in a long time, she knew she was on the right track. Yes, she loved David with all her heart. But if he could never love her, she would survive. She touched her stomach. She had her baby. She had her self-respect. That had to be enough.

David pulled into the garage and turned off the ignition. He heaved a sigh. He'd been so depressed lately, and he'd been working such long, long hours. Tonight, he felt unusually tired and was very glad to be home. Even though his relationship with Tess wasn't what it had been, he still looked forward to seeing her at the end of the day. He knew she didn't feel good, and he knew she thought she looked awful, but he didn't agree.

She'd been on his mind all day today. He couldn't seem to stop thinking about her. Several times he'd even picked up the phone to call her, then regretfully, not wanting to put pressure on her, he'd stopped before dialing the number.

What was it about Tess that was so special? he wondered. He guessed the thing he valued most was her serenity. Just looking at her calm face, her soft gray eyes, and her shining hair was enough to make him feel at peace with his world.

Who had said most men lead lives of quiet desperation? David couldn't remember, but when he'd been married to Leah—especially those last months—he had felt that way most of the time. But this past year, with Tess, he had realized how different things could be.

He smiled. Lifting his briefcase from the passenger seat, he got out of the car. He walked to the door that led from the garage into the kitchen.

He opened the door. Tess, who had been standing at the stove, turned as he walked into the room.

David stopped. He stared at her. For a moment he couldn't believe what he was seeing. Her hair. Her hair was gone. Instead of the gleaming coronet of light brown braids, Tess's hair was several shades darker and had been cut into a short curly style no longer than three or four inches all around. She looked like someone he didn't even know. As he stared at her, she raised her chin in a oddly defiant gesture.

He knew he should remain calm. He knew he had no right to tell her how to wear her hair. But her hair! He'd always loved it so much. Why had she colored it? Why had she cut it? Irrationally, he felt as if she'd cut him right out of her life along with her hair.

The seconds ticked away.

David knew—without understanding how he knew—that whatever he said next was going to determine his future with Tess. He told himself to be careful. To be tactful. Not to hurt her feelings.

He opened his mouth. "What the hell have you done to your hair?"

Chapter Fifteen

Tess hadn't been sure exactly what she would tell David about her hair. But now—looking at the horrified expression on his face, the absolute *disgust*—she knew exactly what to say.

Very carefully, she laid down her wooden spoon. Very carefully, she took two deep breaths. Very carefully, she said, "I've had it cut and I've had it colored. What did you think I'd done to it?"

Then, calmly and deliberately, she removed her apron. She laid it over the back of one of the kitchen chairs. Leaning on the chair for support, she met David's gaze. "You know, David, I'm tired of trying to please you. I'm tired of trying to be Leah. I'm tired of the way you look at that...*damned* portrait, and the way you've completely shut me out. I'm tired, and I'm through. I am who I am, and if you don't like it, well, that's too bad."

In some part of her mind, she was appalled by her behavior. It went against every precept, every principle, she'd ever been taught. Getting angry was not ladylike, she knew that. It wasn't *Collierlike*. But at this moment, Tess didn't care anymore. She had already lost any chance she'd ever had with David. What was a little loss of dignity?

David seemed completely stunned by her words. He stared at her.

She laughed, the sound totally unlike anything she'd ever heard come out of her mouth. "It's ludicrous, really. You want to know what happened? I saw you looking at Leah's picture the other day. I saw how you feel, how much you wish she was still here. And I thought..." She shook her head, still unable to believe she'd been so stupid. "I actually thought I could be Leah. That then you'd love me. So I went to the salon today and told them to cut my hair like hers. To dye it black. I was going to make myself over. Put on bright makeup. Buy a red dress. Be the person you wanted."

"Tess..." He dropped his briefcase, took two steps forward. "I never—"

"No, David." She held up her hands. It was hard enough to say what needed saying. She wasn't sure she could hang on to her control or her anger if he touched her. If he felt sorry for her. Oh, God, she couldn't stand it if he felt sorry for her. She was afraid she'd go to pieces. Break down and start crying. Above all, she did not want to cry. Never again. There had been enough tears. It was time to get a grip. "Don't come any closer," she said. "Just hear me out."

He stopped. His face was pale and tight. His eyes, oh, those eyes... what must he be thinking?

Tess swallowed hard. "But you know what? Something happened to me today. In the middle of trying to make myself into something I'm not, I realized that I'm me. I'm unique. I'm worthwhile. There's not a thing wrong with me except that I'm not Leah. And I can never be Leah. And I don't even *want* to be Leah."

"Tess," he said again. "I don't—"

"Please, David." She could feel tears lurking somewhere. She gritted her teeth. She would not cry. "I've tried to make you happy. But no matter what I do, it hasn't been enough, and it never will be enough. I know you don't love me, and that's okay. I can live with that." She looked away from his eyes, suddenly unable to bear the pity she knew she would see. "What I can't do any longer is live with you." Not looking at him, she began to walk out of the room.

"Tess!"

She ignored him. She continued on out into the hall and up the stairs. Down the upstairs hall. Not thinking. Trying not to think. Into her bedroom—the bedroom that used to be theirs. She yanked open the closet door, grabbed at the suitcase on the top shelf, and almost hit herself when it tumbled off into her arms. Biting her bottom lip, trying to hold on to herself, she put it on the bed, and fumbled with the catch until it sprang open. Then she opened drawers and pulled things out. She threw them into the opened suitcase. Her vision was blinded by the tears that refused to be held at bay.

Stupid. Stupid fool. Crying. Weak. Stupid. Her mind whirled as she cried. She could taste the salt in her mouth. She knew her face was blotched and her eyes would puff out and she would look horrible.

I have to get out of here. I have to get out of here. There's nothing for me here. Even Francesca doesn't need me anymore. She slammed the suitcase shut, then nearly jumped out of her skin as someone touched her shoulder.

"Tess..."

Through the blur of tears and the fog in her head and the careening emotions assaulting her from all sides, she finally heard what David was saying.

"Tess, please look at me."

Tess shook her head from side to side, even as she allowed him to turn her around. He touched her chin, raised her face, and gently wiped her tears with his handkerchief. "No," she sobbed. "Please, David, just let me go. Let me go. You don't have to say things to try to make me feel better."

"I'm not! Dammit, Tess, listen to me, will you? Come over here and sit down." He led her to the bed. Carefully, as if she were a piece of fragile china, he lowered her onto it. Then he sat next to her and took her hands in his.

Tess felt completely drained. Completely unable to put a coherent thought together. The only thing she knew was that she didn't want David feeling sorry for her.

"Look, Tess, I'm sorry I acted the way I did when I saw your haircut. I...I just...it was such a shock seeing you."

"I know," she said, mortified now. Mortified that he knew how pathetic she'd been. What lengths she'd been willing to go to. She must have been crazy. A crazy, seven-months'-pregnant woman desperately trying to make her husband love her.

"I don't think you *do* know, but I'm trying to tell you," he said.

For the first time since David had followed her upstairs, Tess looked at him. Really looked at him. There was an expression in his green eyes that confused her. Suddenly her heart began to thud in slow beats.

"I loved your hair," he said softly. "That was the trouble. I loved your hair." His thumbs rubbed the tops of her hands.

Tess's breath caught. "Y-you're just trying to make me feel better."

He smiled crookedly. "No, I am *not* trying to make you feel better. I am trying, desperately, to make you understand. To make you believe me."

Tess bit her bottom lip. They stared at each other. "You *loved* my hair?"

David nodded. His grip tightened.

"Why didn't you ever say so?"

He sighed, then shook his head. "I don't know. Now my reasoning seems ridiculous, but at the time... well, I thought...I don't know...I guess I thought you knew."

"I knew! How would I know? You never said so!"

He gave her sheepish look. "I know that now. But at the time..."

"Oh, David..." She touched her hair. So short. So different. "If I'd known..." She met his gaze again. She knew this was a time for total honesty. "It was just that I felt so frumpy before. So dull and plain."

"You were never dull and plain."

"Other people think so."

"Who? Name one."

Tess swallowed. "Lots of people. Your beautiful assistant. Leah. I saw it in Leah's eyes every time she looked at me. My parents. Lots of people."

"Tess, you're imagining things. You're a lovely woman. In fact, you're a beautiful woman. There's nothing dull or plain about you." His gaze traveled over her face, then back to her eyes. "Why, Walter Medlock is always talking about how much he admires you. Everyone admires you. I'm proud of you."

"You're proud of me?"

He smiled. "Is there an echo in here? I think I hear an echo in here."

Tess laughed, too, even though she felt like crying.

His face became serious. "I hardly know where to start, but there are so many things I have to say to you."

She waited. The only thing she wanted to hear him say was that he loved her. And she knew that was the one thing he couldn't say. Sure, he said he'd loved her hair. But that wasn't the same as loving her.

"I did love Leah when I married her. At least, I guess I did. But it wasn't the right kind of love. It wasn't love that could last, because she and I never really understood each other. We wanted different things out of life, and we didn't realize it until we'd been married several years."

"R-really?"

He nodded. "Really. The last year we were married, the year before Leah died, well, it was truly awful."

"Awful?"

"There's that echo again," he teased.

She smiled, but her mind spun as she tried to assimilate what he was saying.

"We fought all the time. She hated Collierville, and I think she began to hate me. I know I certainly got to where I dreaded coming home. We were...we weren't sleeping together for months before she died."

Tess swallowed.

"I know to all outward appearances, we looked as if we were the ideal couple. Hell," he added bitterly, "Leah worked hard to give that impression. She didn't give a damn what was really going on between us as long as everyone *thought* we were this mythical perfect family."

And here, all along Tess had thought...

"The day of the accident..." He sighed deeply, his face twisting in remembrance. "That morning, we had a violent argument. Francesca was right. Only Francesca could have no way of knowing exactly what we were arguing about. It was more than that I didn't want Leah to go to New York that day or that I didn't want Francesca to go with her. Leah... she..." He stopped, and Tess saw his throat work. His gaze met hers, and that bleak look, the one she hated to see, the one she'd thought meant he didn't love her, was back in the depths of his eyes. "She told me she wasn't coming back. She said she intended to file for a divorce and keep Francesca in New York with her."

"Oh, David!"

"That's why Leah wouldn't listen when I told her the weather was too bad for her to travel. That's why she insisted I take her to the airport. She said if I didn't, she'd just call a cab." He shook his head sadly. "I had no choice. I knew she'd do it."

"But, David, why would you allow her to take Francesca like that?"

"There was no reasoning with Leah. But I figured that once we got to the airport, there would be no planes leaving, and we'd have to turn around and come home again." He shrugged. "I guess I hoped I'd come up with some kind of plan before she could actually leave." Then he grimaced. "Of course, you know what happened...." He looked down. "I've always felt guilty. I've always felt if only I had been more forceful, more *something,* I could have prevented her death." Then he looked up again, and the bleakness was gone. Now there was just acceptance. "But you know, Tess, I'm beginning to think that there was nothing I could have done. Things were meant to happen the way they happened."

Tess nodded. Sometimes she thought the same thing. Sometimes she wondered why she bothered agonizing over decisions. But at other times, times like earlier today at the salon, she knew she was the master of her fate. Just like Leah had been the master of her fate. She sighed. "This is all so strange. All this time I've thought you really did have the perfect marriage. I've thought that from the first day I met you."

"A more imperfect family would be hard to imagine," David said.

Tess sighed again. She was glad she knew the truth, she guessed, but still... David's confession hadn't changed anything. Not really. He still didn't love *her*, and that's the only thing she really wanted.

She tugged her hands away from his and started to get up.

"Where are you going?" he said.

"David," she said gently. "Nothing's changed. I'm glad you told me about Leah, but I'm still going to finish packing and leave. I'm going to call Hazel and ask if I can stay with her for a few days until I can find a place of my own."

"Tess! You can't leave me! I won't let you!"

"You don't have any choice." *You didn't say what I needed to hear. If you'd say you loved me, I wouldn't go.*

He stared at her. "But, Tess, I love you! I love you, and I won't let you go."

Tess swayed, her eyes drifting shut, and David jumped up and caught her shoulders. He gripped hard, and slowly she opened her eyes. Her heart pounded away.

Boom. Boom. Boom. David loved her? Had she really heard him say the words? Or had she imagined them because she wanted to hear them so badly?

"Tess, I know you don't love me. Not the way I love you. But that's okay. Just stay with me. Please stay with me." He put his hands on either side of her cheeks and gazed deeply into her eyes. "Maybe you could learn to love me."

"But, David, I *do* love you. I love you with all my heart!" she cried.

For a moment he just stared at her. Then he crushed her to him, laughing softly when her stomach prevented them from getting as close as he wanted. He stroked her head. "Tess, we've been such fools." He kissed the top of her head. "God, I love you so much."

Finally she pulled away and looked into his eyes. "You *really* love me, David? You're not just saying so because you feel sorry for me?"

He looked at her sternly. "If you weren't pregnant, I'd beat some sense into you." Then he grinned to show he was joking. "Now, do you have any more questions?"

Tess shook her head.

"Well, I do."

Disappointment welled in her chest. She didn't want to talk anymore. She wanted David to kiss her. She wanted him to say he loved her again. She wanted...

"Where's Francesca?" he asked.

"Francesca?" Tess struggled to switch her train of thought. "S-she's at Jessica's. Jessica's mother invited her to come for dinner."

"When will she be home?"

"About eight, I guess."

He let her go to turn and look at the bedside clock. Its red numerals read 6:45 p.m. He turned back to Tess, smiling slowly, and something about his expression made her heart go wild.

He reached for her again. "In that case, do you know what we're going to do?"

"N-no." Tess wet her lips, and his eyes followed the trail of her tongue. She could hardly breathe.

He smiled—that wonderful smile that always gave her such an odd feeling in her stomach. "Well, first, we're going to go downstairs and into the living room, and while you watch, I'm going to take down that portrait."

Tess's heart leapt. "But Francesca—"

"I'll explain to Francesca that I've stored it away in the attic and that when she's grown and has a home of her own, if she wants it, she may have it."

"But, David, what if—"

Interrupting her again, he said, "I'll also explain that although I loved her mother—you don't care if I say that, do you?—I have a new wife now—one I adore, by the way—and I don't think it's right to have the picture hanging in the living room. She's okay now. She'll understand."

"Oh, David..." Tess's heart felt so full, she thought it might burst. *A wife...I adore...*

"And then..." His smile turned knowing and sexy, and sent shivers down her spine. "Do you know what we're going to do?"

"No, what?" She couldn't have looked away if she'd wanted to. And she didn't want to.

"We're going to come back up here, and I'm going to take off your clothes and then take off my clothes and then..." He paused and his eyes kissed her.

Tess held her breath. *Oh, David, I love you so much.*

"And then, I'm going to make slow... *very slow,* passionate... *very passionate*... love to my silly wife, who thought I didn't love her."

Tess's bottom lip trembled. She couldn't speak. Her heart was too full for words.

"And every five minutes or so... in between kisses and other... things... I'm going to tell her I love her, and I'm going to demand she reciprocate."

"Oh, David, I do love you so very much."

"Thank God," he said. "Thank God." Then he gathered her close and his lips covered hers. He kissed her—a long, deep, thrilling kiss—his lips warm and moist, his tongue demanding and possessive and insistent. Tess closed her eyes and gave herself up to the wonder of the kiss, the wonder of her emotions, the wonder of knowing this man loved her. The kiss went on and on, building in depth and intensity, stealing her breath away. Her heart thundered against his, and she held him as if she would never let him go. When they finally broke the kiss, Tess sighed.

David kissed her nose. "I love you."

"I love you, too."

Still holding her close, he said, "And guess what we're going to do this spring."

"What?" She weaved her hands into his hair and absorbed the feel of him, the smell of him. Her husband. Her husband, and he loved her.

"We're going to put this house on the market, and we're going to get rid of all the furniture that was here before you came—except any pieces you think Francesca might like to have someday—and we're going to find a house of our own. And you can furnish it any way you like."

Tess knew if she lived to be a hundred she'd never fee
as happy and complete as she did at this moment.

Hand in hand, they walked downstairs together.

And later, after David had made good on all hi
promises, and Tess lay in the crook of his arm—warm
and satisfied and oh, so very happy—he said, "I love
you. I love you more than I ever thought I could love
anyone."

And then he kissed her again.

And again.

And again.

Epilogue

"It's a boy, Mrs. Bannister."

A boy! Tess lay back on the birthing table, and her gaze met David's. She knew the same shining wonder, the same glorious exaltation she saw in the depths of his eyes was reflected in her own.

He still gripped her hand tightly. For the past two hours, he'd been with her every step of the way. Each time the nurses said "Push," Tess could feel him pushing with her.

A lusty wail interrupted her thoughts, and Tess laughed. "I hear him," she said.

David nodded, his gaze turned in the direction of the bottom of the table. "God," he breathed, part word, part sigh. "He's beautiful."

Tess heard the awe in his voice, and something hot and thick stuck in her throat. She could feel tears welling in her eyes. She had never felt so happy. So gloriously, wondrously happy.

"Would you like to hold your son?" one of the nurses asked, bringing a little wrapped bundle over to Tess.

Tess nodded, then said, "David, why don't you call Francesca in?"

A few minutes later, Francesca, followed by David, entered the room. "Come and see your little brother," Tess said.

The nurse handed the baby to Tess, and Francesca and David both leaned over to see. The baby's little round head was covered with a knit cap. He was beautiful. Simply beautiful. Fat and red and wrinkled and beautiful. She touched the downy skin of the baby's cheeks.

"David Collier Bannister," David said. "Welcome to the world, son."

"Hello, little brother," Francesca said, touching her fingertip to the baby's nose. She smiled happily.

"Would you like to hold him?" Tess asked.

"Me?" Francesca's eyes widened. "Oh, yes!"

Tess handed the baby to David who cradled him close for a moment, then gently placed him in Francesca's arms.

David looked at Tess then. He leaned over and kissed her. "You've made me so happy," he whispered. "I'd like to do something special for you."

Tess swallowed over the lump in her throat and blinked away her tears. "Just say you love me," she whispered back. "That's all I've ever wanted."

* * * * *

#877 MYSTERY WIFE—Annette Broadrick

That Special Woman!

Sherye DuBois awoke in a hospital with amnesia—and discovered she was married with children. Could the love of her sexy husband, Raoul DuBois, help to unravel the mystery of her life?

#878 SHADOWS AND LIGHT—Lindsay McKenna

Men of Courage

As a marine, Capt. Craig Taggert had faced many trials. Now his greatest challenge was ahead of him—convincing Lt. Susan Evans that this time, hell or high water wouldn't keep them apart!

#879 LOVING AND GIVING—Gina Ferris

Family Found

Finding his real family was just the first surprise in store for Ryan Kent. True love with the beautiful Taylor Simmons would be the second—and best—discovery of all!

#880 MY BABY, YOUR CHILD—Nikki Benjamin

Everything was at stake when Tess McGuire saved the life of Will Landon's nephew—the child she gave up for adoption. Will's tender, loving care proved he wasn't just grateful, but a man in love....

#881 WALK IN BEAUTY—Ruth Wind

Jessie Callahan never expected Luke Bernali—her lost love and father of her child—to return. But Luke was a changed man, and eager to rekindle a love that never died!

#882 THE PRINCESS OF COLDWATER FLATS —Natalie Bishop

Single-minded Samantha Whelan's only mission in life was to save her bankrupt ranch. Prairie-tough Cooper Ryan also had designs on the ranch—and on ex-rodeo princess Samantha!

CONVINCING ALEX

Those Wild Ukrainians

Look who Detective Alex Stanislaski has picked up....

When soap opera writer Bess McNee hit the streets in spandex pants and a clinging tube-top in order to research the role of a prostitute, she was looking for trouble—but not too much trouble.

Then she got busted by straight-laced Detective Alex Stanislaski and found a lot more than she'd bargained for. This man wasn't buying anything she said, and Bess realized she was going to have to be a *lot* more convincing....

If you enjoyed TAMING NATASHA (SE #583), LURING A LADY (SE #709) and FALLING FOR RACHEL (SE #810), then be sure to read CONVINCING ALEX, the delightful tale of another one of THOSE WILD UKRAINIANS finding love where it's least expected.

SSENR

SPRING
fancy
'94

**They're sexy, single...
and about to get snagged!**

Passion is in full bloom as love catches
the fancy of three brash bachelors. You won't
want to miss these stories by three of
Silhouette's hottest authors:

**CAIT LONDON
DIXIE BROWNING
PEPPER ADAMS**

Spring fever is in the air this March—
and there's no avoiding it!

Only from      *Silhouette*®

where passion lives.

MEN OF COURAGE
by
Lindsay McKenna

It's a special breed of men who defy death and fight for right! Salute their bravery while sharing their lives and loves!

Be sure to catch this exciting new series, where you'll meet three incredible heroes:

Captain Craig Taggart in SHADOWS AND LIGHT (SE #878), available in April.

Captain Dan Ramsey in DANGEROUS ALLIANCE (SE #884), May.

Sergeant Joe Donnally in COUNTDOWN (SE #890), June.

These are courageous men you'll love and tender stories you'll cherish...only from Silhouette Special Edition!

MENCI

**WELCOME TO THE
DARK SIDE OF LOVE....**

HANGAR 13

LINDSAY McKENNA

Eerie, *disturbing* things were happening in Hanger 13—
but Major Mac Stanford refused to believe in supernatural
occurrences. He was doubtful about enlisting the aid of
shamaness Ellie O'Gentry, but he couldn't ignore their
undeniable attraction—or his desire to help her challenge
a menacing spirit....

Don't miss bestselling author Lindsay McKenna's first tale
from the dark side of love, HANGAR 13, available in
March from...

As seen on TV!
Free Gift Offer

With a Free Gift proof-of-purchase from any Silhouette® book,
you can receive a beautiful cubic zirconia pendant.

This gorgeous marquise-shaped stone is a genuine cubic
zirconia—accented by an 18" gold tone necklace.
(Approximate retail value $19.95)

Send for yours today...
compliments of ▼ *Silhouette*®

To receive your free gift, a cubic zirconia pendant, send us one original proof-of-
purchase, photocopies not accepted, from the back of any Silhouette Romance™,
Silhouette Desire®, Silhouette Special Edition®, Silhouette Intimate Moments® or
Silhouette Shadows™ title for January, February or March 1994 at your favorite retail
outlet, together with the Free Gift Certificate, plus a check or money order for $2.50
(do not send cash) to cover postage and handling, payable to Silhouette Free Gift Offer.
We will send you the specified gift. Allow 6 to 8 weeks for delivery. Offer good until
March 31st, 1994 or while quantities last. Offer valid in the U.S. and Canada only.

Free Gift Certificate

Name: _____

Address: _____

City: _____ State/Province: _____ Zip/Postal Code: _____

Mail this certificate, one proof-of-purchase and a check or money order for postage
and handling to: SILHOUETTE FREE GIFT OFFER 1994. In the U.S.: 3010 Walden
Avenue, P.O. Box 9057, Buffalo NY 14269-9057. In Canada: P.O. Box 622, Fort Erie,
Ontario L2Z 5X3

FREE GIFT OFFER   079-KBZ
ONE PROOF-OF-PURCHASE
To collect your fabulous FREE GIFT, a cubic zirconia pendant, you must include this
original proof-of-purchase for each gift with the properly completed Free Gift Certificate.

079-KBZ